ACTING
SUSPICIOUSLY

Published by
East Bay Publications

Authors' website
www.the-mulgray-twinsonline.co.uk

Helen and Morna Mulgray have asserted
their right under the Copyright, Designs and Patents
Act 1988 to be identified as the author of this work

ISBN 978-1-84396-549-7

Also available as a Kindle ebook
ISBN 978-1-84396-485-8

A catalogue record for this
book is available from the British Library and
the American Library of Congress.

Typesetting and pre-press production
eBook Versions
27 Old Gloucester Street
London WC1N 3AX
www.ebookversions.com

Other books by the authors in the DJ Smith and Gorgonzola series

No Suspicious Circumstances
(Scotland - Edinburgh and the Lothians)

Under Suspicion
(Tenerife)

Who Would Suspect? (former title Above Suspicion)
(Scotland - Islay, the whisky island)

Suspects All !
(Madeira)

No. 1 Suspect
(Scotland – Edinburgh, Fife, East Lothian)

Acting Suspiciously
(Scotland – Edinburgh and Fife)

This book is dedicated to my twin sister, without whom this book could not have been written!

Many thanks to...

Norman Bissett, poet and artist, for his inspired thumbnail sketch on the cover of Sherlock Gorgonzola in action.

Alanna Knight MBE for drawing our attention to Antonia Fraser's fascinating biography of Mary Queen of Scots with its contemporary accounts of events in that tragic queen's life, published initially by Weidenfeld & Nicholson Ltd and more recently in paperback by Phoenix, imprint of Orion Books Ltd.

Irvine Morrison of Inwood Garden, Carberry, who used his extensive knowledge of historic Carberry hill to lead us in a muddy reconnoitre in search of that perfect spot needed for the plot. And who volunteered to delve into the interior of his Mercedes to check that what we had written was in fact feasible.

Harry McNulty, Master Piper, a fund of knowledge about the mysteries (to us) of the Highland bagpipe and the skill necessary to play them. We take no responsibility for the view of some of the characters in this book that the sound of Scottish bagpipes is painfully discordant and something to be endured!

Jim and **Joan Flett** for allowing us to use their photo of their delightful Papillon, Tutyak Day Dreamer (Danny), who features as Hermione Fielding's little darling Mephistopholes (Meffy), Gorgonzola's sparring partner.

The Society of Authors Literary Representative of the Estate of Alfred Noyes for their kind permission to quote three lines from his poem *Edinburgh*.

We are very grateful to **Historic Environment Scotland** for allowing us to use for our front cover the view the imprisoned Mary Queen of Scots would have had from a window at Lochleven Castle.

Twinny thanks to **Craig** and **Charlie Reid**, **The Proclaimers**, for permission to quote from their lyric *Sunshine on Leith*

ACTING SUSPICIOUSLY

The Mulgray Twins

EAST BAY PUBLICATIONS

Chapter One

Geoff Grantham, undercover agent for Her Majesty's Revenue & Customs, stood in the shadows, eyes scanning for the slightest movement, ears taking in the sounds of the night – the whisper of the wind ruffling the needles of the imposing two-hundred-year-old Scots pine tree that towered over the grey-stone shooting lodge, the squawk of a roosting bird disturbed by some predator, the gurgle of clear brown water tumbling over the stones in the burn in its haste to reach the sea. Overhead, a full moon was sailing through the cloud layers as if it too had no time to lose. Geoff Grantham himself was in no rush. He would take as long as it took.

Satisfied at last that he was alone, he moved across the courtyard to the stables where the van was garaged, his rubber soles silent on the flagstones. The mortise locks on the wooden door were no barrier to his pick-tools and in a few seconds he was inside with the door closed securely behind him. Only then did he risk switching on his torch to play it over the white Act It Out minibuses spray-painted on their sides with characters famous in Scottish history, and next to them, a sleek black Mercedes. Grantham consulted his watch. A rigorous search of the minibuses for a secret compartment to transport drugs shouldn't take more than an hour. Yes, there'd be time.

Three quarters of an hour later, he found it. Big enough to take a large consignment of drugs, the space had been so skilfully built into the bodywork that he'd almost missed it, been just about to give up, in fact. He smiled to himself. Job done. His controller Gerry Burnside would be pleased with this contribution to Operation Red Grouse. He glanced at his watch again. There'd just be time to cover up all signs of his search and get back to his room. Wouldn't do at all if anyone noticed he was missing.

Half a minute after the garage door closed behind him, the motion-activated CCTV camera switched itself off.

Chapter Two

Edinburgh, October

In the next couple of minutes, in two minutes and forty seconds to be precise, the door facing me would open… It didn't. The briefing had been scheduled for ten o'clock, but it was now nine minutes past ten and the door facing me was still firmly closed.

I'm DJ Smith, undercover agent for Her Majesty's Revenue & Customs, waiting in my controller's outer office to be briefed on the next dangerous mission, waiting to learn the direction my life would take for the next few weeks or months. It's always a time of heightened tension. Drugs worth millions of pounds are involved, so the risk of injury or death is high, but to me the adrenalin rush of undercover work is addictive.

Impatient to find out what Gerry Burnside had in mind for me this time, I shifted restlessly on the hard leather seat and glanced once again at the large digital clock on the wall. Punctual to perfection himself, he demanded the same punctuality from others – to the extent that on the occasion when I had arrived a mere half a minute late, he had looked pointedly at his watch in silent rebuke.

Tension building – nothing short of an emergency, such as an agent in jeopardy, could have caused this delay – I jumped up, paced across to the window… back to the chair… across to the window. The HMRC office is situated on the second floor of one of the elegant nineteenth-century Georgian houses in Edinburgh's New Town. Biting my lip, I stood looking over the autumn brown and gold of the trees in Queen Street Gardens, over the grey slate roofs of other townhouses, to an equally grey Firth of Forth and beyond to the distant dark smudge of the Fife coast.

At last the door behind me opened. I swung round. The dark-haired man with rimless glasses who beckoned me into his office didn't fit the popular conception of an undercover agent – none of us did. That was the whole point. Even Gorgonzola, my talented drug-detecting sniffer cat, attracted no attention to herself. A pedigree Red Persian by breeding, her patchy coat gave her a scruffy appearance that fitted perfectly with her undercover role. Gerry Burnside motioned me to a seat, his sombre expression confirming my fear that he had indeed been dealing with an emergency.

Dispensing with the usual preliminary chat, he handed me a newspaper. 'Page seven.'

He walked over to the window and stood looking down at the russet leaves scattered on the pavements and gathered in little mounds against the railings of Queen Street Gardens. The loud rustle of newsprint as I thumbed through the pages, somehow made his silence more unnerving.

I folded the paper open at page seven with its typically tabloid headline:

COUNTRY HOUSE DEATH HORROR

and skimmed through the graphic eyewitness account of how, yesterday evening, at a country house near Edinburgh, Geoff

Grantham playing the part of Polonius had died tragically during a private performance of Hamlet. In the scene in which Hamlet kills the eavesdropping Polonius by thrusting his sword through the wall tapestry, the actor was fatally stabbed. Something had gone terribly wrong.

Interviewed, one of the shocked house-guests gave this account. 'Hamlet shouted, "How now! A rat? Dead for a ducat, dead!" We heard choking groans and what we thought was stage blood seeped through the curtain. Then, just as in the play, Polonius's body toppled out and Hamlet dragged the body off stage. The first we realized that something awful had happened was when from the next room we heard a scream. "Oh, my God! Oh, my God! He's dead. I've killed him!" '

The newspaper report ended with the statement that police were investigating how a non-theatrical sword had found its way among the props hired from a theatrical supplier.

I re-read the account, more slowly this time, and after a moment broke the silence. 'I take it that this is part of my briefing?'

With a sigh, Gerry turned away from the window and sat down at his desk. 'Geoff Grantham was working undercover for us in a drug investigation into a company called Act It Out. Heard of it?'

I shook my head.

He held up a small brochure. 'It's an outfit specializing in small-group tours to castles, palaces, and stately homes. Their unique selling point is the dramatic re-enactment of an historical event tailored to each place they visit. What is of interest to us, is…?' He raised his eyebrows in enquiry.

He was well aware that I hated his irritating insistence on

'Exercising the Brain' as he called it, a method of forcing his listener to make an in-depth analysis of a problem. I usually react by volunteering an exasperatingly obtuse answer that forces him to rephrase his question. But on this occasion, when the death of a fellow agent was involved, such a game of wits was inappropriate.

After a moment's thought I said, 'Of interest is the correlation between their itinerary and a dramatic increase in the volume of class-A drugs being distributed in the areas the tour visits.'

'Er... right.' He'd expected me to engage in the usual amicable repartee. After a moment he continued. 'I've had difficulty in finding a replacement for him and that is what has delayed your briefing. I had a very different mission in mind for you, Deborah, but due to this development,' he gestured towards the newspaper, 'we need a fully experienced replacement agent, one of our best, to take on the investigation. All suitable agents, apart from yourself, are well into their missions and cannot be withdrawn.' He fell silent.

I too was silent, thinking it over. When an assignment is known to be extremely hazardous, we are given the opportunity to refuse without detriment to our record of service. He was giving me that opportunity. It didn't take long to come to a decision. When I'm offered a mission with a challenge, adrenalin always wins.

'If it wasn't for–' I sensed his disappointment and realized he thought I was declining the mission. I said quickly, 'I mean, I'd accept the mission if it wasn't for the fact that there are two obstacles: firstly, I wouldn't be any good as a stage actor. And secondly, there's the problem of Gorgonzola. We always work together and how could I explain bringing a cat with me to the company?'

For the first time Gerry's mood lightened. 'In undercover work agents are always putting on an act, are they not? In recent missions you have acted the part of a hotel guest, a personal assistant to a property developer, a travel rep, and a butler – or house manager, as I believe the post is called nowadays.' He tapped his pencil on the desk as each role was mentioned, ticking them off. Point rejected. 'As for the mog problem, leave that to me.'

Two days later, a special messenger delivered a bulky packet. It contained documents necessary to establish my role in Operation Red Grouse: my new identity as Shelagh Macbeth working for the Scottish Tourist Board and Historic Scotland to search out quality attractions for those organisations' web pages, and a booking confirmation for myself on Act It Out's Tour 3, 'In the Steps of Mary Queen of Scots.'

Curious to see the tour Gerry had lined up for me, I studied the accompanying brochure. It seemed I could look forward to a pampered stay at a country house hotel with daily excursions to castles and palaces where key historical events would unfold through compelling re-enactments by actors of the company.

Pampered stay! Whatever lay ahead of me, one thing was certain: next week would subject me to discomfort, stress and danger.

Always thorough, Gerry had supplied me with mug shots of Act It Out's manager and actors, and background material needed for this new mission – the souvenir guides for places visited in Tour 3. I tipped the booklets out onto the table:

Stirling Castle, Lochleven Castle, St Andrews Castle, and the Royal Palaces at Falkland and Edinburgh.

On a yellow post-it note attached to the top booklet, he'd written, 'Ignorance is not bliss. Herewith, essential knowledge for your cover role. You've five days to mug up on these.'

Not a problem. That was plenty of time for me to memorize the lot. So that was me organized, but what about Gorgonzola, indispensable to me in drug investigations? What had Gerry arranged for her? I frowned. Perhaps he had scribbled something on the back of the post-it note. Blank. It was unlike him to promise something and not to deliver. There must be another note inside the padded envelope. I fished inside and pulled out a small leather collar (cat size) bristling with realistic-looking rubber spikes. Had Gerry flipped, gone mad?

Attached to the collar was another post-it note. 'N.B. See small print on back page of brochure re pets. The exorbitant additional charge has been paid. Receipt enclosed.'

I looked at the receipt. The taxpayers had most certainly dipped deep into their pockets to fund G's working holiday. The fact he'd sanctioned the expense meant he was telling me to pay special attention to the conditions so as not to jeopardize Operation Red Grouse by infringing them. Dutifully I studied the small print on the back page.

'Carriage of pets. Due to the fact that most hotels and tour companies do not cater for pets, many pet-owners are unable to take a tour that lasts more than a day. As animal lovers ourselves, we have made special arrangements, subject to a few necessary conditions, that will enable your pet to accompany you on one of our week-long tours at a modest extra charge.'

I laughed. 'Modest if you're a millionaire! Now pay attention to this, G.' I waited till she had paused in her grooming. 'Condition 1. Pet owners are responsible for feeding their pets.' She looked up at me expectantly. 'No problem, G. I always keep a week's supply of your favourite tins in your small holdall.'

Condition 2 was a bit more troublesome. 'For the safety and the convenience of other passengers, while travelling in our minibus, pets must be...' I trailed off. 'Confined in a carrier' were words guaranteed to cause a strop.

'Conditon 3. All pets must be well-behaved and of a non-aggressive nature.' I looked down at Gorgonzola now engaged in savaging a squeaking rubber mouse, her favourite reward for a drug find. Well-behaved? Non-aggressive? Only if it suited her. Cats are independent creatures.

'You'll be sweetness and light itself, won't you, G?' I stroked her head. She dropped the squeaky mouse and wrapped herself round my legs with an affectionate *purrr*. 'Unless another cat positively asks for trouble,' I added as she pounced on the mouse and shook it in a blur of movement.

Uneasily I recalled a previous mission when G had trashed and left for dead a robot cat and a thuggish pedigree Persian. No problem on this tour, though, for what were the chances of her meeting pets like that on the tour? Nil.

'So that's all right, G, we can meet all these conditions. Now let's see how you look in this rather odd collar.'

As I unbuckled it to fasten it round her neck, I noticed that the nameplate was engraved *Lady*.

'You, a lady, G! You're no more a lady than I am.'

Then I understood Gerry's little joke. Smiling, I pounced on her, and carried her over to the mirror, mouse still dangling from her jaws. Together we stared at our reflections.

'I'm Shelagh Macbeth, and you, G, are the formidable Lady Macbeth, the perfect publicity mascot for Historic Scotland and the Scottish Tourist Board.'

Chapter Three

At four o'clock in the afternoon, precisely the time detailed on the itinerary, the Act It Out luxury twelve-seat minibus drew up outside my Edinburgh hotel. Two minutes later, G's cat carrier in one hand, I hurtled out onto the pavement, rolling behind me my trolley suitcase. A small holdall bulging with cat food tins was balanced not too securely against the handle. This made steering a trifle difficult, which was why I didn't notice at first that the minibus already had one passenger.

I was handing the suitcase and holdall to the driver to stow in the luggage compartment at the rear, when a sharp *tap tap tap* on the minibus window made me turn round. A silver-haired woman with dangling earrings was mouthing something through the glass and stabbing a finger in my direction.

Puzzled, I stared at her. 'What? Me?' I mouthed back, raising my eyebrows to mime enquiry and pointing at myself.

The head nodded vigorously, causing the tiny dog figures on the end of the earrings to swing and twist as if a snarling dogfight had suddenly broken out. Slow and exaggerated movements of her lips formed the words, 'Dr… o… pp… ed some… thi… ng.' And I had. Lying on the pavement behind me was a small grey object, Gorgonzola's much-chewed squeaking mouse. It must have fallen out in my last-minute rush out of the hotel as I struggled over to the minibus with luggage and cat carrier, at the same time attempting unsuccessfully to soothe an angry Gorgonzola after a frustrating battle of wills. She had refused point-blank to go into the cat carrier, so far from being ready with plenty of time to spare when the minibus drew up, I had had to resort to desperate, and I have to admit, underhand measures. I'd placed the toy mouse inside the carrier with its tail hanging out through the back bars, lured her into the hated prison, and with one swift movement slammed the carrier door shut and pulled the mouse out, stuffing it into my pocket.

I snatched it up from the pavement, careful this time to zip up my jacket pocket. G was making clear her resentment by presenting her rear end to the carrier door. This and silence, not yowling or hissing, were her selected weapons of retaliation. Designed to make me feel a heel, they denoted a cat wounded to the heart by shabby betrayal – and would guarantee that in due course I would ply her with placatory rewards.

The saviour of the mouse was sitting in the middle row of seats. She fluttered her fingers in greeting as I edged down the bus towards her, holding the cat carrier in front of me.

'Thank you so much.' I sank onto the aisle seat opposite her and took the chance to practise using G's new name. 'Lady would never have forgiven me for losing her favourite toy.'

'I know exactly what you mean.' The dangling earrings swished as she nodded vigorous agreement. 'Life just wouldn't be worth living if I mislaid my little Meffy's pink,' she lowered her voice to a stage whisper, 'r-a-t. Must spell it out, if I say the word it'll set him off.'

She leant forward to peer through the cat carrier grid at the mound of reddish fur, all that was visible of Gorgonzola. 'What breed is your dog? Let me guess… she's a Yorkie, is she?'

'Well… let's put it this way,' I said, wondering how this would go down with Meffy's owner, 'how does your dog get on with cats?' *Yip yip yip yip.* The wicker basket on the seat beside her quivered and bounced. A pointed nose and a feathery-fringed ear pushed through the bars. *Yip yip yip yip.*

'Naughty, naughty, Meffy,' she cooed. 'I'm afraid he has a complete aversion to c-a-t-s. It's most unfortunate that your pet is a c-a-t, but "sufficient unto the day is the evil thereof".' She held out a hand, each finger encumbered with a huge gemstone set in gold. 'Let me introduce ourselves. Hermione Fielding and Papillon Mephistopheles.' She stroked the dog's fringed ear affectionately. 'You are such a little a devil, aren't you, Meffy!'

Yip yip yip. Acting up to this description as if he understood what was being said, Meffy performed his own introduction.

'I'm Shelagh Macbeth. And this is–'

Gorgonzola whirled round, sulk abandoned for something she couldn't resist, terrorizing a small dog. I made a grab for the cat carrier that had suddenly developed a life of its own and threatened to topple from my lap into the aisle. Her face was now pressed against the grid of the carrier with a 'Let me get at it!' look in her copper eyes.

Yip yip yip.

For a long moment, dog and cat sized each other up. G made the first move, a wide disdainful yawn, showing off to perfection her razor-sharp eyeteeth. Sharp claws hooked onto the grid.

Yip yip yi– The feathery ear and pointed nose withdrew into the depths of the wicker basket.

Hermione beamed. 'Look, they're friends already. There's

going to be no trouble at all with them getting together.'

I knew differently. I'd have to ensure that they never met outside their carriers. If Meffy was trashed and left for dead, Operation Red Grouse would be too. I smiled and nodded but was saved from answering by the driver getting into his seat.

He half-turned to address us. 'I'm Gordon Russell, owner-manager of Act It Out. No doubt you will have heard of me.' Not a question, a confident statement.

Hermione obviously hadn't, for she remained silent. I certainly had. I'd been fully briefed with his background, complete with photo of this balding man with horn-rimmed glasses. The hopeful pause lengthened embarrassingly. We were not, however, to be allowed to remain ignorant of his celebrity status for, undeterred by our lack of response, he continued, 'I can modestly say that I'm not without fame in the theatre world. My productions have been praised by the likes of the world-famous Royal Shakespeare Company.'

Non-committal murmurs and nods from both of us.

Satisfied, he turned back and switched on the engine. 'But now we must be on our way. Just another three guests to pick up, and then its straight to our country house hotel, the Shooting Lodge, which will be your base for all the excursions.'

The minibus moved smoothly off from the kerb. Operation Red Grouse was up and running.

Chapter Four

At first, I took her to be one of Act It Out's actors standing at the kerbside waiting for the minibus. The red-haired young woman in ankle-length black skirt, short black jacket, was wearing what looked remarkably like a starched white medieval ruff at her neck. She would not have looked out of place in the sixteenth century. Except for the tall four-wheeled suitcase at her side, that is.

'Ah, this will be Marie Stuart.' Russell ticked off a name on his list and got out to stow her case in the luggage compartment.

'*Bonjour, Mesdames.*' She settled herself, spreading her gown-like skirt over both seats. 'The weather of Edimbourg is not as pleasant as that of France, *n'est-ce pas?*'

'Welcome to Scotland, Marie.' Hermione extended a bejewelled hand. 'My dog, Meffy, is in a way, French too. He is of the Papillon breed. I must say that you speak very good English for a foreigner.'

'That is because I am not a foreigner.' A tinkling laugh. 'I am Scottish. I was born in Linlithgow near to Edimbourg, but I was brought up in France for nearly twenty years.'

'Just like Mary, Queen of Scots,' I said. 'And your name's the same, more or less.'

'That is because I *am* Mary, Queen of Scots. Reincarnated,

bien sûr. But there's no need to address me as Your Majesty. You may call me Marie, that will be quite all right.' With that, she took a small leather-bound book out of her pocket and, head bowed, lips moving, began to read.

Hermione and I exchanged covert glances, but neither of us could come up with a suitable response. We sat in astonished silence as the minibus drove on.

Outside the Premier Inn a young man and woman were standing hand in hand beside two large red suitcases, obviously newly-purchased since they bore as yet no scuffs and marks of travel. As the minibus drew up, the couple stepped forward.

Russell consulted his clipboard. 'Mr and Mrs Templeton?'

A momentary hesitation. 'That's us, Tony darling, Mr and Mrs.'

The girl giggled, stood on tiptoe and kissed her husband on the lips.

Russell ticked off their names on his list and rolled the suitcases to the rear of the bus. Laboured grunts followed by two heavy thumps indicated that he was finding the honeymoon couple's luggage extremely heavy. The new Mr and Mrs Templeton had been quite unable to part themselves from a huge haul of wedding booty.

'Come on, Val, ups-a-daisy.' The young man held out a hand to assist his wife into the bus, seizing the opportunity to snatch a hug and a kiss. A tell-tale speck of confetti drifted to the floor when they came out of their clinch. As they edged past her to the back seats, Hermione smiled up at them.

'I take it that congratulations are due, Mr and Mrs Templeton. Or can I call you Tony and Val? I'm Hermione.'

'And I'm Shelagh,' I said.

Marie said nothing. Her head remained bowed over what appeared to be a small prayer book, lips moving silently, fingers caressing a rosary of gold beads with a pearl-studded figure of Christ on the cross.

'Yeah, Tony and Val, that's fine by us. Hi, guys.' They flopped down on the back row of seats, looking into each other's eyes, lost in their own little intimate world.

Hermione rolled her eyes in their direction, then at Marie. 'Seems like we're destined to have a *conversation à deux* on this trip, Shelagh.'

She was about to say more, when Russell, breathing heavily from his battle with the suitcases, subsided into the driving seat. 'One more pick-up and then we head over the Forth Road Bridge to the Shooting Lodge. He reached into the glove compartment. 'Here's the illustrated itinerary for the week.' He swivelled in his seat and handed some thin booklets to Marie. 'If you'd care to pass these round, Ms Stuart…'

Eyes closed, lips moving, fingers caressing the rosary, she held the booklets till we took them from her. I thumbed through my copy, a more detailed version of the company's brochure with a whole page devoted to each day of the excursion. On the first page was an illustration of the Shooting Lodge itself, an imposing grey-stone building framed by the lower branches of a majestic old Scots pine. Below was a small picture of a smiling Ralph and Arabella De la Haigh, owners of the Shooting Lodge, and a short paragraph of welcome.

The minibus slowed and I looked up to find we were drawing up outside the Holiday Inn. No one came hurrying out with suitcase or holdall. The glass doors remained obstinately closed. Drumming his fingers impatiently on the wheel, Russell waited with the engine running. A small group was gathered round a bearded piper in tartan kilt of red and black squares. A plaid in the same tartan draped over one shoulder half-covered a coarse linen shirt laced at the neck. No one showed any interest in the arrival of the minibus.

'Ooh, look!' Val untwined herself from Tony's embrace. 'A piper, just like at our wedding. You'd look great in a kilt, Tone. You've got the legs for it.'

'Shaddup, Val. I'd get a divorce first.'

'Tone, we're having our first married tiff!'

Her wail filled the confined space, provoking a *yip yip yip* from Meffy and a mischievous *yowoowll* from Gorgonzola.

I winced. Marie Stuart didn't even look up from her book.

Hermione clamped her hands over her ears, then mouthed, 'Uncalled for! Young people! Such histrionics nowadays!'

I smiled and nodded in agreement. There was something overdone about Val's outburst. Were the Templetons merely revelling in the novelty of being newly wed? Or, an interesting train of thought, were these newlyweds as fake as myself?

Meffy and Gorgonzola, having had their moment of fun, sank down, eyes bright, awaiting the next opportunity.

Russell switched off the engine. 'There's always someone keeps me waiting!' With a heavy sigh he threw open the driver's door and muttering, strode towards the hotel entrance.

The piper switched to a spirited rendition of 'Flower of Scotland' and with a jaunty swirl of his kilt marched off in step with Russell. The automatic foyer doors opened to receive them and closed, cutting off the din. The normal sounds of everyday life surged back.

Hermione sniffed. 'I'm not a fan of the pipes, and this

confirms it. Reception won't be able to hear a word Russell says!'

Two minutes later, the foyer doors swished apart, spitting out a somewhat flushed Russell lugging a heavy holdall. Strapped to it was an instrument case. The piper strolled in his wake, bagpipes mercifully silenced and tucked under his arm.

Hermione sighed. 'That man's not coming on the tour with us, is he? He'll assault our ears with a *frightful* racket morning and night!'

The bus door slid open with a crash. 'Cheers, everybody! The name's Rob, Rob MacGregor.' He subsided heavily into the double seat opposite Marie, placing the pipes beside him, handling them as carefully as a mother her helpless infant.

Russell climbed behind the wheel. 'One other guest has been delayed and will be joining us at the Lodge. We'll be there in just under an hour. Now, some Scottish music to while away the time.'

'Oh, right.' MacGregor stretched out an eager hand towards his pipes.

Forestalling him, Russell slipped a CD of traditional Scottish tunes into the player and turned up the volume, effectively putting an end to ordeal by bagpipe, or indeed to any conversation. To the accompaniment of 'I'll tak' the high road… ' and 'By yon bonnie banks… ' the Act It Out minibus sped on its way.

If the honeymoon couple imagined the Shooting Lodge to be a small, intimate hideaway surrounded by dense forest, they were due for a disappointment. The approach was up a winding drive edged both sides with tall dark-leaved rhododendron bushes, abruptly opening out to reveal a wide expanse of lawn, its central feature a tall spreading Scots pine. Even in the gathering dusk, the Shooting Lodge itself was an imposing Victorian building, the grey-stone, solid, no-nonsense plainness embellished with little turrets on its many gables. Warm light spilled from its ground floor windows with the promise within of log fires, leaping flames, leather armchairs and mulled wine.

'Ye banks and braes of bonnie Doo–' The track died in mid-bar as Russell switched off the engine.

'Well, here we are. Welcome to the Shooting Lodge, your comfortable base for the next seven days.' He walked round to the rear of the minibus and began to unload the luggage.

Marie Stuart closed her little book. She hesitated at the door of the bus, feeling with her foot for the step hidden by the folds of her flowing ankle-length gown.

'Careful does it.' Russell hurried round to offer a supporting hand.

Next out, Rob MacGregor tucked his pipes under his arm, fingered the chanter and puffed out his cheeks to inflate the bag.

Russell swung round. 'Not now, sir. Perhaps later. I'll see if I can arrange it with the De la Haighs.'

Hermione manoeuvred the large wicker basket down the aisle and held it out to MacGregor. 'I don't want to drop Meffy, so if you would be so kind…'

Intentional or not, that ensured the bagpipe player was doubly thwarted from assaulting our ears. Well done, Hermione, I thought. I joined her on the forecourt, putting G's carrier down at a safe distance from cat-chaser Meffy's basket.

Russell put his head inside the minibus. 'Mr and Mrs Templeton? We're here.'

'OK. Right!' Tony leapt to his feet pulling Val with him as they tumbled out, still hand in hand as if super-glued together.

A man came hurrying towards us across the gravel. Hair greying at the temples, tailored Savile Row suit, striped shirt and regimental tie, all spoke 'successful hedge-fund manager'. Or perhaps, in view of his link with the suspect Act It Out company, 'successful drug baron and money-launderer'. I reserved judgement.

'Welcome, everybody, welcome to our home.' A professional smile. 'I'm Ralph De la Haigh. My wife and I wish to treat you as our friends paying us a visit. You will find here, therefore, some obvious differences from hotels run merely with an eye to profit. Yes, indeed. We aim to provide the ambience of a home.' His gaze rested momentarily on each of us in turn, the pause designed to let that attractive aspect sink in. 'Names, not numbers, for the rooms. And, of course, all meals are family affairs eaten round the same table.' An immaculately manicured hand picked up Gorgonzola's carrier and held it aloft. 'Dogs are an integral part of a home.'

Miou-o-ouw. G expressed her loud displeasure at the sudden lurch into the air.

De la Haigh rephrased quickly. 'And cats, of course.' A weak smile, then the polished performance resumed. 'Ah, here's my wife, Arabella.'

A woman, diamond bracelet at wrist and pearls at neck, had appeared in the open doorway of the Shooting Lodge. Smiling, she descended the shallow entrance steps and advanced towards us. 'I'll show you to your rooms. Don't worry about your luggage. That will be with you very shortly. You'll have an hour to settle in before meeting together for a buffet supper in the dining room. After that, Mr Russell will give a talk on the history behind tomorrow's re-enactment at Falkland Palace.'

We trooped after Mrs De la Haigh into a shadowy oak-panelled entrance hall complete with the seemingly mandatory antlered stags' heads and a glass case containing a bright-eyed red grouse, a superb example of the taxidermist's art. An appropriate bird, really, in view of the code name for my mission. All the rooms were on the ground floor: the lounge (sofas and armchairs tastefully upholstered in green hunting-tartan); breakfast/dining room (oak-panelled with oak refectory table seating fourteen); and guest bedrooms (doors with green tartan nameplates).

Arabella De la Haigh paused outside one of the bedrooms. 'This is to be your room, Mrs Fielding.'

Marie pushed past me. 'Oh no, there is some mistake, *un erreur sérieux*. Has it not Clan Stuart on the door? I, Marie Stuart, must have this room, for it has my name.'

'Well… er…' Arabella, somewhat disconcerted, looked enquiringly at Hermione who lifted up the wicker basket for a face-to-nose consultation.

'We don't mind. Marie can have this room, can't she, Meffy?'
Yip.

'You see he agrees. Go ahead, dear.' She stepped aside to allow Marie to take possession. The rest of us trooped after Mrs De la Haigh.

Hermione winked and whispered, 'Meffy's barks are to be interpreted like the Delphic Oracle. I read into them whatever the situation demands.'

'The Clan Robertson room, Mrs Fielding.' Arabella held open the door. 'You, Ms Macbeth, are next door in the Clan

MacIntosh. And Mr MacGregor, you'll be in the Clan Campbell.'

MacGregor scowled. 'No way am I sleeping in a Campbell bed! These rats stole our lands by treachery five hundred years ago. The massacre of our MacDonald kin at Glencoe will for ever stain their hands.' He swung the chanter pipe out from under his arm and put it to his lips. 'I'm minded to play the Glencoe lament.'

As the first plaintive notes ricocheted off the corridor walls, Arabella De la Haigh raised her voice. 'I'm sure that–' Drowned out by the wail of the pipes, she tried again. 'I'm–' Then, accustomed to coping with awkward guests, she rose to the occasion, pointing to the room that was to have been mine, and flung open the door.

Absorbed in playing the plaintive lament, he marched in, oblivious to the pained expressions of his listeners. She quickly closed the door behind him. Faintly through the thick timbers, the tune dirged on, and as his next-door neighbour, I could only hope that the adjoining walls were adequately soundproofed.

Having ascertained that I had no hang-up about the Campbells, Arabella turned to Tony and Val. 'I've put you in the Clan Armstrong. This way.' They disappeared round the corner of the corridor.

I set the cat carrier down on the green tartan carpet. When I opened its door, G didn't even poke her head out though she normally shot out like a bullet. She was again making clear her displeasure at being tricked into the cat carrier. It had been a big mistake to use the mouse to lure her into the carrier and then perfidiously whip it out. If a cat can't trust its 'lord and master' (in my case 'lady and mistress'), who could she trust? I should have let her keep the mouse, I thought guiltily. I unzipped my pocket and left the grey mouse where she could see it, hoping that curiosity about her new surroundings and the prospect of appeasing titbits would tempt her to forgive – if not forget.

While I busied myself unpacking my small suitcase, I thought about my fellow guests. Which, if any, of them would be of interest to Operation Red Grouse?

Marie Stuart was an oddball. Could anyone *genuinely* believe they were a reincarnation of a famous person from the past? Well, yes, I had to admit that there were some well-documented instances. On the other hand, it could all be an act. Whoever was organizing the drug ring might have planted her and others on the tour to facilitate the distribution of drugs or money. Yes… each of the suitcases Russell had loaded into the back of the minibus could hold a hundred thousand pounds worth of drug packages. Even G's bulging holdall would be big enough to hold a valuable consignment of drugs.

Hermione Fielding seemed genuine and likeable. Who would appear more above-board and innocent than an elderly lady with her little lap dog? But she too could be playing a part.

And what about the newly-weds, the Templetons? If they were actors, they weren't very good ones, hamming it up, over-acting the role of Young Love's Sweet Dream. I had to admit, however, that young people were often over-intense in their personal relationships.

Piper Rob MacGregor was another one worth investigating. His behaviour, too, was somewhat exaggerated – though musicians *did* tend to be totally focused on their instrument. And Russell had marched straight past him into the hotel, apparently not recognizing him, but this lack of recognition might also have been an act.

Would it be so ridiculous to think that tour guests, the Shooting Lodge managers, and possibly even the Act It Out actors, were acting a part, just like myself? I pursued this train of thought as eagerly as a bloodhound, nose to the ground, following a fresh scent. That show of hospitality by the De la Haighs was as much a performance in its way as one of Act It Out's re-enactments. I stared at my reflection in the wardrobe mirror. It wouldn't do to concentrate on that line of thought, thus closing my mind to other possibilities. All the same, I let the possibility linger at the back of my mind.

Chapter Five

When I'd finished unpacking, which didn't take long, I wandered over to the window. At the rear of the Lodge, a man was unlocking double wooden doors in one of the low buildings ranged round a flagstoned courtyard. He disappeared inside. A moment later, a minibus bearing the Act It Out logo backed slowly out. From across the courtyard another two men appeared wheeling a clothes rail hung with theatrical costumes. I moved further back into the room to observe without being seen as they transferred the costumes from the rail and folded them carefully into a trunk in the back of the minibus. After one of them had driven the bus back into the garage, they closed and locked the garage doors. All three made their way back across the courtyard towards the Lodge and I lost sight of them. Buildings used for storage and garaging would be ideal hiding places for drug consignments awaiting distribution. A snoop there during the hours of darkness was definitely on my to-do list.

First on my to-do list, however, was to unpack the tins from G's holdall. I was ready for my lunch, so Gorgonzola should have been more than ready for hers, but she was still sulking in the carrier. My heart sank.

'Come on, G. I'm sorry. I won't do that again, I promise.'

No resentful *miaow*, no forgiving *purrr*. Obviously, I'd not sounded penitent enough. 'Sorry, sorry, sorry, *sorry*.'

The only response was a worrying silence. Worrying because when she was in a mood like this, she expected me to deluge her with abject apologies, offer favourite titbits, and stroke and caress her for as much as ten minutes. I didn't have ten minutes. In five, I would have to leave to join the others in the dining room, and if I hadn't placated her before then, she would take it as positive proof that I wasn't sorry at all. A Mega Sulk would be on the cards.

Trained animals work only when they are happy. With just a week to investigate Act It Out and its base, the Shooting Lodge, I couldn't afford to miss any chance to use her nose and this afternoon would be my first opportunity. I'd already decided to give Russell's history talk a miss, pleading a migraine, and take her with me to visit the bedrooms of my fellow guests.

I opened a tin of salmon, tipped it into her bowl and moved it to and fro in front of the carrier so that its fishy smell would waft temptingly in. If that didn't make her nose twitch and elicit from her a pleased purr, nothing would.

Nothing did. Again, no forgiving *purrr*, not even a resentful *miaow*. I laid the bowl on the floor and peered into the carrier. No disdainfully taunting rear, the equivalent of the rude gesture of a mooning youth. No slitted eyes narrowed in anger.

The carrier was empty. A long ginger hair was the only evidence she'd ever been there. While I'd been concentrating on what was going on outside the window, she'd sneaked out of the carrier, spiriting away the grey mouse from where I'd placed it.

Then, from behind my left foot came the sound of the greedy wolfing of fish. I looked down to see half the salmon gone, and G's head and shoulders poking out from under the bed valance.

'That's a girl,' I said, toadying ingratiation in every syllable. '*Forgiven*, am I?'

A momentary pause in the chewing while she considered, then she snatched a couple of mouthfuls and I was left looking at a swaying valance. From beneath the bed came a provocative *squeak squeak* as the mouse received the treatment she deemed *I* deserved.

I glanced at my watch. I couldn't delay any longer, but as she had asserted her independence, I was confident that we were on good terms again. She'd start scoffing the rest of her food as soon as I locked the door, and I'd find an empty bowl when I returned.

It was then that I discovered that there was no way of locking the bedroom door. There was a lock with a keyhole, but no key. Was it just that this was his home as Ralph De la Haigh had said, and he was treating us as family friends, not paying guests? Family friends shouldn't feel the need to lock their bedroom door. In fact, the host would be most insulted if they did. The De la Haighs had asked us to feel we were family friends, but in reality we were complete strangers paying for a hotel room. If, as I suspected, the Shooting Lodge was indeed a drug distribution centre, the lack of locks would make it easy to snoop on guests and discover if they posed any kind of threat. Snoop as much as they liked, I was confident that they'd find nothing to tie me in with Her Majesty's Revenue & Customs.

It would be vital to know, however, if anybody had been in while I was away – and there was a way to find out. I screwed up a piece of paper tissue into a tiny pellet, went into the corridor, closed the door till it was open a mere crack, and inserted the pellet at the hinge, a foot from the floor where it would fall to the ground unnoticed by an intruder. Then I closed the door and made my way towards the dining room to join the others.

'Hi, I'm Brad.' Bearing down on me from the direction of the entrance hall was a dark-haired man in his early thirties, wearing calf-length cargo pants and an Aran sweater over a check shirt. He set down a canvas holdall. 'Are you one of us?'

'One of us?' I echoed, puzzled. On the Mary Queen of Scots tour, do you mean?' Remembering Russell's mention of a delayed guest, I added, 'You must be the guest who missed the minibus pickup.'

'Yup, that's me.' He grinned. 'Blotted the old copybook there. Just arrived. Am I in time for the eats?'

I nodded. 'In the dining–'

Before I'd finished, he picked up his holdall, brushed past me and loped off round the corner of the corridor towards the other bedrooms. I looked after him. Odd. How did he know where the bedrooms were? And was his, 'Are you one of us?' merely asking if I was on the Mary Queen of Scots tour? Yet… A little later that idea didn't seem quite so far-fetched. I was standing in a little queue for dessert. In front of me were the Love Birds who had decided to share a dessert but seemed unable to make up their minds which to choose.

Behind me, I heard Brad say, 'Hey, it's just clicked. Hermione… Hermione Fielding, am I right? Brad Peterson's the name. Weren't we in the same show five years ago?'

'Five years ago? That was then, this is now. I'm afraid I don't remember you. So many roles, so many fellow actors… I've long since given up treading the boards.' She gave a little chuckle. 'But once an actor, always an actor. I'm here on the tour because...' I didn't hear Hermione's explanation. At the critical moment Tony and Val had finally come to a decision.

'Ok, Val. We'll take the cheesecake and the apple tart, and we can feed each other spoonfuls.' They bore away their plates leaving me at the head of the queue. I didn't want Hermione and Brad to be aware that I'd been listening in to their conversation so I busied myself with pouring cream over my slice of lemon cheesecake and moved away.

I sighed. I was little the wiser. Hermione Fielding and Brad Peterson might very well have booked on the tour simply because, as actors, they had a professional interest in seeing history brought to life by fellow actors. The fact that she didn't remember him, might mean something – or nothing.

When it came time for the history talk, I pleaded a migraine and escaped back to my room. As I opened the door, no tiny piece of paper fell to the ground. The paper pellet had already been dislodged. The lingering scent of jasmine and the presence of an illustrated visitors' guide to Falkland Palace told me that my visitor had been Arabella De la Haigh. Not in itself suspicious, but it would have given her the opportunity to search my luggage and go through the pockets of my coat.

In my line of work, covert snooping was only to be expected so I always take precautions to allay the suspicions of others. To give the appearance of having nothing to hide, I'd left my empty case unlocked and G's holdall open to reveal the cat food tins. In full view, hanging round one of the bedposts was her spiky rubber collar with transmitter concealed within the 'Lady' nameplate. In the inner pocket of my Gortex jacket was an official pass for Historic Scotland and the letter from head office asking me to find out whether Act It Out would qualify to be included on the web pages. I'd booby-trapped the pocket with a small piece of fluff in such a way that it would be impossible to remove the letter without the fluff floating out with it. The fluff had gone.

G's collar was still hanging on the bedpost at precisely the angle I'd left it. But G herself was no longer under the bed where I'd left her. Well aware that pillows were forbidden territory, she was testing my reaction. In a provocative feline challenge, she was stretched out on my pillow completing a wash-and-brush up after scouring clean her bowl. Not a trace of fish remained. When she saw me, she broke off her ablutions to place a large paw protectively over the squeaky mouse. I made no attempt to snatch away the mouse or heave her off the pillow, and she knew she'd won. Honours were even. We were a team again.

I had fifty minutes before Russell's illustrated talk finished, giving me forty minutes to search the other rooms before I returned to lie on the bed in my darkened room as if felled by a migraine. But always act in accordance with the role you are playing – and for the first ten minutes I did exactly that. I closed the curtains, lifted G gently off the pillow, and lay flat on the bed with a hand towel over my eyes. A prostrate body with covered eyes should fool anyone checking up on me out of concern – or suspicion. Ready to snooze off her meal, G curled up beside me.

I had set my phone to vibrate in ten minutes and it must have been after five that I heard the faint click of the door handle as it turned the latch, and felt G raise her head. I kept my breathing regular, resisting the temptation to peer with half-closed eyes to see who it was. The seconds slowly passed. Was somebody still there, standing by the door, watching me? G's body language told me the answer was yes. Her head remained up, her body tense. I heard the faint creak of floorboards, the soft brush of shoe on carpet, as someone approached the foot of the bed. Mustn't give any indication that I knew someone was there, mustn't alter my breathing, mustn't suddenly sit up, hands at the ready to defend myself. It wasn't likely that I'd already aroused suspicion and that I was about to be attacked. I focused on that thought and lay still.

After what seemed an age, I again heard the brush of shoe on carpet, the creak of floorboards. The door closed softly. Beside me I felt G relax, and at last I did too. Who was my silent visitor? No hint of jasmine perfume, so probably not Arabella De la Haigh. Tony and Val appeared too absorbed in each other to have thought for anyone but themselves, and Marie was too engrossed in her reincarnation fantasy. Probably not Brad Peterson or Rob MacGregor. From the briefest of encounters I judged neither of them to be the caring type. Hermione was, so it might have been her. Nevertheless, I had the feeling that the silent visitor had been checking up, not on my health, but on my whereabouts.

I sat up and reached for the spiky collar on the bedpost. 'Get ready to test for drugs, G.'

I opened the door, screwing up my eyes as if the light hurt them, ready with the excuse that I was making a brave attempt to attend the history talk, but there was no need, the corridor was empty. With G on her lead, my first stop on the suspect trail was the Clan MacIntosh room next door. I didn't have to put my ear to the door to find out if Rob MacGregor was there. The unmistakable skirl of bagpipes was loud even through the thick wood. He was another escapee from the history talk, but why would he book a historical tour if he wasn't interested in a talk about the history of one of the places he was going to visit? I had my reasons for not attending, but what were his?

The Papillon's sharp *yip* as I eased open the door of Hermione Fielding's room warned me to move on before a crescendo of yips attracted attention. I'd have to seek another opportunity. I closed the door quickly before Gorgonzola could make it a duet.

I'd seen Marie arranging her flowing skirts as she took up her position on a settee in the lounge ready for the talk. But was she still there? Never assume. Assumptions have been my downfall on more than one occasion. A gentle tap on the door evoked no response and in I went. A quick but careful search of her room left me none the wiser as to whether she was genuine or not. Although all her outer clothes were sixteenth century, make-up and underwear were modern, as was to be expected. What I didn't expect to find in a drawer was an Apple iPad in its protective case. Further investigation of the files and emails on it would definitely be on my to-do list.

Next on my list was the Clan Armstrong room where Arabella had installed the Templetons, but when G and I rounded the corner, something more interesting attracted my attention. A silk cord hung across the foot of the staircase leading to the De la Haigh's upstairs domain marking it off as private territory. As a second line of defence against a guest too obtuse to take the hint, hanging from the cord was a white-painted board bearing the words STRICTLY PRIVATE. Despite the impression Ralph De la Haigh had given when he welcomed us to the Lodge, it was apparent that guests would not, in fact, have free run of the house.

For me as an HMRC agent these words whispered temptingly, 'Investigate Now'. With no way of telling if anybody was upstairs, it was far too risky to step over the rope and creep up to nose around. Far easier to explain away a straying cat. I unclipped the leash and gave the order, 'Search!' Eager to reassert her right to the reward of the rubber mouse, Gorgonzola darted up the carpeted stairs and disappeared into the shadows above. I retreated to the corner and waited.

A few minutes later I heard the hoped-for drug-detecting croon, followed almost immediately by a roar of, 'What the hell's a bloody cat doing up here?'

Thump. A heavy object hit floor or wall.

I withdrew round the corner, whipped the ultrasonic cat whistle out of my pocket and summoned G. Wooden treads *creak creak creaked* as someone pounded down the stairs. There was no chance of me getting back to my bedroom before G's pursuer rounded the corner. I stayed where I was.

'Lady! Lady, where are you?' I called out, injecting a note of exasperation. 'This is not doing my migraine any good at all. Come here at once, you naughty cat!'

Too late I realized that 'naughty' and the exasperation in my voice would confuse her by sending the wrong message. She had followed orders, achieved a result, and would expect her due reward. What to do? The moment I saw her running towards me, I tossed the rubber mouse in front of her. She pounced on it.

I scooped her up, hugged her and whispered in her ear, 'Well done! Clever cat! Fish tonight.'

Aloud, I cried, 'There you are!'

Round the corner, hot on G's heels, came Ralph De la

Haigh, face flushed with exertion. On seeing me, he stopped short. 'Oh! Ms... er...'

'Macbeth, Shelagh Macbeth.' Then, as if I'd suddenly registered his agitation, 'Oh dear! Has Lady been up to mischief, stolen something from the kitchen? I *do* apologize. My fault! My migraine was so much better that I thought I'd catch a little of the Falkland Palace talk after all, and she shot out of the bedroom the minute I opened the door.' I screwed up my eyes as if experiencing severe pain. 'Ooooh! I'll just have to go and lie down again.'

Without giving him a chance to ask awkward questions, I tottered off, face buried in G's fur. All the way to my room I could feel his eyes on me, boring into my back. Had I talked my way out of the tricky situation? If so, why was he still standing there watching me?

Chapter Six

Russell drummed his fingers impatiently on the steering wheel and revved the engine of the minibus.

'I'm afraid we can't wait much longer for the missing guests.' He pushed back his cuff and consulted his watch. 'I'll give them another two minutes, then we have to set off for Falkland Palace. The schedule's already a bit tight.'

'Oh dear! Marie'll be so disappointed if she...' Hermione pressed her forehead against the window and stared hard at the Lodge door, willing her to materialize.

'Quarter past bloody eight! Crack of dawn.' Brad yawned ostentatiously. 'The sun's barely up! I could have had another hour in bed'. He made a big show of settling back in his seat with his eyes closed.

Tony winked. 'Same with us, eh Val? We'll have to make up for it tonight.'

She giggled, leaned her head on his shoulder and whispered something in his ear.

I unbuckled my seatbelt. 'I'll go and look for them. Won't be a minute.'

'A minute's all you've got.' Russell's eyes were on his watch, counting down the seconds. 'We really do have to go. Our private re-enactment must be completed before eleven o'clock when the Palace opens to the public.' A *poop poop* of the horn and a rev of the engine underlined the urgency.

Reluctantly I refastened the seatbelt and settled back in my seat. I couldn't risk being left behind. Keeping the actors and the minibus under close observation was what I was here for.

'Here they are!' Hermione tapped on the glass and beckoned urgently.

Rob MacGregor in red and black tartan trousers and black jacket had appeared on the front steps. A solicitous hand hovered near Marie's elbow. She was wearing the same old-fashioned long black skirt and short black jacket, though this time the folds of a black veil concealed her face.

Val broke off from nuzzling Tony's ear. 'Look at that, Tone!' adding with unfortunate timing just as MacGregor helped the veiled figure up into the bus, 'You'd think she was going to a funeral, wouldn't you!'

Marie marched up the aisle and stopped, the veil inches from Val's face. 'Madame,' she hissed, 'please to show respect. I was delayed at prayer, for today I am visiting the very room in Falkland Palace where my father died.'

Lost for words, Val stared at her open-mouthed as she glided back down the aisle to a seat as far removed as possible from the young couple. Fastening her seat belt, she bowed her head over her little book, withdrawing into her own private world behind the veil.

Recovering, Val rolled her eyes heavenward.

'Screw loose.' Tony tapped a finger against the side of his head.

'Tut tut! Young people these days!' Hermione made a moue of disapproval. 'Quite uncalled for.'

Brad flung his arms in the air and yawned noisily. He winked at Tony, then with a 'watch the expert at work' look, leaned across the aisle towards Marie. 'Don't bother about them, *ma chérie*. I'm so awfully sorry about your father's death. Recent, was it?'

'1542.' The muffled reply emerged from under the veil.

'Er, right…' For once at a loss for words, Brad slumped back into his seat, silenced.

Rob sat down on one of the two remaining seats and placed his bagpipe case on the other, carefully securing it with the seat belt.

He caught my eye. 'You're wondering why I've brought my pipes with me? The MacGregors and the Stuarts were partners in her dad's time.' He pressed his lips together. 'Though not later. The lassie here,' he indicated the bowed head, 'asked me to play a lament at Falkland in memory of her dad. I couldn't say no, could I?' He reached over and patted her shoulder.

This had the opposite effect from that intended, eliciting low sobs from Marie. The rest of us exchanged embarrassed glances.

The minibus moved off. Russell slid a CD into the player. 'Yesterday, traditional: today modern Scottish music.'

My heart is broken, my heart is broken – Sorrow…sorrow… sorrow – the mournful words and music of The Proclaimers' *Sunshine on Leith* burst from the loudspeakers perfectly in tune with the mood of the reincarnation of Mary Queen of Scots.

Russell took a hand off the wheel in an expansive gesture. 'Here we are, then. The Royal Burgh of Falkland.'

We were driving up the main street, past buildings of

traditional Scottish architecture: house walls, grey stone or whitewashed; small windows, multi-paned and framed with sandstone slabs, sometimes in contrasting colour to the walls; corbelled roofs of grey slate or terracotta pantiles.

'And this is the Palace Gatehouse.'

Set no further back from the street than a modern house with a front garden, the Gatehouse dwarfed in scale the simple cottages in the village street. A combination of castle, fortified house and French chateau, complete with twin towers capped by conical turrets, its grey façade was pierced with heavily grilled windows of all shapes and sizes.

For the first time on the trip Brad Peterson showed some interest. 'More like a prison than a palace.'

I peered at the forbidding exterior leavened only by three small brightly painted heraldic stone panels. 'It's certainly no light and airy fairytale palace.'

Hermione frowned. 'Well, it looks imposing enough for the entrance to a palace, but where are the surrounding grounds? Why on earth would someone build a palace right beside the road?'

Marie lifted her head from studying her book. 'When my grandfather started to build, this was countryside. There were no houses. At sunrise he and my father hunted the wild boar and deer through the trees.'

From the back seats came a suppressed giggle and a splutter.

'Shut up!' I hissed, apprehensive that Marie Stuart would decide the Mary Queen of Scots tour was not for her, pack her bag, go home, and reduce us to below the minimum number for the tour to run.

Russell switched off the engine and heaved himself up out

of his seat to open the passenger door.

MacGregor unclipped the seatbelt securing the precious bagpipes in their case and leaned over to Marie. 'Would you like me to pipe you in through the Gatehouse to mark the return of the daughter of King James to her royal home?'

She smiled and nodded, but before she could reply, Russell stamped firmly on the suggestion with a brusque, 'No time for that now. The re-enactment is due to start. We're running late, so we'll have to go straight to the Real Tennis Court.'

MacGregor bridled. 'What's the hurry? Don't tell me it will make a whit of difference if the re-enactment starts a couple of minutes late!'

'No time to argue!' Russell pulled down the step of the minibus. 'There'll be plenty of time afterwards to play the pipes in the Palace and explore the village. We leave here at three-thirty. Please don't be late.'

Hermione muttered a most unladylike, 'Bossy bastard. Meffy would soon sort him out.'

Oh dear, tempers fraying already. And this was only day one. I was first out of the bus, eager to see Real Tennis – this unusual cross between modern lawn tennis and squash. The others seemed in no hurry. Tony and Val, reluctant as ever to un-clinch, were last out. Russell stepped forward to lock the bus doors.

'Wait a mo!' Val brushed past him. 'I've left our jerseys in the bus.'

He waited impatiently for her to retrieve a large duffel bag lying on the back seat, then slid the door shut with a bang. 'The re-enactment begins in five minutes. We'll have to get a move on.' Calling over his shoulder, 'Follow me,' he set off at a brisk trot through the Gatehouse arch and along the edge of a large expanse of lawn towards the East Range, a roofless three-storey stone frontage with empty rectangles of sky where once had been window glass.

Marie gradually slowed her pace and soon lagged some way behind the group. Whatever she had in mind, she didn't want anyone to notice. We passed through a gap in a yew hedge flanked by two giant stone urns on pedestals and entered a small enclosed garden with its rectangular low-walled pool.

I let the others forge ahead and stepped to one side so that I was screened from Marie by the hedge. Making the pretence of shaking a stone out of my shoe, I waited for her to appear. But she didn't. Through the gap in the hedge I saw her black-veiled figure moving swiftly back across the lawn towards the herbaceous borders and the ruined East Range of the Palace. Was this how Act It Out operated – someone assigned to make a drug drop while the rest of the group were watching a re-enactment?

When she had gone up a flight of steps and was lost to sight, I sprinted across the grass after her, trying to think of a plausible excuse if she saw me. But Marie Stuart seemed to have vanished into thin air. She could only have gone through a small door at the end of the flagstone terrace.

I opened the door to see narrow steps spiralling upwards and hear the soft scuff of shoes on stone. My rubber soles making no sound, I crept up after her, stopping to listen every few steps. The scuffing stopped. I stopped, one foot on the tread ahead. Had she sensed that someone was following her? Would she be standing at the next turn of the stair, looking back to see who was there?

According to the booklet, this stair led to the King's Bedroom, and above it, the Queen's. Whipping out the guide provided in my undercover role pack and pretending to read, I tiptoed up the last few steps and stood to one side of the entrance to the room, ears strained to hear the murmur of voices, eyes ostensibly studying the guide to the Palace.

'*Non non no-o-on!*' Again, '*Non!*' Agonized, despairing, desolate.

'What's wrong? Can I help?' I rushed in through the doorway calling out as a warning signal to the attacker that somebody was coming to the rescue.

There was no attacker, nobody else at all with her in a room hung with faded tapestries, a room surprisingly small for a king's bedroom, made smaller by the huge cupboard-chest along one wall. She was kneeling by the side of a richly carved, gold-ornamented and canopied four-poster bed, sobbing and pounding her fists on the damascene coverlet, completely unaware of my presence.

Wondering if her distress was all an act, I knelt down beside her. 'What on earth's the matter, Marie?'

She flung back the veil to reveal a tear-stained face. 'I came here to kneel in prayer beside the bed on which my father died, run my hand over the covers, be in touch with his departed soul.' A sob. 'But in this room there is too much that is not the same as I remember when I lived here. My father does not speak to me. He is not here. *Pourquoi* is this so?' The tears coursing down her cheeks dripped onto the pale coverlet to form a damp patch on the fabric. If she was indeed acting a part, she was a very fine actor.

The time spent in study of my guidebooks came in useful.

'You do not feel his spirit here, Marie, because your father now lies in Holyrood Abbey. Don't you remember? His body was taken there after he died.' I put a gentle hand on her shoulder.

She trembled as if she had been struck. 'Oh!' She stared at me, mouth open, wide-eyed. 'Yes… you are right. And in only two days we go to Holyrood, *n'est-ce pas*?' As if a tap had been turned off, the tears miraculously dried up. She pulled out a small white handkerchief, wiped her eyes and rose to her feet. 'Now I can go with a light heart to the tennis court where I had such fun.' She sailed past me out of the room and down the stairs.

Taken aback by this abrupt change of mood, I stood looking after her. Was she deluded, or was it all a deception? Mary Queen of Scots had lived in Holyrood Palace for several years, so how could Marie have forgotten that her father had been buried in the Abbey, sited only a few yards from Holyrood Palace walls? I had the sudden sinking feeling that her stealing away from the group might have been a clever ruse to distract an agent from Drug Enforcement while a drug swap was taking place at the Real Tennis Court.

Curious to hear how she would react if she was faced with a direct question about her 'reincarnation', I hurried after her and caught up with her as she made her way along the terrace.

'I find it strange to hear you talking about King James the Fifth as your father, Marie. He's someone who lived five hundred years ago.'

She glanced at me, relaxed, no hint of unease in her eyes. 'It is simple. From my earliest years I have known I am Mary Queen of Scots, living today in the body of a woman born in the twentieth century. So, of course, King James is my father. I have been to *séances* and spoken to the Queen and she to me. Her thoughts are my thoughts.'

She pointed towards a high wall of irregularly-shaped sandstone blocks. A board over a low doorway proclaimed 'Royal Tennis Court' in gold lettering.

'This is the tennis court built by my father. He was an expert at the game and it was my favourite too. Perhaps Monsieur Russell will allow me to play.'

I hesitated in the doorway, letting my eyes adjust to the faint light in the passageway. Ahead of me, her black-clothed figure merged with the gloom, as insubstantial in the semi-dark as her claim to reincarnation.

After a short distance, light flooded in as, cloister-like, the left-hand passage wall lowered to waist-high with the roof supported by black marble pillars. The long rectangular court was open to the sky, enclosed on the other three sides by smooth black walls that must be all of thirty feet high. In place of a modern net, a tasselled rope stretched across the centre of the court. Heavy-mesh stretched the length of the viewing gallery to protect spectators from flying tennis balls.

The re-enactment of the Tudor game of tennis had already begun. Four actors in sixteenth-century dress of doublet, padded breeches, stocking hose and tall hats were energetically smashing a hard ball against the walls. Another two, less richly dressed, were standing watching. One of the players lobbed the ball high in the air to land with a loud thump on the sloping roof of the viewing gallery.

To my surprise, a court official raised an arm in the air.

'Point to server!'

Hermione enlightened me. 'When the ball bounces off the roof that's a point scored, Shelagh. The Presenter, the Tudor gent standing against the back wall keeping the score, told us all about it in the introduction, don't you remember? Oh, I forgot. You weren't here then, were you.' She lowered her voice. 'Was anything wrong?'

'No, no,' I said quickly. 'It's just–'

At that moment the ball came flying towards us at head height. Instinctively we all ducked. All except Brad. As the protective netting ballooned inward, he stood his ground with not even a sideways twitch of his head.

We were treated to a Masterful Male smirk. 'No need to press the panic button, guys.'

Mr Show-Off, I thought. Aloud I said, 'There wouldn't have been a net six hundred years ago and a spectator could have lost an eye. You were lucky. The mesh has already been broken in two places.' I pointed at the twine. 'Look, it's frayed here, where the ball hit.'

'Perfectly safe. Did the calculations, just like that.' A snap of his fingers to illustrate the lightning quickness of his mental processes.

Unimpressed I turned my back. 'Hermione, these vertical green lines, crowns and numbers painted on the wall must mean something. What are the rules?'

She shook her head. 'I haven't a clue! Val will be able to tell you. The Presenter explained it all, of course, but it went in one ear and out the other.'

Val shrugged. 'Same with me. All those funny French words! Boring, boring, boring! So I nipped off to the Gift Shop for some retail therapy, had a quick nosey round, and bought,' she patted the duffel bag, 'some snazzy tea towels and–'

'Want to know the rules, ladies? Anxious to regain the limelight, Brad interrupted. 'I'll look them up on the internet.' He tapped commands into his phone.

Hermione peered over his shoulder. 'Rob missed the explanation too, Brad. That's three people who want to know. Make it four, I'm not too clear about the rules either.'

So both Rob and Val had left the group. Should I have been keeping them under surveillance rather than Marie? Had I missed a handover of drugs transported in Val's duffel bag or Rob's bagpipe case?

'So what were you looking for in the gift shop, Rob?' I made a joke of it. 'A Falkland Palace sticker for your bagpipe case?'

'Didn't go anywhere near the shop. I thought Marie had skipped the re-enactment as she was upset at not being played into the Palace. So I went looking for her to give her a wee tune on the bagpipes. Didn't find her, though, so I came back.'

How much of this was true? Had he been listening to our conversation in the King's Bed Chamber, reluctant to intrude on an emotional scene? Or was it his role in the drug gang to keep tabs on those of us who were genuine tourists? If so, I was in the clear. My words and actions had shown concern for Marie, nothing more.

'You haven't been listening, have you, Shelagh!' Brad seized my arm and steered me over to the pillared gallery wall. 'See that crown painted on the back wall there? Well that means... He consulted his phone. 'Yes, it's used in the awarding of points and...' He elaborated at tedious length. I could feel my eyes glazing over.

I was rescued by loud cries of alarm from the tennis court.

'Oh, no!'

'My God!'

'Are you OK, John?'

I rushed over to join the others peering through the netting. Racquets were lying abandoned on the court, thrown down in mid-game, the actors clustered round someone lying motionless on the ground.

'First real bit of action.' Tony sounded positively gleeful. 'The ball hit him smack on the head.'

'Oh!' Hermione's hand flew to her mouth. 'That must have hurt.'

One minute Brad Peterson was standing beside us, the next he was striding confidently across the court, calling out, 'Stand aside, there. I'm a doctor.'

Rob snorted. 'Poser! Doctor of what?'

'If he's a medical doctor, I'm the Queen of Sheba!' Hermione snatched out her phone and punched in 999. 'Send an ambulance... violent impact on side of head... man unconscious...'

The casualty was barely visible through the forest of legs. Could this be another HMRC colleague who had aroused suspicion?

Val stood on tiptoe to get a better view. 'Do you think this is part of the play?'

As we stood in silence watching what was obviously real-life drama unfold, Russell came running, pushed past us and joined the group in the centre of the court. After conferring with the players, he came over to address us.

'I really must express my regret that this unfortunate mishap has cut short the planned re-enactment. I will, of course, be accompanying the young man to hospital, but the minibus will still leave at the scheduled time of three-thirty to give you the promised leisurely visit to the Palace, time for lunch, and exploration of the picturesque village of Falkland.'

At three-thirty, we took our seats in the minibus. Russell stood at the door clearing his throat. The nervous removal and replacement of his glasses telegraphed bad news.

'As we are now not one, but two, actors short, I'm afraid that this most unfortunate accident to a second member of the cast has put into serious doubt the continuation of the Mary Queen of Scots Tour.'

'You can't do that!' Tony leapt to his feet, banging his head on the low ceiling of the bus. 'It's… it's…' He spluttered to a halt.

Val pulled him back down into his seat and burst into tears. 'That's our honeymoon spoiled!'

Marie muttered something. Her words, muffled by the veil, sounded angry.

Hermione, too, looked as if she was about to cry. 'You mean I have to go home now? I was *so* looking forward to all the places we were going to visit and the promised re-enactments. Few holiday tours will take Meffy. Please, please, reconsider.'

The premature end of the tour would be the death blow for Operation Red Grouse. Perhaps the need for a reputable organisation to endorse the tours might make Russell reconsider. I added my voice to the chorus of protest.

'Oh dear, I'm afraid I've not seen nearly enough yet to convince Historic Scotland that they should put Act It Out's re-enactments among the list of attractions on their website.'

Rob backed me up. 'Shelagh's right. One re-enactment! We

haven't seen very much for our money so far. I want a refund. And that goes for the others too. You'll just have to recruit more actors. That's what should be done. If you're stuck, I'll take a part. One or two rehearsals and I'll have the lines off by heart.'

'Oh yes!' Hermione clapped her hands. 'I'm a trained actress. I could take a part too.'

Brad, 'Problem solved. So no need to cancel the tour. Isn't that right, guys?'

'It's not up to me to decide. Other factors...' Russell started the engine and slipped a CD into the player. The loud plaintive notes of a bagpipe pibroch lament blasted out, cunningly designed to make our complaints inaudible and prevent further rebellious discussion. Rob sat back fingering an imaginary chanter and obviously enjoying the music, but for the rest of us, the journey back to the Shooting Lodge was a somewhat sombre affair.

Chapter Seven

The late afternoon sun was gilding the frontage of the Lodge and burnishing the windows as the minibus rolled to a stop in the long shadow cast by the dark spreading branches of the Scots pine in the Lodge forecourt. As Russell cut the engine, the CD bagpipe lament playing on repeat died in mournful mid-wail, putting us out of our misery.

Yip yip yip yip.

'Oh, that's Meffy!' Hermione craned her neck to pin down the source of the hysterical barking. 'What can be wrong?'

'There he is! Over there, under the Scots pine.' From my side of the bus I had a clear view of the Papillon leaping up and pawing at the rough bark of the trunk in baffled frenzy.

Arabella De la Haigh, flustered, pink in the face, untidy wisps of hair straggling from her perfectly groomed coiffure, was making ineffectual grabs at the dancing dervish that was Meffy. Abandoned a short distance away were his wicker basket and Gorgonzola's overturned cat carrier. I scrambled out of the bus close on Hermione's heels.

'I'm so… sorry.' Arabella gasped an explanation. 'You see… I let Meffy out… for his little walk as… as we'd arranged.' She put up a hand to push a strand of hair from her eyes. 'I'd put the cat carrier down over there. Then… then… Lady was suddenly out. I don't know how it happened.'

I knew exactly how it had happened. Gorgonzola, bored, bored, *bored* by her long incarceration in the carrier and desperate for some entertainment, had seized the opportunity to provoke the small dog. She'd hurled herself against the side of the carrier to unhook the catch. Once free, she'd strolled casually towards Meffy and allowed him to 'chase' her up the tree, keeping just ahead to spur him on. Once safely up the tree, she'd set about goading him beyond endurance.

Yip yip yip yi– Hermione pounced.

The three of us stood beneath the spreading branches. Our eyes travelled up… up… up to where G crouched smugly in the fork between a giant limb and the trunk, far, far higher than was necessary to escape slavering jaws.

'Naughty, naughty, Meffy!' Hermione held him up to view the scene of his crime. 'Just see what you've done! The poor, poor dear! She's so frightened.'

Yip yip yip yip.

'That's quite enough. Back you go into your basket. No treats tonight.'

Feeling more than a little guilty that the dog was shouldering all the blame, I said, 'I don't think Lady's too frightened. She'll come down when Meffy's back indoors.'

But she didn't. Or rather, couldn't. After several tentative clawings to secure a grip on the trunk for her descent, her Cheshire Cat grin faded, to be replaced by a long-drawn-out miserable *miao-ow*. Like a terrified climber frozen into immobility on a rock face, unable to move up or down, G was completely and utterly stuck. I turned to Mrs De la Haigh. 'Oh dear, I think the fire brigade will have to be called.'

Since it wasn't exactly an emergency, by the time the fire brigade arrived, had set up a ladder and rescued Gorgonzola, dinner had long been eaten – but not by me.

Hungry and in a foul mood, I made my way along the corridor to my room with G safely in the cat carrier. As I passed the Clan Robertson room, Hermione's voice came clearly through the closed door. Gorgonzola wasn't the only one in deep disgrace.

'Shelagh will be at the talk in an hour's time. How can I possibly face her! Into your basket you go now. Tonight you'll not sleep on my bed.'

Sheepishly I crept by, hoping G wouldn't make a sound to start Meffy off again. Once in my room, I plucked G out of the carrier and held her up, looking straight into her eyes, and gave her a good talking-to.

'While I was away, you were to be on your best behaviour. But what do I find when I come back? I find…'

I was in full indignant flow when I heard footsteps coming along the corridor. They stopped outside and a piece of paper was pushed under the door, then the footsteps continued along the corridor. Investigation of the note could wait. I continued with my harangue.

'… I find the poor little dog about to have a heart attack. Meffy might have dropped down dead because you wanted a little fun! And it would have been entirely your fault. Think of that.' I gave her a little shake. 'And it's not you, but Meffy, who is being punished. He's been sentenced to spend the night in his wicker basket instead of on Hermione's comfy bed. So tonight you will sleep in the cat carrier.'

Fired with righteous indignation, I shoved her into the

carrier and securely fastened the hook to ensure that no amount of shaking would work it loose. That done, I picked up the note that had been pushed under the door.

It was from Ralph De la Haigh.

Dear Guests

Let me start with the Good News! I am delighted to tell you that tomorrow's visit to Stirling Castle, the childhood home of Mary Queen of Scots, will take place as planned. That will be a marvellous opportunity for you to step back into the sixteenth century through meeting the Castle's own costumed performers in the Royal Apartments. This evening' s talk will enable you to get the best out of your visit.

Since Mr Russell will be engaged in the recruitment of actors to replace the missing members of the company, he will not be able to drive you to Stirling. Your driver tomorrow will be your hostess, Arabella De la Haigh.

Unfortunately, however, there is also bad news. The Company now being two actors short, it is after much painful consideration and with much regret that I have to make the difficult decision to inform you that after tomorrow's visit the Mary Queen of Scots tour will be cancelled. Therefore, on Wednesday the minibus will transport you back to Edinburgh. We will, of course, be pleased to offer compensation in the form of a voucher for a future tour of your choice.
Ralph De la Haigh

I tossed and turned, staring up at the panelled bedroom ceiling. Weighing on my mind was the fact that tomorrow G and I would be heading back to Edinburgh in the minibus, no doubt to the accompaniment of the so appropriate Proclaimers' mournful refrain. A couple of hours later I'd be reporting to Gerry that Operation Red Grouse was dead in the heather, killed off by a Real Tennis ball.

Sleep eluded me. I watched as a strip of moonlight inched almost imperceptibly across the red lines and dark green squares of the tartan carpet. The minutes crawled by... The measured *tick... tick... tick* of the wooden wall-clock irritated rather than soothed. I pulled the duvet over my head. *Tick... tick... tick* drilling its way relentlessly through the layer of filling till I felt like screaming. I'd have to silence that damned clock. Perhaps if I wrapped it up in the tartan throw... Flinging back the duvet, I swung my legs over the edge of the bed and padded over to lift the clock off the wall. I interred it in the thick woollen bed-throw. That should do it. I waited.

Tick. A pause as the second hand struggled to move against the hampering wool, then *tick.* The sound was definitely fainter, but the wait for the next tick even more irritating. Removal of the battery was the only solution. I hung the disembowelled clock on the wall. Blissful silence. I should have thought of that in the first place.

I turned to go back to bed. The strip of moonlight was shining through the window onto the cat carrier. In its depths were two glowing green spots, the reflective layer at the back of G's eyes. She was awake and silently watching me.

'Awake too, eh G?'

No mew of acknowledgement, no loud demand to be let

out to reclaim her rightful place on the bed. Just that steady, unblinking gaze.

'No need to sulk. After all, you were–'

I frowned. If she'd been sulking, she'd have been facing the other way in the carrier, presenting her rear. Yes, she'd provoked Meffy. That was definitely in character. But it was also in character for her to get carried away by the excitement of the moment. Had I not been carried away myself on occasion? A pang shot through me. Perhaps being trapped up the tree had genuinely traumatised her.

Or perhaps she was merely trying it on. That was in character too. I'd test her by opening the carrier door. If she rushed out and leapt onto the bed, I'd know I had been tricked. I undid the latch and stood back. there was no movement inside the carrier, just a faint, sad mew, the equivalent of a human sob. All doubt dispelled, I reached in, gently lifted her out and hugged her to me, walking back and forth whispering reassurances, then stood at the window stroking her till at last her rough tongue tentatively licked my hand.

I stopped in mid-stroke. A movement out in the courtyard had caught my eye. Someone was moving slowly and furtively from the direction of what must have been the servants' annexe. The figure kept close to the rear wall of the Lodge, paused for a moment before leaving the shadows, then darted across the moonlit stretch of flagstones towards the range of low buildings that housed the garage and storerooms. I was too far away to make out any detail except that it was a man, tall and thin, with hair gelled into spikes. Was he an actor? One at the Real Tennis re-enactment had been taller than average, but as they had all been wearing wigs and hats, I couldn't tell if this was the same man.

'What's he up to, G?' I whispered.

He fiddled with the lock of the garage door for a couple of minutes, much longer than needed to insert and turn a key. The garage door swung open.

'I think he's using a picklock. Now why would that be? Interesting, eh?'

She turned her head to look and her ears flicked forward.

He slipped inside and the door closed behind him. I stood watching, waiting for him to re-cross the moonlit stretch of courtyard on his way back to the Lodge. When he did, he'd be coming towards me and in the bright moonlight I'd have a good view of his face.

Ten minutes later he hadn't reappeared. I turned away from the window. 'He's acting suspiciously, G. There's something in there worth investigating, so you and I will have to have a look – but not now. Don't know about you, but I'm getting cold.'

While Gorgonzola prowled up and down on the bed, selecting just the right spot to curl up, I pulled the duvet round myself and snuggled down, putting all thought of the pending cancellation of the tour firmly aside. She, too, immediately settled down, nestling into the small of my back with a loud triumphant *purrr*. It drifted into my mind that her traumatised behaviour in the cat carrier had just been an act. It was my last conscious thought.

Chapter Eight

I was the young Mary Queen of Scots playing in a Real Tennis match at Falkland Palace. *Thwack*. My racquet stroke sent the heavy padded ball rolling down the sloping penthouse roof to bounce on the ground on the other side of the net. My opponent, Brad Peterson in tall hat, doublet and breeches, lunged with outstretched racquet to return it, and missed. I bowed, acknowledging the applause of the spectators in the side gallery.

A courtier bearing a remarkable resemblance to Ralph de la Haigh stepped forward. 'I declare the game null and void. Your Majesty, it is not fitting for a lady to be wearing men's breeches.'

'Bah!' I cried, snapping my fingers. 'I do as I please. Am I not the Queen?'

'No, you are not!' A black-veiled figure swept onto the court, her black gown trailing behind her. 'You are an impostor. I, Marie Stuart, am the true Queen of Scots.'

'Off with her head!' The chant from the spectators echoed round the high walls of the tennis court. 'Off with her head! Off with her head!'

I woke with a start, caught between half-remembered dream and reality. For a moment disorientated, I gazed wildly round the room trying to remember where I was. Tartan throw... tartan carpet... suitcase... cat carrier... Of course! I was in the Shooting Lodge in an undercover role for Operation Red Grouse.

And while I slept, my subconscious brain had found a solution that just might possibly prevent the cancellation of the tour.

Breakfast was not a cheerful affair. My fellow guests, gloom on every face, were coping with their disappointment in different ways.

'Might as well get my money's worth.' Brad made the most of the full Scottish breakfast by filling not one, but two bowls with porridge, and ordering a double helping of kippers.

Marie had discarded the veil for the practicalities of eating and was dabbing periodically at her eyes with a lace-edged handkerchief. Hermione was toying with her food. As for Tony and Val, they hadn't yet appeared, perhaps prolonging the honeymoon experience for as long as possible.

They were not the only absentees. Outside the dining room window, the wail of bagpipes swelled and faded as Rob marched up and down, kilt swinging, cheeks puffed out, face crimson with effort, playing a lament for the tour that was not to be – or possibly continuing in Queen Victoria's tradition of having a piper play while she breakfasted at Balmoral.

I helped myself to porridge and carried the bowl over to sit opposite Hermione. 'I've decided not to go on the Stirling Castle trip today because–'

She looked down at her plate, not meeting my eyes. 'It's because of Lady, isn't it! She's been traumatised by Meffy chasing her up the tree. You're waiting for the vet, aren't you?'

'No, no, Lady's fine, quite recovered. It's just that–'

'I can't say how sorry I am about his appalling behaviour yesterday.' She patted my hand. 'Now, you mustn't miss the trip to Stirling, but since Arabella is driving the minibus, if we both go, there won't be anybody to look after Lady and Meffy. So I'll stay behind to look after them. *You* go to Stirling. I insist.'

Going to Stirling was precisely what I didn't want to do. 'That's very generous of you, Hermione. But as I work for Historic Scotland I've been there many times, and you've never been to Stirling Castle. Besides...' I leaned forward conspiratorially, 'I've got a plan that just might allow the tour to continue.'

I stood on the front steps of the Shooting Lodge waving off the minibus. Then I went back to my room, fitted G with her spiky collar and lead, and went off in search of Russell. I had expected to find him in his office, engaged in a desperate effort to find replacement actors to prevent next week's tour being cancelled, but he wasn't there. I was wondering where to try next, when from a room further along the corridor came the sound of raised voices. 'It's quite simple. Just re-script the parts, Samantha.' This delivered in a near shout.

'But, Mr Russell, allocating the part of presenter to Mark won't work. I keep telling you that we need four men for the Holyrood Palace re-enactment, and now that John is in the Royal Infirmary with a suspected fractured skull–'

I crept along, making not a sound as I glided up the corridor, and listened with interest. I'm pretty good at ear-to-keyhole, if I say so myself.

'Really, Samantha, I'm losing patience. I tell you, the tour can't go on without a presenter.' Just what I wanted to hear.

'Then give the part to Sophie.' Russell's tone brooked no argument.

My heart sank.

'But that's ridiculous! Sophie's red hair makes her ideal to play Mary Queen of Scots. Jacqui's too fat for the part, and at fifty years old, she looks more like Queen Victoria than the young Mary! As for Chloe, she's a great actress, but at five foot four she's not tall enough. I've given her the part of Lady Argyle, Mary's lady-in-waiting.'

My hopes rose. Once again to be dashed.

'Let me point out then, Samantha, that Jacqui is the obvious candidate for presenter. So there's no problem at all. Just calm yourself, my dear.'

'Calm yourself, my dear.' Words guaranteed to inflame the female of the species. The condescendingly soothing tone infuriated even me, the eavesdropper. I drew in a deep breath. Had the man no sense?

'Out of the question!' Samantha's voice rose in a shriek. 'As wardrobe mistress she does an excellent job, but her only acting experience is in small walk-on parts. She'd never manage to cope with your script. There's not one, not two, but three pages to memorize.'

'Well, it'll have to be you, Samantha. Now let's hear no more about it.'

In a couple of seconds she'd reluctantly agree and my offer to be presenter might very well come too late. Russell struck me as a man who would be reluctant to alter a decision once made. He'd take it as a sign of weakness. Time to act. I knocked loudly and opened the door. The fate of Operation Red Grouse rested on the next couple of minutes.

'Mr Russell, I thought I heard your voice.' I looked from the one to the other. 'Oh, I do hope I'm not interrupting. It's just that I've had an idea. You see, with my knowledge of the historical background of the places you'll be visiting, I could stand in as presenter, thereby releasing an actor for the re-enactments. And, of course, my cat, Lady, wearing her mediaeval collar is just the sort of thing that audiences will love.'

I twitched sharply at the lead so that G's head came up displaying the spiked collar to perfect advantage. Incensed at the rough treatment, Gorgonzola made a sound as near a growl as a cat can make.

'A wonderful idea!' Samantha jumped at the chance to win the argument. 'That solves our problem, Mr Russell.'

'I suppose...' He rubbed his chin, obviously convinced, but not willing to credit me with an idea better than his own. 'Well, I'm having a crisis meeting with the actors in a few minutes. Let's see what they say about it. Follow me.'

His short tubby figure seemed to bounce rather than walk as he made his way briskly along the corridor ahead of us. 'We're all one big happy family here, Shelagh. No formality, first names are the order of the day. I'll introduce you to the cast.' He flung open a door. 'Here they are.'

I hooked Gorgonzola's lead over a piece of fancy iron scrollwork on the banister of the stairs – her introduction could wait till later – and followed him, confident everything would go smoothly, totally unprepared for the hostile reaction that met me the minute I stepped into the room.

Someone called out, 'Who's this then? Not *another* reporter, are you? If so, you can leave right now.'

Indignant cries followed thick and fast.

'My God, have we not been pestered enough!'

'We've had it up to here with the press!'

Russell turned to me with a muttered explanation. 'They're still in shock, you see. It's barely a week since that awful accident to our actor Geoff Grantham. Reporters descended on us like vultures. No sensitivity at all. Telephoto lenses trained on faces… cars in hot pursuit of the minibus… allegations of jealousy and rivalry in the company. We've all been shaken by it.'

Another shout. 'What rag is she from?' The shouts of protest redoubled.

Through the secretly taken mug shots supplied to Gerry Burnside by the murdered Grantham, I could put a name to each of the angry people staring at me. Perched on the window ledge was Chloe Inglis, unmistakable in Goth makeup and outfit of aggressive spiked collar, studded leather waistcoat and tight stone-washed jeans. Samantha Palmer, producer/scriptwriter, and middle-aged Jacqui Fowler, wardrobe manager, were in possession of the only chairs. Sophie Taylor, identifiable by her red hair, was sitting cross-legged on the floor. The male actors were standing or leaning against the walls. Mark Carpenter, hair gelled into spikes and noticeably taller than the others, was of particular interest to me. He fitted the height and build of the furtive figure I'd seen visiting the garage last night. But Gordon Russell was the only one definitely on my list of suspects. As owner-manager he'd be in an ideal position to organize the shipment of drugs. A calculating and astute criminal brain might lie concealed behind his inept handling of my introduction to the cast and his apparent inability to manage people.

Conscious that he was losing control of the situation, Russell held up both hands, palms outward, a diminutive Canute attempting to fend off a tidal wave of protest. It engulfed him leaving him spluttering incoherently, 'Just a… wait… let me…'

At that moment, the cavalry came galloping – or rather, wandering casually – to the rescue.

'Oh my God, what's that? Jacqui was staring at something behind me. 'Look, it's wearing a collar just like yours, Chloe!'

A burst of laughter released the tension.

I swung round. A large paw, G's tufty head, and the spiked collar had appeared in the gap between the door and the jamb. She stared about her inquisitively and from her throat came the growling purr that told me she'd detected the scent of drugs on someone's clothing.

Smiling, I stepped forward, grabbed the trailing lead and scooped her up. 'Meet Lady, the new publicity prop for Act It Out. And I promise you that I'm not from a newspaper or anything to do with the media. I'm Shelagh Mac–'

'Just a minute, Shelagh. I've an important announcement to make.'

All eyes focused on Russell. Taking out a white handkerchief, he polished his glasses and replaced the handkerchief tidily in his pocket. Confident that he was now the centre of attention, he fingered his black tie, cleared his throat and addressed the cast. 'How this terrible accident to Geoff could possibly have happened is still not clear. For the last seven days we've done our very best to help the police with their investigations.' Tone sombre and measured, that would have done credit to a funeral undertaker, but with no genuine feeling for the dead man. 'It's all most unfortunate, *most* unfortunate. But the show must go on. The scheduled performances will take place. Yes, the show will go on. That's what Geoff would have wanted.'

'A terrible accident,' he had called Grantham's death, but it was no accident, it was murder and one or more of those in the room had to be implicated. There's always a motive for murder – almost certainly, in this case, the money generated by illegal drugs.

Covertly, I studied Jamie Cruikshank, lead actor in performances requiring a romantic role. Fresh-face, designer stubble, engaging smile, he didn't look like a murderer. None of them did. Shakespeare was right, 'there's no art to find the mind's construction in the face'. I turned my attention back to Russell as his eyes swept over the assembled actors.

'Yes, the show must go on, but time is short. I have to remind you that our next scheduled performance is tomorrow.'

'Where is the new actor, then?' Jacqui Palmer jumped to her feet. 'As wardrobe mistress I've got to know whether to alter the costumes or make up new ones. It's not all done in a minute, you know. Sam's damn well right. It's impossible.'

'I'm the boss. It's up to me to make decisions and I've decided that we don't need another male actor.' He put an arm round my shoulder and drew me forward. 'And that's because I've asked Shelagh, here, to join the company.'

I expected smiles of welcome. Instead I became the target of furrowed brows, hostile stares and cries of, 'Should have been consulted. Always need more men than women. Crackpot decision! Can't be serious!'

Russell plucked the handkerchief once more from his pocket and mopped his brow, unintentionally giving the impression of a beleaguered general waving the white flag of surrender.

There was only one way to defuse the situation and keep the mission running. I unclipped G's lead and set her down on the floor.

'Search!' I whispered.

Motivated by the thought of beating up the squeaking rubber mouse as a reward, G made straight for one of the men lounging against the wall and sat at his feet crooning softly.

Gorgonzola had 'fingered', or more accurately pawed, Jamie Cruikshank.

'You've got a lady admirer, Jamie.' Chloe, the Goth, hooted with laughter. 'Must be the kipper you had for breakfast.' That broke the tension.

There was indeed something 'fishy' about Jamie, not the smell of kipper, but the whiff of drugs from his clothes. It might mean something – or nothing. He could merely be a recreational drug user.

I tossed Gorgonzola her mouse-reward and stepped forward. 'I think there's been a bit of a misunderstanding, everybody. I'm definitely not an actor – or a reporter. Mr Russell has engaged me as presenter to introduce the re-enactments.'

'That's what I've being trying to get through your thick heads.' Wiping his glasses, he tucked the flag of surrender back into his pocket. 'We don't now need to employ another male actor because I've engaged Shelagh as presenter. But changes in roles, of course, have had to be made and you'll just have to accept them.' Whether you like it or not, went unsaid but hung heavily in the air.

I wanted to shriek in his ear. 'Appeal for their co-operation, damn you!' But I could only stand there with sinking heart awaiting their reaction.

Russell consulted a sheet of paper. 'You as scriptwriter, Samantha, will need to work it out.'

She leapt to her feet. 'But just a minute, that means I'll have to rewrite most of the scenes and... and...'

'It's what I pay you for, Samantha.' He waved his hand as if swatting away an irritating fly, and swept on. 'Any other objections?'

Unable to come up with an alternative solution to the problem of being a male actor short, no one spoke up.

'Well, that's agreed then.' A self-congratulatory nod of satisfaction for matters well-handled, and he was gone.

I breathed a sigh of relief. Operation Red Grouse, so nearly derailed, was back on track.

But, alas, not for long. And this time, it was me, DJ Smith who nearly brought about disaster.

Chapter Nine

At first, all went well with no hint that anything might go wrong. The atmosphere lightened with Russell's departure. One by one the cast came forward to shake my hand and welcome me to the company.

'Just love those spikes! Shows class!' Chloe pounced on Gorgonzola, hugged her tightly and flicked the collar with her finger.

Outraged by being handled without her consent, G wriggled free from her grasp, snatched up the mouse and made a swift escape via the half-open window.

'Nothing personal,' I soothed as Chloe eyed the scratch on her hand. 'It's just that she got a bit of a fright when you picked her up suddenly like that. Lady's a very nervous cat.'

Nothing, of course, was further from the truth. G had nerves of steel, but she was sending a stern message to Chloe. 'I will decide when to be friendly.' Cats hate being grabbed and held tightly by strangers.

'Her name's Lady, did you say? Some lady!' She dabbed at the trickle of blood with a paper handkerchief. 'Queen Boudicca's more like it. She's even got claws like scythes to prove it.'

'Her name's not just Lady, it's Lady Macbeth,' I said, thinking Chloe might feel better disposed towards her if she knew G bore the name of one of Shakespeare's more famous characters.

That's when things went horribly wrong.

'What on earth possessed you to give your cat that name?'

I stared at her, nonplussed. 'What's wrong with that? Lady's my cat, and I'm Shelagh Macbeth so–'

'You've done it again!' Chloe shrieked. 'Surely you know never to mention that name in the theatre or in the company of actors? It's *such* bad luck!'

Samantha's voice shook with anger. 'Haven't we had enough bad luck already with… with what happened to Geoff?'

Cue for accusing looks and cries of, 'She'll have to go!'

'With a name like that we can't possibly have her as our presenter.'

'Sure to bring disaster!'

'That bastard Russell kept her name from us. Didn't want us to find out before the next performance, did he?'

Bastard indeed for not warning me. If he'd done so, I'd have told the cast that my name was Mack or MacIntyre – anything, even Smith. Russell hadn't warned me. He had been so desperate to hire someone, anyone, to keep the show on the road, as he'd put it, that he'd taken me on, gambling that when the cast discovered my ill-starred name, they would jettison superstition in favour of employment and cash in the hand. It seemed he'd miscalculated.

Alan jumped up onto Samantha's vacated chair. 'If that woman stays, we go on strike. Let's take a vote on it.'

With only seconds to make them change their minds, I cried, 'The cat's name is Lady but not Lady M–' only just preventing myself from saying the forbidden word. 'I'm so sorry. I thought it was a clever idea to add that… that… extra name because we would be working with actors. I'll call her something else, like…' I frowned, desperately racking my brain. '… like, let's say… Gorgonzola.'

A burst of laughter gave me a few more vital seconds of thinking time.

'Actually, the… er… M name was my married name. Now that I'm divorced I'm Shelagh Smith again.'

Alan exchanged glances with the others, then jumped down from the chair. 'Just a mo' while we have a council of war.'

If there was some arcane superstition among actors involving the name Smith, Operation Red Grouse was doomed. I had nobody to blame but myself – and Gerry Burnside – for when I had made that ill-omened choice of cover-name and he had agreed to it, neither of us had for a moment considered the superstitious world of the theatre.

They went into a huddle, heads together. My hopes rose and sank with each word or phrase that drifted my way.

'… something to be said for what she…'

'… don't like it. Sure to be another accident if…'

'… but that means more days without pay.'

'We've no other choice, have we?'

At last, they came to an agreement and the huddle broke up. Stay or go, what was the verdict?

Jacqui stepped forward. 'We have decided that' – theatrical pause to prolong the suspense – 'Shelagh Smith and the formidable Lady Gorgonzola can join the company as presenters of enactments.'

'So pleased to be able to help you out,' I said with just the right degree of enthusiasm. 'Now tell me exactly what I've volunteered for as presenter.'

Mark-of-the-Gelled-Hair shook my hand. 'Thanks for rescuing me from that role. Good luck! You'll be responsible for outlining the historical background at each location and setting the scene in an interesting way – pretty impossible with Russell's boring script. It's in my room. Come with me and I'll give it to you.'

He led the erstwhile Lady Macbeth and myself upstairs to the rooms allocated to Act It Out in the original servants' quarters at the rear of the Shooting Lodge. His room was sorely lacking in comfort compared with mine. It was sparsely furnished: two single beds with blankets and quilt, a couple of rugs on white-painted floorboards, and on the wall a cheap sun-faded print of a Victorian lady and gent. An electric kettle, a couple of mugs, a battered biscuit tin and a box of teabags stood on a tray on top of a chest of drawers. Washbasin, wardrobe, small table and two chairs made up the rest of the contents.

'Here's the script.' He thrust the pages into my hand with a breezy, 'Russell's compiled the necessary historical information. It's his pride and joy. Don't dare to change a word of it, not a word. Read, digest, memorize, and have the presentation perfect in time for tomorrow's re-enactment in Holyrood Palace. By the way, if you decide to stay on after this week to help us out for a bit, the room next to mine will be yours. Want to see it?'

He turned the handle of the room next door, then paused in the doorway. 'Not superstitious are you, Shelagh? This room's definitely got a jinx on it. Poor old Geoff shared it with Robbie, our props man. Now one's dead and the other's a nervous wreck.'

Just in time, I stopped myself from revealing that I knew exactly what he meant – a fatal error if he was part of the drug organisation.

'Oh,' I said, 'what happened? When he was introducing me to the actors, Mr Russell did refer to some terrible accident.'

'Geoff was stabbed with a faulty prop while playing the part of Polonius in a Hamlet re-enactment.' He closed his eyes for an instant as if to shut out the scene. 'Props man blames himself.'

He didn't elaborate and I didn't press him. This room was a carbon copy of his own, even down to the same cheap faded print on the wall.

I walked over to the window. 'I'll definitely be staying till you get someone else. And I think I'll make a start on reading the script right now. It's nice and quiet up here, no interruptions.'

'You've got till rehearsals at two this afternoon to memorize the script. Good luck, or break a leg, as we actors say.' He paused in the doorway. 'If I were you, I'd seriously consider changing your mind about volunteering. You know what they say, bad luck comes in threes. There has to be a third accident – and the third unlucky sod could be you.' This said without the trace of a smile.

The door closed quietly behind him and I heard him clattering his way down the stairs, whistling a dirge-like tune as he went, perhaps recalling that only eight days ago his fellow actor, Geoff Grantham, had left this very room for the evening re-enactment, never to return. The thought sobered me too, but dwelling on the risks run by HMRC agents was a waste of time. After all, it was my chosen career. I felt pretty confident that my cover was still intact. Nevertheless, in view of what had happened to Geoff Grantham I'd have to be very careful, very careful indeed if I wanted to avoid the same fate myself. Better to concentrate on working out how my fellow agent had aroused suspicion.

I sat at the window, the sheaf of script papers in my hand still unread, my thoughts elsewhere. Besides Russell, two of the company were already worthy of investigation. Jamie Cruikshank's drug-contaminated clothing had been targeted by Gorgonzola. If drugs were being transported in a hidden compartment of the minibus or in a suitcase, Cruikshank as the driver would surely know about it. The other obvious suspect was Mark Carpenter of the spiked hair. What lawful reason could he have had to creep to the garage in the middle of the night, and what had kept him there so long?

The clatter of footsteps on the stairs and the sound of a nearby door closing reminded me that the afternoon rehearsal was only a few hours away and I'd have to get down to reading the script. Judging by this morning's set-to with the cast, it was obvious that Russell was a man who took any divergence of opinion from his own as a challenge to his authority, so I set about memorizing the script word for word.

It was hard work to inject life into something so boring. An hour or so had passed when I heard footsteps on the stairs and Mark Carpenter's door open and close. Too intent on committing to memory Russell's turgid script, three pages of historical introduction featuring the murder in Holyrood Palace of Rizzio, Mary Queen of Scots' Italian secretary, I didn't pay much attention to the indistinct murmur of voices on the other side of the wall. Was I word perfect? I launched into my speech in front of a captive audience, a well-fed Gorgonzola lounging at ease in a shallow depression on the quilt. After a couple of minutes I slowed to a halt. This deadly script wouldn't hold the attention of *any* audience.

'It's dull, dry as dust, boring,' I sighed. 'What do you think?'

A gentle snore drifted up from the furry heap on the bed. Even the most discreet changes of wording would antagonize Russell. And that would be a bad move. The script would have to remain as it was. I decided to give up, have a cup of tea and nibble on a biscuit.

As I stood beside the kettle waiting for it to boil, something more interesting than the script caught my attention, raised voices on the other side of the thin partition wall.

'Load of tosh, Jamie!' Mark's voice, exasperated. 'I think you're just being bloody-minded. Give me the keys of the garage and the van so I can load the props into the minibus tonight. It'll make all the difference. You know what a hassle it is if everything's left to the last minute.'

'No! What part of the word 'no' do you have difficulty with, Mark? I've told you why I'm not giving you the keys.' Each word rapped out slowly and clearly as to a child of limited understanding. 'But I'll tell you again in words of one syllable. If you load the props and I am not there to show you how to stow them, it will make more work for me, take me more time, a lot more time. No means *no!*'

I was impressed. Two whole sentences using words of only one syllable!

Carpenter must have turned away because his voice dropped to a murmur. A few seconds later, the flimsy wall shook as the door of the adjoining room slammed shut. Footsteps hurried past my room and down the stairs.

I dipped a teabag in and out of the mug of boiling water, picked a slightly stale digestive biscuit from the tin, and nibbled at it while waiting for the tea to cool. Carpenter's desperation to gain access to the garage tonight indicated that he hadn't found what he'd been looking for last night.

And what was behind Jamie Cruikshank's adamant refusal to allow him unsupervised entry to the garage? Everyone likes his own way of working, but did Cruikshank really think that Carpenter would be incapable of loading the van properly?

Much more likely that there was something in the garage or minibus that he didn't want anyone to see, perhaps drugs that had been transferred to the minibus during the hours of darkness.

I'd keep watch from my window, so there'd be no sleep for me tonight. Which did not augur well for my debut as presenter for the re-enactment at Holyrood Palace. Forgetting my lines, making mistakes and stumbling were forgivable during rehearsals, not before an audience. But tomorrow morning would be time enough to worry about that.

Meanwhile opportunity knocked while the minibus was away on the trip to Stirling Castle. It was the chance to find out if the garage or the neighbouring buildings were being used to store drugs for onward transportation. I'd take Meffy, then G, for a walk in the courtyard. I looked at my watch – only an hour before I had to join the actors for lunch. No time for separate walks. I'd have to find a way of taking them out together on my reconnaissance mission.

I gave G a gentle poke. 'Walkies.'

I dangled the mouse invitingly, and clipped on her lead while she yawned and stretched. That was the easy bit. On my way to the guest bedrooms in the main lodge I worked out tactics to prevent Meffy and G inflicting grievous bodily harm on each other. It wouldn't do for Hermione to return from Stirling to find her beloved Meffy scratched and bleeding.

Back in my own room, I unclipped G's lead, leaving the spiky collar round her neck to underline to her that she was still on duty, then unlocked the sash window, pushing it up a fraction to leave enough of a gap for my fingers to prise it up from outside. Their first face-to-face meeting would be through glass. If I stood outside the window holding Meffy firmly so he'd feel safe from attack, and tapped to summon Gorgonzola, all should be well.

Whispering reassurances, I pushed open the door of the Hermione's room to be greeted with a volley of suspicious *yip yip yips*. It's difficult to know what cats are thinking, but dogs are open books. They love to be petted, and respond accordingly. So, ignoring this challenge, I picked Meffy up and after a few cuddles and endearments he stopped squirming in an effort to escape, and relaxed, content to view the world from the elevated position of my arms. Before I left the room, I pocketed his toy, the much-chewed pink rat, for emergency use as a distraction.

All went according to plan. Cat and dog stared at each other warily through the glass, then each recalling the dismal consequences of yesterday's fun and games, airily pretended the other did not exist. I put Meffy down on the ground and while he was sniffing around, pushed up the window. When Gorgonzola poked her head and shoulders out onto the sill, I pressed the radio button disguised as the nameplate on the collar and pointed in the direction of the garage. 'Search!'

I fussed and petted Meffy while G was making her way across the courtyard. When she was close to the garage, I strolled leisurely off in the opposite direction with Meffy on his lead. To anyone watching, Shelagh appeared to be listening on an earpiece to music on her mobile phone while walking

Hermione's dog. In fact, the earpiece and its wire trailing into a pocket was the radio receiver to bring in G's signal. I didn't have long to wait.

Croooo…

Casually I tugged at Meffy's lead and turned back towards the garage. Gorgonzola was sitting in front of the doors, confidently anticipating her rubber toy reward. As we approached, I tossed it to her. A mistake. Meffy lunged forward in pursuit of the mouse. Just in time I hauled hard on his lead, pulling him up short. G got there first, snatched up her prize and shot round the side of building.

Yip yip yip yip.

'Shut up, Meffy!' I clung onto the lead, digging hurriedly in my pocket with my free hand to extricate his pink rat.

Yip yip yip yip. The frustrated yelps of protest redoubled in volume.

'Shelagh! Meffy!' At that inopportune moment, Hermione and the minibus had returned.

The afternoon rehearsals went far better than I'd expected, so I was confident all would go smoothly tomorrow at the re-enactment of the murder of Rizzio, Mary Queen of Scots' secretary. As I snuggled down under the duvet that night, I congratulated myself on the progress I'd made with Operation Red Grouse. I'd ascertained from G's reaction that the garage was indeed being used for the storage of drugs, and I was more convinced than ever of the likelihood that some or all of the guests on this tour were pseudo-tourists, a means to enable drugs to be transported round the country. Perhaps most promising of all, I'd been accepted into the company. And that left the door open to make further discoveries.

Chapter Ten

Next day, when my fellow guests set off for a tour round Edinburgh culminating with the evening visit to Holyrood Palace, I wasn't with them as Gorgonzola and I were to travel with the actors. When Jamie swung open the garage doors, I was interested to see a black Mercedes standing alongside the empty space previously occupied by the tour minibus. While Jamie was manoeuvring the actors' minibus out of the garage, I wandered over, pretending to admire the car's polished gleaming bodywork, but in reality searching for an imperfection to identify the vehicle even if the number plates were changed. And I found one, a tiny chip in the glass of the nearside rear indicator light.

The interior of the garage was empty of boxes or packages. I looked down at G on her lead, sitting at my feet. This time, no croon. The drugs had been moved.

Jacqui paused, one foot on the step of the minibus. 'Come on, Shelagh, jump in. We're on a tight schedule. I've got to get everybody dressed and made up. Can't be done in a rush, you know. It all takes time.'

The only vacant seat was in the back row beside Mark Carpenter. As I sat down and made G comfortable on my knee, he was staring out of the window, face set in a scowl, and didn't even acknowledge my presence with a smile or greeting. Chloe leaned across with a friendly smile. 'Don't take any notice of him. Nothing personal. He's been in a foul mood with all of us since he had some sort of a burst up with Jamie yesterday.'

'He's a prat!' Mark's scowl deepened. 'Insisting on loading the props all by himself! That's why we're running fifteen minutes late this morning. Didn't listen, did he? If he'd let me make a start last night, we–'

The engine revved and the minibus jolted forward as Jamie put his foot down heavily on the accelerator. He was in a bad mood too. Fertile ground for an agent to pick up information. Things are often said in anger that should be left unsaid.

We'd been driving for perhaps five minutes when Gorgonzola shifted restlessly in my arms. Nose twitching, she climbed up onto my shoulder, stepped carefully over the back of the seat and started sniffing round the assorted boxes of props stowed in the luggage compartment of the minibus.

'She's a real busybody,' I said with a laugh as the best way of making her actions seem harmless. 'I should have called her Nosy Parker.'

I twisted round to see which of the boxes she'd home in on. After a cursory sniff at the costume trunk, she lingered for a few moments at a piece of carpet between two wicker baskets, then moved on to investigate the rest of the props before returning to sniff again at the carpet. I waited for the croon.

None came, confirmation that drugs had been stored in the minibus but were no longer there. Were the drugs now in the guests' minibus for one of them to pass on to street dealers? More than likely.

'Here, Lady.' To distract her I held up the grey mouse,

dangling it invitingly by its tail.

With G sitting once more on my lap and patting happily at the mouse, I stared thoughtfully out at the passing scenery. When Val had left the group at Falkland Palace with the excuse that the gift shop was more interesting than a boring game of Real tennis, had she too used a distraction tactic on her return? She had left carrying a duffel bag and had made a point of drawing attention both to her absence and to the duffel bag. At Holyrood I'd be on the lookout for Val – or anyone else – slipping away from the group.

The re-enactment was to take place at eight o'clock this evening to replicate as closely as possible the time of Mary Queen of Scott's fateful supper party, with candlelight and darkness adding an enjoyable frisson to the scene.

The actors had told me we'd need two hours to prepare for the performance, so our minibus arrived just after the six o'clock closure of the Palace to the public. Even though I'd driven past the building many times on the occasions I'd been based in Edinburgh, I'd never seen it look so splendid. A spectacularly fiery sunset reflected in the tall multi-paned windows was staining the stone of the chateau-like frontage and turrets blood-red, appropriate in view of the bloody event we were about to re-enact.

The drama was lost on Jamie as he drove across the vast stretch of forecourt, his only comment being, 'We've got special permission to park at the Queen's front door.'

He rounded an ornate stone fountain and drew up with a squeal of brakes in front of a door rather small for a grand entrance, but rendered impressive by double pillars soaring the height of the building and the massive royal coat of arms sculpted in stone above the lintel.

First out of the bus, Samantha led the way into the Palace. 'We'll leave the men to haul the boxes to the rooms allocated as dressing rooms, while we take you upstairs to show you the Bed Chamber, the Supper Room and where Rizzio's body was found.'

With Gorgonzola on the lead, I followed the three of them past the inner courtyard, up the main staircase and through a succession of rooms with panelled walls hung with portraits and lined with tapestries until we reached a small dimly-lit room dominated by a sombre portrait of Mary Queen of Scots dressed in black and holding a crucifix and prayer book. Inset in the dark background of the picture was a disturbing vignette of what the future held for her: an executioner with axe raised, her head on the block, blood streaming from her neck.

Chloe sighed. 'Love this picture, all that black and gloom. Got a print of it on my wall. She's an honorary Goth in my book. Be sure to stop here on the tour, Shelagh, to get the clients in the right mood.'

'Shut up and leave this to me, Chloe. It's the producer who gives the instructions, not the actors.' Samantha turned to me. 'Stand here so that they look at the portrait while you give your introduction, then you take them up to Mary's Bed Chamber and the Supper Room for the first part of the re-enactment by Sophie, Mark and Chloe. Now lead the way up the stairs, Shelagh, as if we're the guests.'

A narrow twisting stairway with iron handrail took us up to a spacious Bed Chamber with curtained four-poster bed, walls hung with heavy tapestries depicting classic scenes, and wood-panelled ceiling. For the occasion, a fire had been lit in the blue-and-white tiled fireplace and imitation candles shed a soft light.

'So this is the Supper Room.' Cosy, I thought, yet with a sinister history. 'This is where Rizzio was murdered.'

'Oh, no, we're in the Queen's Bed Chamber.' Sophie pointed to a curtain beside the door to the stair. 'The Supper Room is behind that. It's where Mary and Rizzio – that's Mark and me – will be talking and laughing when Tarquin, Alan and Jamie rush in and Mark gets dragged away.'

She held the heavy curtain aside for me to step into a tiny room hung with tapestries, one wall taken up by a tiled fireplace, another by a window. A carved oak table, a high-backed chair and a padded stool filled most of the floor space.

'I'm Lady Argyle, Mary's lady-in-waiting.' Chloe subsided onto the stool. A knowing wink and a leer in Sophie's direction. 'And chaperone.'

Pretending not to notice Sophie's flush at the hint of a relationship between herself and Mark, I sat down on the chair to warm my hands at the fire.

'Candlelight and a flickering fire – how cosy and romantic. I suppose this is the sixteenth century equivalent of the snug. When Darnley and the soldiers rushed in, there couldn't have been much room for so many–'

Jacqui poked her head through the door curtain. 'Better get changed. The wardrobe box and props will have been carried up from the bus by now. It'll take time for us all to get into costume, especially you, Shelagh, as you've not done this sort of thing before.'

I stood up. 'At least G's ready. She's in her costume.'

As if she understood her moment of stardom was

imminent, G stretched first one foreleg, then the other, to show off to advantage her menacing spiky collar.

In the room assigned to the women as a dressing room, I stood surveying myself in the mirror. For the presentation I'd somehow assumed that I would be wearing my own twenty-first century clothes. Now here I was, the very image of a sixteenth-century lady of the court in a long gown with tight bodice and puff sleeves. A close-fitting crescent-shaped cap with a trailing hood concealed my short twenty-first-century hairstyle. I ran my finger round my neck in an attempt to ease the stiffly starched ruff, wondering how the women of the past put up with the discomfort. Gorgonzola sat at my feet, gazing with some suspicion at her reflection in the mirror, debating whether that cat was an intruder asking to be trashed. To distract her, I stooped, gathered her up, and turned away from the mirror. Together we'd make the perfect introduction for the dramatic scene about to be acted out.

Sophie and Chloe similarly dressed to myself, only more luxuriously as befitted the Queen and her lady in waiting, were applying their make-up, while Jacqui in doublet, short slashed breeches and thigh-length boots for her part as a conspirator, was having some trouble gluing on a short beard and moustache.

Samantha looked up from gathering Sophie's hair into a knot. 'You won't need make-up, Shelagh. Give us a shout when the tour bus drives through the gates. That'll give us half an hour to finish and get into position.'

I wandered over to the window. By now it was dark, the looming bulk of Arthur's Seat barely visible, the courtyard patterned by rectangles from the lighted windows of the royal apartments open for Russell's exclusive tour. By craning my neck I could see the two ornate lamps shedding pools of welcoming light at the main entrance.

I didn't have long to wait. Headlights blazed through the wrought-ironwork of the gates on the other side of the courtyard as a vehicle drew up. Act It Out's guests had arrived. It would be easy for any one of them to linger in a room examining the tapestries or portraits until the rest had moved on, then wander off from the others. Tonight there'd be little chance of spotting a drug transfer.

I put G down and attached her lead. 'That's the bus now. I'll go along to wait in the Great Gallery for Mr Russell to complete his part of the tour.'

Samantha looked at her watch. 'It's five past eight. We'll be in position in the supper room at a quarter to nine. When the tour arrives at the foot of the stairs you'll hear Mark playing the lute. It's the signal that we're ready.'

G and I were waiting in the Queen's AnteChamber when Russell led the fellow guests towards me.

'Sorry we're a little behind schedule. I allowed everyone to take their time as we went through the rooms. I'm afraid some became a little too engrossed…' He turned to the group. 'This is where the re-enactment begins. I'll leave you in Shelagh's capable hands.'

'Is that really you, Shelagh?' Hermione's surprise turned to admiration. 'That gown is simply gorgeous.'

Val bent to scratch Gorgonzola gently between the ears. 'And isn't Lady sweet!'

Brad and Rob were studying the ornately plastered ceiling, paying me no attention, taking my changed appearance for granted. Marie Stuart said nothing. She wasn't there.

As Russell strode away, I called after him, 'What's happened to Marie? Have I to wait for her before I begin?'

'No, no.' He barely paused to reply. 'She prefers to visit her father's grave in the Abbey. I'm deferring to her wishes by taking her there while the re-enactment is in progress. She's waiting downstairs for me. A guest's wish is our command.' With that he moved briskly away.

Val frowned. 'Why on earth does she want to go and look at a tombstone now, when she could see it any time?'

Hermione sighed. 'Perhaps she couldn't bear to see her dear Rizzio murdered again.'

A snort of derision from Brad. 'As soon as she saw the Palace, she spouted enough tears to fill a bucket. Typical hysterical female. And Rob encouraged her by marching up and down playing his bloody pipes. No offence, but that screech is enough to make anyone burst into tears!'

Rob glowered. 'Offence taken!' His fists clenched.

Marie's absence confirmed my theory that the guests were couriers. At Falkland it had been Val and Rob; at Holyrood it was Marie. And tomorrow at Loch Leven, someone else.

With G on her lead, I signalled the group to follow me through to that dark little room with the sombre portrait of Mary Queen of Scots inset with its sixteenth-century thumbnail sketch of her execution. I launched into my presentation, keeping strictly to Russell's uninspiring introductory script in case he was lurking within earshot to check up on me.

When I finished, a surreptitious glance at my watch hidden under the lace cuffs of my costume revealed that it was now ten minutes to nine, five minutes after the notes of Mark's lute should have drifted down from the Supper Room. Something must have gone wrong. For a few minutes more I did my best to play for time: asked for questions (none), directed them to peer more closely at the portrait, (they'd done that already), and to examine the embroidered coverlet of a bed in a glass enclosure (of interest only to Hermione).

Sensing an increasing restiveness among my captive audience, I beckoned the group over to the foot of the stairs leading to the Bed Chamber and set the scene for the re-enactment in the Supper Room, spicing things up with a couple of quotes from the poet Alfred Noyes.

'You are now in the ancient palace of Holyrood "where the blood rust sears floors a-flutter of old with silks and laces". I pointed dramatically to the portrait of Mary Queen of Scots. 'See! There she is, "gliding, a ghostly Queen, through a mist of tears." It's the night of the murder, the ninth of March 1566. In a room at the top of these stairs, that romantically tragic figure and her secretary and court musician, the dashing David Rizzio, are enjoying an intimate meal together. Imagine… candlelight, logs crackling in the fireplace.' Dramatic pause. 'Let us go up and observe.'

I picked up Gorgonzola. Hoping that by now the problem, whatever it was, had been sorted out and the scene I'd conjured up was indeed what we would see, I led my little party up the narrow twisting stairs and pushed open the door of the Bed Chamber.

Through the heavy curtain closing off the entrance to the Supper Room, I could hear the crackle of logs sparking and spitting in the fireplace, but disquietingly, no murmur of voices, not even the lightest strum of a hand brushing lute strings.

I put G down and drew aside the curtain. In the small

inner room the flames in the fireplace cast a rosy glow over the pewter wine goblets and the table set with platters of food. No actors. No Mary. No Rizzio. No Lady Argyle.

Whatever had gone wrong, the explanation would have to wait. Now it was up to me to dramatize the events of that terrible night. I stood aside and motioned for the others to enter the Supper Room. For a few moments I allowed them to soak up the atmosphere, then dropped my voice to a whisper.

'Rizzio is sitting at Mary's feet playing the lute. A romantic and peaceful scene. But listen... Do you hear the soft scuff of footsteps on the stairs? The murderers are even now creeping towards this room.' My eyes swept over the little group, pleased to note that they were hanging on every word. 'In less than three minutes, Rizzio will be...' I lowered my voice, '...dead.'

A satisfyingly sharp intake of breath from my audience.

Encouraged, I let my imagination rip. 'The door crashes back against the wall. Mary's jealous husband, Lord Darnley, and his armed men rush in. Lighted candle, wine goblets, roast goose, tumble to the floor from the overturned table...' I swept both hands downwards in graphic illustration. 'Mary screams. Rizzio clings in desperation to her skirts.' I fell to my knees and grasped empty air in desperate supplication. 'But he is dragged from here, his heels ploughing through the rushes on the floor.'

I leapt to my feet and darted across to a door at the far side of the Bed Chamber, beckoning them to follow. 'And through there, in the outer chamber of the Queen's Apartments' – a long pause heightened the tension – 'he is stabbed fifty, sixty times.' Violent stabbing motions.

'Yes, in the next room,' I slowly turned the door handle, 'in a pool of blood lies the lifeless body of David Rizzio.' Sending up a silent prayer that the actor playing the dead Rizzio was in position, I flung open the door to the murder room and stood aside as the group crowded past me, followed by an inquisitive Gorgonzola, never one to pass by something to investigate. Would Rizzio's 'body' be lying in a pool of fake blood or would they merely see the brass plaque marking the spot where his body had been left five hundred years ago? Gasps, a little scream, told me that the murder re-enactment was of a very professional standard indeed. This scene, at least, had gone to plan.

On the far side of the room they were gathered round the 'body'. All I could see of Mark was his feet.

Excited murmurs, 'Very lifelike.'

'Fooled me for a moment.'

I relaxed. Even Gorgonzola had been taken in by the realistic corpse, for she had stopped in the doorway, standing rigid, fur raised. I gave the group a couple of minutes to indulge their morbid fascination with death.

'Tone, stand beside the corpse and make like you're one of the murderers.' Val held up her mobile phone. 'That's right. Go for it! Stab! Stab! Stab!'

Hermione came over to join me in the doorway. 'This is extremely well done, Shelagh. The make-up is particularly good, the face quite, quite pallid, but it's all a little too realistic for my liking.'

'Tone, stop that play-acting and get a look at this!' Val had wandered over to the middle of the room and was peering into a showcase displaying royal mementos.

I clapped my hands to attract the group's attention. 'Mary Queen of Scots, never forgave her husband, Lord Darnley, for

Rizzio's death. And a year later, almost to the day, Darnley was murdered by unknown hands. And how do you think it was done?'

Val and Tony looked at each other. 'Poisoned?'

'Same way as Rizzio, I'd say.' Brad made a stabbing motion. Hermione pursed her lips.

'Was he shot?'

'You're all wrong.' Rob's confidence challenged anyone to argue. 'He was blown up. No doubt about it.'

Ever the diplomat, I said, 'A tremendous explosion did indeed demolish the house at Kirk o' Fields where Darnley was staying. And that is certainly the story put about at the time. But it wasn't the explosion that killed him... His body was found in the garden. Strangled. It's a five-hundred-year-old Mystery Whodunit.'

I cut through the buzz of speculation. Mark Carpenter had managed to remain heroically corpselike up till now, but he wouldn't be able to hold that position much longer.

'That's the end of the re-enactment. Go back through the Bed Chamber and down the spiral staircase. A Palace official will take you to the Palace shop where you'll find books about Mary Queen of Scots and the murder of Darnley. You've half an hour to browse before the minibus picks you up.'

When my group had chattered its way down the stairs, I approached the corpse.

'Good show, Mark. You'd win an Oscar for acting dead. What's the secret of keeping so still and appearing not to breathe?'

No change in his expression, not a flicker of an eyelid, not a twitch of a muscle.

I couldn't keep the irritation out of my voice. 'Why were you not in the Supper Room playing the lute, and what happened to Sophie, Chloe and the rest? That could have been a disaster.'

No response.

'Your audience has gone, joke's over. No need to overdo it.' I looked down at Mark Carpenter and took a deep breath.

That patch of blood near his heart looked disturbingly real. Alarmed, I felt for a pulse at his neck. No heartbeat, but his skin was still warm. The actor's make-up had disguised the pallor of skin that comes with death.

Gorgonzola was still rigid in the doorway, fur raised.

'You knew he was dead, didn't you, G? You weren't fooled.'

I'd left my phone in the dressing room with my twentieth-century clothes. My sixteenth-century costume might be elaborate and richly decorated, but it had one big defect – no pockets. He was beyond the help of paramedics, but the sooner the police arrived to protect the crime scene the better.

I gathered up Gorgonzola and as quickly as the hampering folds of the heavy gown would allow, hurried off in search of a Palace official and a phone. Through the Bed Chamber… down the spiral staircase… along the passage towards the front entrance. Nobody in the Queen's apartments. In the Great Gallery, the red carpet stretched emptily ahead. Nobody in the King's apartments.

Nobody in the Drawing Rooms or the Throne Room. I paused at the foot of the main staircase. Where were the Palace staff, where were the actors? Everyone seemed to have melted into thin air. Surely there must be somebody in the building, even if just the caretaker to lock up after the re-enactment.

'Hello? Anybody there?'

The stone of staircase and walls swallowed the sound. However loudly I shouted, they wouldn't hear me in the Palace shop located across the expanse of forecourt.

'Hello? Anybody there?'

No answering call, no approaching footsteps. Nothing.

Then faint, so faint that I almost missed it, a *thump... thump... thump* coming from across the quadrangle to my left. I pushed open a door and recognised it as the corridor allocated to Act It Out for their dressing rooms.

'Hello?' I shouted again.

'Help! We're locked in!' A man's voice muffled by the thickness of the wood came from two doors along.

I stooped to let G jump from my arms and ran forward. The key was in the lock. At the sound of the key turning, an angry voice yelled, 'This is one stupid joke too far, Mark, you bastard!'

I flung open the door.

'Bloody well ruined the–'

'What the hell–?'

The male actors stared at me in astonishment.

Tarquin was the first to recover. 'Give it to us straight, Shelagh. All day Mark's been in a foul mood. Still was, when he left to get into position in the Supper Room. And he locked us in to ruin the re-enactment, didn't he? Now he's too yellow to come and let us out.'

'Russell will kill him for this.' Jamie seemed to relish the prospect.

Somebody had indeed killed him, I thought grimly.

To them, I said, 'I don't know if it was Mark who locked you in, but he's had a serious accident, very serious. Who's got a phone?'

'Had it coming to him, eh, guys!' Jamie looked round at the others for agreement.

'Give it a rest, Jamie.' Tarquin was rummaging through the pile of shirts, jeans and jackets on the floor. 'Look at Shelagh's face. This is really serious.' He found a mobile and looked at me, eyebrows raised. 'Ambulance?'

'And police. He's been stabbed. He's dead.' That sobered them. Even Jamie.

I stood in front of the door to prevent any of them leaving. 'There's nothing we can do for him,' I sighed. 'It's a crime scene. All we can do is stay here till the police come.'

We waited in silence.

Who had had the opportunity to kill Mark? All the male actors had an alibi, likewise the female actors who must also have been locked in their dressing room. My fellow tour guests had gone from room to room together escorted by Russell. And when he left me, he too had created an alibi for himself and Marie by announcing for all to hear that he was going off to the Abbey ruins to show her the grave of King James the Fifth.

Then the realization hit me. Everybody had an alibi. I didn't.

The finger of suspicion for the murder of Mark Carpenter was definitely pointing at me.

Chapter Eleven

'Now, Ms Macbeth, perhaps you could go over that once more...'

I'd lost count of the times I'd had to repeat my version of what happened. The police were looking for inconsistencies in my account so they could pounce – normal technique for interrogating a suspect. They made a point of informing me that I was the only one on the premises whose movements could not be verified. As I'd thought, all the other actors had been found locked in their dressing rooms; Russell and Marie had furnished each other with an alibi; and Russell's tour group had vouched for each other, as had the few Palace staff on duty for the evening.

'But,' the detective leaned forward and stared into my eyes, 'nobody saw you from the time you left the dressing room to the time you started your presentation in the Queen's Ante-Chamber. Tell me exactly what you did in those twenty-five minutes?' Over and over again that casual question designed to trap.

I sighed and for the umpteenth time repeated my account of how I had passed the time. 'Well, as I've told you already, I spent some minutes studying that striking picture of Mary Queen of Scots – the one with the grisly execution scene in the background.'

'And then?' As if not paying much attention to what I was saying, having heard this many times before, the detective leaned back in his chair and fixed his eyes on an irregular brown stain on the ceiling. Another interrogation tactic in the hope that I might make a mistake, change something in my account that would indicate I was lying.

'As I've told you,' I tried to keep the irritation out of my voice, 'I was going over in my mind the main points of the coming presentation.' Even to me, my story seemed thinner and less convincing every time I repeated it.

He lowered his gaze from contemplation of the ceiling, scepticism in his eyes. 'So during this time, the twenty-five minutes when you were alone, you would have had ample opportunity to arrange to meet Mr Carpenter, perhaps on the pretext of going over your script. That's what happened, wasn't it?' he said softly.

'No, it damned well wasn't!' Despite having been trained to remain calm in situations like this, my voice rose to a shriek. 'Whoever killed Mark, it wasn't me!'

He sighed and pressed the button to switch off the recording machine. 'I'm afraid we'll have to ask you to spend the night at the police station, Ms Macbeth. Expect further questioning in the morning.'

I wasn't surprised.

So G and I spent the night in custody. G slept peacefully, curled up next to me, an occasional gentle snore indicating sweet untroubled dreams. I tossed and turned, kept awake by the questions churning in my head. Who had killed Mark Carpenter? The murder must be linked to the drug ring. So how relevant was Carpenter's row with Jamie Cruikshank over loading the minibus in the garage? And what about...? I wasn't aware of my eyelids closing.

The next morning, to my surprise, there was no further questioning. Something had convinced the police that I was telling the truth, and at midday I was free to go. On one condition: I, along with everyone who had been at Holyrood Palace last night, must remain at the Shooting Lodge until permission was given to leave.

I had a lot to think about. Now that guests and the Act It Out actors were at the centre of a murder investigation, the present tour would without doubt be cancelled, bringing to an end my successful infiltration of the company. There was nothing I could do to rescue Operation Red Grouse. The murder of Mark Carpenter had dealt it a fatal blow.

I had been allowed to change into trousers and sweater before leaving the Palace last night – not to save me embarrassment, but because the gown was required for forensic examination. It was no consolation that on my release from the police station I could walk through the streets of Edinburgh in my twenty-first century clothes rather than the sixteenth-century court gown complete with stiffly starched ruff. The police hadn't taken any interest in G or her costume, the transmitter collar with the rubber spikes.

I hailed a taxi to take us to the HMRC office discreetly situated in the elegant townhouse in Queen Street. Any forlorn hope that the murder of Mark Carpenter would not yet be public knowledge was soon dashed. A media frenzy was already raging, guaranteed to have the staid citizens of Edinburgh rushing to read the lurid details. As the taxi idled in heavy traffic, there was more than enough time to read the newsagents' poster-boards:

MURDER IN HOLYROOD PALACE
KILLER STALKS HOLYROOD PALACE
KILLING IN QUEEN'S APARTMENTS

Undercover agents, by definition, aim to do their work in the background, must not attract attention to themselves in any way. But Shelagh Macbeth, the actor who had discovered the body and been held overnight for questioning, would become the target of newshounds seeking interviews and digging into my past. To Gerry Burnside, this would be a definite no, no, no. And though I couldn't be censured for discovering Mark's body and so becoming directly involved in the murder investigation, I would most certainly be rapped over the knuckles for not informing him that I had volunteered to take up an active role with the company as presenter of the re-enactments. I sighed. In the words of the original Lady Macbeth, 'What's done cannot be undone.'

While I waited for Gerry to carpet me, I busied myself writing a report bringing him up-to-date on events leading to my grim discovery of the murdered actor in the Queen's Apartments.

'You see,' I looked Gerry straight in the eye, hoping that a slight stretching of the truth would escape his notice, 'the tour was about to be cancelled after one of the actors was injured at the Real Tennis re-enactment. But then Russell... er... offered me the role of presenter. I *had* to accept, as it was the only way to save Red Grouse.'

He wasn't taken in. 'The ability to obfuscate the facts is an admirable talent in an agent, Deborah.' He stared at me stonily.

'On this occasion perhaps you'd care to rephrase that last sentence?' Picking up a pen, he doodled a line of spiky accusing question marks.

My heart sank. I should have known that when I'd said I'd been 'offered' the job, he would guess at once that the truth had been somewhat embroidered.

I hastily rephrased. 'That is to say, once I'd suggested that taking me on as presenter would prevent the tour being cancelled, they offered me the job and I accepted.'

His pen twirled in a neat circle converting the last doodled question mark into a smiley face. 'Excellent. The fact that it was you who offered to take the post, indicates to me that you are in the clear, that your cover is intact.'

I frowned, puzzled. 'I don't see...'

'If your cover had been blown, they would have offered you the post – and there would have been two deaths in Holyrood Palace last night.'

It took a moment for the implication to sink in. 'Are you telling me that Mark Carpenter was an HMRC agent? That there was another agent besides myself undercover in the company?'

I failed to suppress a squeak of outrage that he'd not trusted me with the information. But I shouldn't have been surprised. Gerry Burnside's briefings to agents were on a need-to-know basis, and on second thoughts, I had to admit he was right. What you don't know, you can't reveal. My attitude to Carpenter would have subtly changed if I had been aware that he was a fellow agent. Body language can betray just as fatally as words. I had the comfort of knowing that nothing I had said or done had led to Mark Carpenter's death.

I stared at Gerry. Several little things now made sense.

He didn't meet my eye. *Click click.* He fiddled with a retractable pen and gazed thoughtfully at the ceiling, then transferred his gaze back to me. 'I was about to say…'

He hadn't been. This was nothing more than a tactic designed to change the subject. I was as good as he at detecting untruths.

Click click of the pen. 'I see from your report you have not managed to pinpoint exactly who is involved in this drug ring. Russell, or indeed, any one of your fellow guests, could have been responsible for killing Carpenter.'

'But that's not possible! I was in position long before any of them could have reached the stair to the Bed Chamber. Nobody could have got past me without me noticing. And that's the only way to the room where Mark's body was found.'

'Making an assumption, Deborah, is a little weakness of yours, if I may say so. I've studied the floor plan of the Palace. There are, in fact, two doors to the murder room, one your group entered by, and one on the opposite side of the room. That door leads directly down to the interior courtyard of the Palace. It would take only a few minutes for anyone lingering in the Dining Room or the Throne Room to run down the entrance stairs to the courtyard and up from there to confront Carpenter and kill him.'

Crestfallen, I met Gerry's gaze. 'But I was told that the group were to return the way they'd come. I… er… assumed that the other door was locked.'

He allowed a short silence for me to reflect, then continued, 'Nevertheless, your theory that the drugs are being distributed by some of the guests booked on the tours brings us a considerable step forward.'

Gerry always managed to boost an agent's morale when things had gone badly. Though my role in it was over, Operation Red Grouse was still running. How I hated it when I had to leave a mission before it reached a conclusion. All that effort put in and never to know the outcome. I dragged my attention back to what Gerry was saying.

'... so the murder of two of our agents working undercover in the company indicates that this is no small outfit, but large-scale organized crime. And that means...?'

I sighed. Why was he asking me that question as if I still had a role to play in Operation Red Grouse? We both knew that my part in it was at an end.

'Means?' I furrowed my brow in puzzlement.

Click click. That biro pen clicked irritatingly on and on. It wouldn't stop clicking until I was forced into an answer. I surrendered and gave him the answer I thought he expected.

'The murder of two of our agents means that if you put in a replacement, the risk for that agent rises from amber to red.'

'I'm not thinking of another agent.'

He was asking me if I wanted to continue, letting me make up my own mind. There would be no disgrace in refusing. We both knew that a resumption of an undercover role with Act It Out would be considerably more hazardous.

The silence lengthened, broken only by the creak of upholstery as Gerry shifted in his chair. I came to a decision.

Fellow agents Geoff Grantham and Mark Carpenter had given their lives for Operation Red Grouse. I felt I owed it to them to see their murderers brought to justice. Besides, as I've said, when I'm offered a mission with a challenge, adrenalin always takes over.

I broke the silence. 'Tell me what you want me to do, Gerry.'

A little nod was the only sign he was pleased. 'The murder of Mark Carpenter means you must be on your guard, play safe at all times, Deborah. To comply with police instructions you must go back to the Shooting Lodge, but' – he leaned forward to emphasize the importance of what he was about to say – 'however much you are tempted, on no account are you to carry out any further investigation at this point. It is vital for the operation and your safety that your undercover role is not compromised. The tour will, of course, be cancelled, but they'll want to carry on with the distribution of their drugs after as short an interval as possible, so my bet is that quite soon they'll offer you and the others another tour, free, in compensation. Only at that point do you continue your investigation.'

'But they've killed two of our agents.' I blurted out. 'They must know that we have them under surveillance.'

Some controllers would have shown their irritation at a lowly agent questioning something they had just said. Gerry merely continued to doodle a circle with a smaller one balanced on top.

'Let me tell you how I see it, Deborah.' A triangle was added on the top of the smaller circle… and then a second one. 'I'm pretty sure they'll consider Mark and Geoff to have been members from a rival gang who tried to muscle in on their territory – a common occurrence and to be expected – and with their deaths that rival drug organisation has been warned off.' A squiggly line attached itself to the larger circle. 'As I said, they will want to resume the drug distribution as quickly as possible, and that will make them careless. They've gone to a lot of trouble to recruit the guests on this tour and the quickest way to restart the drug distribution would be to use these same guests. And that includes...' Three little lines sprouted on each side of the smaller circle. The finished doodle was a cat.

In preparation for my reappearance at the Shooting Lodge, I made a beeline for the cosmetic counter in a store near the HMRC office and asked for their lightest shade of long-lasting concealing make-up.

The assistant frowned. 'But, madam, that's *much* too pale for your skin tone. People will think you're ill!' Exactly, I thought, and handed over the cash.

By looking unnaturally pale when I turned up at the Shooting Lodge I hoped to give the impression that I was still suffering from the shock of discovering Carpenter's dead body. That's how ordinary members of the public would react to finding a body, wouldn't they?

During my very costly taxi ride back to the Shooting Lodge, a source of satisfaction was that Gerry had agreed with my theory that some of Act It Out's guests had been recruited as couriers pretending to be genuine members of the public. I pondered Gerry's assessment of the risk I was taking. His judgement was always spot-on and he had deemed the risk acceptable – the level acceptable for an undercover agent, that is.

I relaxed. This tour would definitely be cancelled, but in a week or so, I'd be offered a place on the next tour in my present role as an assessor from the tourist board. When the police gave permission, all I had to do was pack my few belongings and say goodbye to the other guests till I met them again on the tour offered in compensation.

What could possibly go wrong?

Chapter Twelve

As the taxi swept up the Shooting Lodge's winding drive, I considered the best way to react if a rerun of the tour was offered. Act It Out would be eager to have the tour endorsed by a representative of the Scotish Tourist Board and Historic Scotland to make their company seem above board. I would let them persuade me to accept. Decision made, I relaxed.

Until, that is, G struggled free from my arms and leapt out onto the gravel as soon as I opened the taxi door. By the time I'd paid off the taxi, she'd shot across the lawn. Showing more sense than on the previous occasion, she clawed her way up the Scots pine only as far as the lowest branch and settled down on the lookout for prey – bird, rodent, or a small dog.

'Oh, it's you Ms Macbeth!' Arabella De la Haigh came hurrying towards me down the entrance steps. Evidently she had no qualms about using that unlucky name. 'Ralph and I were absolutely devastated to hear of last night's terrible event.' A theatrical wringing of hands followed. 'A most unfortunate thing to have happened. *Most* unfortunate!' Hardly adequate words when an employee has been murdered. Obviously, Carpenter's death meant nothing to her.

If Mrs De la Haigh was putting on an act, I could too. I allowed my lips to tremble in what I hoped she'd construe as a valiant attempt to hold back tears. It seemed to work. She grabbed my hand, patted it, and led me inside.

'There, there, my dear. You're so pale, obviously still in shock. And on top of that awful experience of finding a body, to find yourself held in the police station overnight!' She turned to face me, eyes now sharp and questioning. 'Did you see something that might help solve Mark's murder?'

'Nothing. Nothing!' I gulped. 'Just because I found him like… like that… the police seemed to think that I had something to do with it.' I bit my lip as if holding back a sob. 'They kept asking me if I'd seen anybody between the time I left the dressing room and when I started my presentation to the group.'

She turned away and ran a casual finger across the top of the glass case, coffin of the bright-eyed red grouse. 'And did you?' She inspected her finger for dust.

'No!' I wailed.

For a moment she said nothing.

Was I over-acting? I blinked my eyes rapidly as if trying to hold back the welling tears and stared fixedly up at the stags' heads lining the oak-panelled walls. The glass eyes of the dead deer gazed blankly back. No help there. I took a deep shuddering breath and closed my eyes, waiting for the reaction that would tell me I'd convinced her that I wasn't a danger.

A brisk, 'Well, we'll hear all about it later.' In her tone, more than a hint of 'Pull yourself together!' And something else. Relief.

I'd passed the test.

She slipped her mobile phone from the pocket of her Angora wool jacket. 'Mr Russell has gathered the rest of the cast in the rehearsal room. I'll let him know you've returned.' She tapped the screen and held the phone to her ear. 'Gordon, Ms Macbeth's just arrived back.' She listened for a moment. 'No, she says she didn't. Right, I'll tell her to join you.' It seemed that Gordon Russell, too, was anxious to know if I'd seen something incriminating.

If I'd expected sympathy from the actors when I pushed open the door of the rehearsal room, I didn't get it. I was met with even more hostility than I'd encountered two days ago.

'Clear off! You've put a curse on us!' Chloe's outburst was the first of many, all with the same message – if more politely couched. That message was clear – Shelagh Macbeth brought nothing but bad luck.

Jamie scowled. 'Chloe's right. First Geoff died, now Mark. Whose funeral will be next if Shelagh stays on as presenter? I say, if she stays, we go!'

A chorus of agreement from the others. Unfriendly looks were cast in my direction. Superstition is a powerful force. I realized with a sinking heart that the blight cast by the name Macbeth had proved an insurmountable barrier. On any compensatory tour, there would be no chance at all of me being even in the audience with the other guests.

To make myself heard above the ensuing storm of protest, I shouted in Russell's ear, 'There's no question of me continuing as presenter. I've just come back to collect my things.'

That, I thought with some satisfaction, would leave the insensitive bastard with an even bigger headache – he now had three positions to fill. As I closed the door behind me, I glimpsed him, back to the wall, under siege.

Leaving him to his fate, I sought out my fellow guests to discover their reaction to a murder committed almost before their very eyes. Marie's reaction was easy to foretell. Her visit to Falkland Palace, where her father had died peacefully, had left her in tears, so how much more would she have been affected by the violent death of her beloved Rizzio?

A chat with her was a priority. If I said casually, 'Being by yourself in the Abbey ruins in the dark must have been awfully scary, Marie', she might tell me if Russell had left her alone in the Abbey, giving him the opportunity to kill Mark Carpenter. Would she tell me the truth? Was Marie Stuart, a superb actress or a genuine believer in reincarnation? She couldn't be ruled out as a suspect. If she'd been left alone in the ruined Abbey, she could certainly have had the opportunity for murder. Did she have a motive?

But I never did have that chat. Though all the others were sitting around in the lounge poring over a pile of assorted newspapers, there was no sign of Marie Stuart.

Brad was the first to catch sight of me standing in the doorway. 'It's Shelagh! Come on, give us the low-down on what it's like to spend a night in the clink. They've let you out, so who do they think did it?'

Val giggled. 'Where's the cat? They didn't arrest it as your accomplice, did they?'

I had expected Tony to make some sort of comment, but he was intent on poring over the sports pages of a couple of tabloids spread out side by side on the table.

'A dreadful business, this.' Hermione shook her head, pressing her lips together. 'And how must you be feeling, my dear, after getting to know him in rehearsals!' She picked up the handbell on the table and rang it vigorously. 'What we all need is a stiff drink.'

'A drink to the stiff, eh? Count me in.' Brad Peterson, like Val, seemed to care little that a man had been murdered.

Rob looked up from a half-completed Guardian cryptic crossword. 'That's not funny. Have a bit of respect for the dead.'

Along the corridor in the Clan Stuart room, Marie Stuart lay on her bed staring up at the ornate plaster cornice on the ceiling. To think that her fellow guests had looked forward to witnessing the distressing re-enactment of the murder of her dear Rizzio! The very thought of him lying in a pool of blood, just as he had five hundred years ago had made her shudder.

The visit to Holyrood Palace last night had started off so well. Mr Russell had kept his promise to arrange for her to slip away from the others to pay her respects at the tomb of her father. It had been a bit scary, of course, when she'd stepped outside from the well-lit Palace into the dark of the ruined Abbey, but his powerful torch had ensured she didn't trip on the uneven flagstones. When they'd rounded a corner of the Palace, the moonlit nave had stretched ahead, roofed only by the sky. But gone were the familiar statues of saints, the gold and silver ornamentation, the very altar itself. She stifled a sob: the once magnificent Abbey was now a bare shell, the south window reduced to a skeleton tracery of stone astragals, the imposing fluted columns greened by more than two centuries of rain.

Footsteps loud in the silence, they'd made their way down the arched-and-columned side-aisle towards the darkness at the far end of the nave. The beam of the torch had picked out the uneven walling and stone-slabbed roof of the royal tomb. Another tear dampened the pillow. That cheap monument was no fitting mausoleum for a king of Scotland.

She'd lit the candle she'd brought with her. 'Leave me here, I wish to be alone to pray,' she'd told him and watched as the light of the torch bobbed away and disappeared as Mr Russell rounded the far corner on his way back to join the tour. With darkness pressing in on the flickering flame of the candle, she'd knelt in front of the studded wooden door of the tomb, hands steepled in prayer. Only that door separated her from her father and the infant brothers whose bones lay within. Bowing her head, she'd poured out her heart and felt them reach out to her. At length, lips barely moving, she'd whispered, '*Nunc dimittis servum tuum, Domine.* Lord, now lettest thou thy servant depart in peace.'

Rising to her feet, she'd made the sign of the cross and touched her lips to the royal flag of Scotland on the commemorative plaque. At that moment she had indeed felt at peace. If only she could blot out what had happened next.

Shielding the candle with her hand, she'd made her way back towards the Palace. The fluttering flame threw grotesque shadows, distorted and menacing, on the wall. She'd stumbled and the sudden movement had extinguished the flame. Fingers brushing the cold stone of the wall, heart beating faster, she'd crept on, feeling with a foot for any unevenness in the paving that might trip her up.

Somewhere ahead, a door had opened, then quietly closed. Relief had flooded through her. Mr Russell with his powerful torch was coming back to escort her to join the rest of the party.

She'd been on the point of calling out to him, when the

moon slid out from behind the clouds and moonlight flooded the nave. A figure had passed quickly across the top of the aisle, a man, much taller than Gordon Russell. Then she'd recognised him. But what was he doing in the ruined Abbey? Mr Russell had told her that only she and himself had been given special permission to be here. As she watched, something in the tall man's manner had frightened her. She was safe now in her bed in the Shooting Lodge, but just reliving that moment made her breath catch in her throat. She'd shrunk back, pressing against the base of a column, her black gown merging with the shadows. Not daring to look, scarcely daring to breathe, she'd listened to his footsteps, stealthy on the gravel of the nave.

The footsteps stopped. Silence. Then had come the scrunch of gravel being dug up, the scrape of metal on stone, a muffled curse. More sounds – of gravel being cast aside, of rapid breathing. Despite her fear, she'd risked a brief glance. He was kneeling between the two central columns, concentrating on – what? Without warning he'd stood up and smoothed the gravel with his shoe. If he turned towards her, he couldn't fail to notice the pale blob of her face. A sudden movement would catch his eye. Slowly... slowly, she'd turned her head, pressed her face into the cold stone of the column, and prayed.

She'd heard his footsteps move away across the gravel, not towards the door into the Palace, but towards the double door in the outer wall of the Abbey. She'd remained there, trembling, for a long time after she'd heard the door close. What if he hadn't gone, as she'd thought, and was still standing there watching, waiting for anyone who had been spying – for her – to come out of hiding?

After what seemed an age, she'd heard Mr Russell calling

her name, seen the powerful beam of his torch playing over the flagstones ahead. He'd seen how frightened she was and asked what was wrong. She'd led him to believe she was trembling because her candle had blown out, leaving her feeling her way in the dark. He had taken her back through the Palace and across the entrance courtyard to join the rest of the group in the Palace shop, but just as she'd joined them, the police had driven in through the gates, blue lights flashing. They'd interviewed each of the group separately. Obviously something awful had happened, but when she'd asked, all they'd said was, 'We're the ones who ask the questions.'

'Where were you?' they'd asked her. Quite brusque they'd been. 'Can you prove that?' Accusingly, over and over again, as if they thought she was a criminal. She'd said that Mr Russell had gone with her to the Abbey to show her the royal tomb. She hadn't told them that Russell had left her alone. They didn't ask, so not to mention it wasn't a lie. After that, they'd stopped asking her questions.

A crime must have been committed, but she hadn't wanted to accuse falsely and cast suspicion on the man she'd seen acting so strangely in the Abbey. There must have been a legitimate explanation for his presence, something to do with the re-enactment. Yes, that was it. And then, this morning Mr De la Haigh had gathered the guests together and she'd learned the awful truth. Tears coursed down her cheeks and fell onto the pillow. Rizzio, dear Rizzio, murd– No she couldn't say that word, even to herself.

She ached to find out the latest developments, discover if the police had made an arrest. She got up, washed her face at the basin. With her hand on the door, she paused. The other guests would be there in the lounge, reading aloud the sensational bits from the newspaper, revelling in the gory details. She couldn't bear that... But if the police had made an arrest, that would bring some comfort, she'd be able to sleep. She would have to find out. How?

As if in answer, the faint boom of the lunch gong travelled along the corridor from the front hall. She'd wait ten minutes to make sure that the others had left for the dining room, go along to the lounge and switch on the television. Then she saw that the hands of the clock on the wall pointed to half past one. The tears flowed down her cheeks. The Scottish news was about to begin, and in ten minutes she'd have missed all mention of the murder and how the case was progressing. She dabbed at her eyes.

It was when she opened a drawer in search of another lace handkerchief that she saw her iPad, used only to access the internet for more information about the places on Act It Out's Mary Queen of Scots' itinerary. Modern machines made her nervous. Tentatively she switched it on and navigated to the BBC live news page. She was just in time to hear the signature chords of BBC Scotland News.

'Here are the news headlines.' The newsreader gazed sombrely into the lens of the camera. 'Police Scotland announce a breakthrough in their investigation into the murder in Holyrood Palace. The Scottish Government faces questions on...'

She sat on the edge of the bed, hands twisting nervously, body tense, her mind in turmoil, waiting impatiently, paying little attention to the other headlines, until the screen filled with a shot of the exterior of the Palace. Her attention focused on the reporter standing outside the entrance gates, microphone in hand.

'There's been a significant breakthrough in the investigation into the Holyrood Palace murder. At first light this morning, a fingertip search by police in the ruined Abbey found signs of disturbed ground beside a central pillar, leading to the discovery of a knife, now being subjected to forensic examination. According to a police spokesman, they are confident that an arrest will be made in the next few days.'

She sat there, frozen with shock. What she'd seen in the Abbey last night must have been the murderer hiding the murder weapon. With trembling fingers she closed down the iPad.

Now she knew what to do. In 1567, Rizzio's death had been avenged by the death of his murderer, Darnley, and five hundred years later, Rizzio's murderer would again be brought to justice. Tomorrow morning she would confront that man, tell him she'd seen him in the Abbey, savour his fear as he watched her call the police on her mobile and denounce him as the murderer they were seeking.

Chapter Thirteen

The morning following my return to the Shooting Lodge, I woke rested and relaxed. My bed here in the Clan Campbell room was soft and comfortable, so very different from last night's hard, narrow mattress in the police cell. Chafing against Gerry's restriction on further investigation at the Shooting Lodge, I talked it over with G who was sitting on the window sill looking longingly out, clearly with frustrations of her own.

'Any time now, the police will make an arrest and tell us we are free to go our own way, so I'll have no chance to find out what's going on here.'

Her eyes half-closed in thought.

Encouraged, I elaborated. 'But if I could have a little chat with Marie, I might just learn something to pass on to Gerry. Do you think I'm right?'

She gazed inscrutably back. It wasn't a 'no', so I took it as a 'yes'.

'The trouble is, there's a problem. She's shut herself up in her room since she came back from Holyrood Palace.'

G opened her mouth in a long leisurely, ya-a-wn clearly signifying, 'Am I bothered? That's your problem.'

Next moment, she'd swivelled round to tap smartly on the window with her paw, sending a small bird fluttering up in panic from the ground. She turned her head to fix me with a look that plainly said, 'You think you're frustrated, what about me?'

A light knock on the door and, 'Ms Macbeth?'

Before I had the chance to call out an answer, the handle turned and Arabella De la Haigh stood framed in the doorway.

'Sorry to interrupt your convers–' She stopped.

She'd been listening at the door. How much had she heard? 'Just talking to my cat.' I smiled weakly, as if all that was bothering me was the embarrassment of being caught holding a conversation with an animal. 'This terrible… er… incident at the Palace will have been particularly upsetting for Marie Stuart, won't it? How is she taking it?'

'Yes, terrible, terrible,' then she swept on, ignoring my questions. 'I'm just going round the guests to summon everyone immediately to the lounge. My husband has an important announcement to make about the future of the tour.' A perfunctory smile and the door closed.

The non-future of the tour, she'd meant. My offer to be presenter had prevented cancellation after the Falkland accident, but this time…

'That was a message of doom for Operation Red Grouse, G,' I said. 'Our part in it is about to come to an end.'

Five minutes later we were all gathered in the lounge – all except Marie, that is.

Ralph De la Haigh consulted his watch. 'There's just Ms Stuart to join us.' He turned to Arabella. 'Perhaps you could go along to her room, my dear, and tell her we're waiting for her.'

Each lost in our own thoughts, nobody spoke. I could feel the tension. A small tic in De la Haigh's cheek betrayed that he too was nervous, presumably because the Shooting Lodge and everyone in it were now under the police microscope.

Hermione broke the silence. 'I do hope she's all right.'

Rob tapped his fingers impatiently on the arm of his chair and suddenly burst out with, 'You're going to tell us that the tour is cancelled, aren't you?'

'All in good time. It would be a discourtesy not to wait for Ms Stuart.'

Rob scowled and was about to make an angry retort, when Arabella's heels click-clicked back along the corridor and she appeared in the doorway, alone.

'Ms Stuart doesn't feel able to join us, so I thought it best to give her the information and let her rest.'

'Thank you, my dear.' He held up a piece of paper. 'I received this email a short while ago from Police Scotland. I'll read the relevant part.

"… In view of the ongoing investigation into the murder of Mark Carpenter, we must request that all those present on the evening visit to Holyrood Palace, both clients and actors, remain at the Shooting Lodge to hold themselves available for further questioning." '

He looked up, the nervous tic on his cheek more pronounced. 'Of course, your stay here will be made as comfortable as possible. Though the company would have wished to stage a re-enactment at another venue, I'm afraid that will not now be poss–'

Face flushed, Rob sprang to his feet. 'We've paid for a week of re-enactments, and I don't see why we can't have them. As long as the police are told in advance that we're together and where we all are, it shouldn't matter.'

Brad drawled, 'Sounds good to me.'

'Oh, yes!' Hermione clasped her hands anxiously. 'Please ask them if that would be possible.'

I was confident that Gerry Burnside would be maintaining close high-level contact with Police Scotland and use his influence to ensure such a request was granted. The more voices in favour, the better, so I seized the chance to increase the pressure on De la Haigh to agree.

'Rob could be right. There's nothing to lose. If we don't ask, we don't get. We won't be any worse off. They can only say no.'

De la Haigh looked relieved, nervous tic gone. 'That was a very helpful suggestion from Mr MacGregor. It is certainly worth a try.'

He'd be doubly relieved: the planned drug distribution could continue, and if the guests and actors moved to another location, both he and the Shooting Lodge would escape police scrutiny as police interest lay only in those who had been at the Palace. And if the tour continued, G and I would be able to resume our undercover role.

I didn't have long to wait to find out if my optimism was justified. Arabella De la Haigh caught me in the corridor as I was coming back from a stroll in the grounds with G on her lead. 'Ah, Ms Macbeth, tremendous news! The police have indeed agreed that the tour can go on, with the proviso that our guests stay together. So pack your case and be ready to leave at two o'clock. My husband and I will be holding a short meeting in the lounge in five minutes to give you details of the reinstated tour and answer any queries.'

'Thank you for letting me know, Mrs De la Haigh.' In fact, I had no intention of attending the meeting, for how could I miss what would definitely be the last opportunity to investigate the De la Haigh's apartment upstairs? What choice did I have in the matter? None.

I opened a tin of trout for G and while she nibbled daintily at it, argued myself into the right frame of mind, resolutely repressing the thought that I'd be ignoring Gerry's express order not to do any further investigation at the Shooting Lodge.

'As you know, Gerry's usually right, G. But when the situation changes, sometimes one's got to adapt, don't you agree? It's of the utmost importance to investigate their apartment at the Shooting Lodge while I can, isn't it?'

She stopped in mid-nibble, turned her head, and gave all the appearance of considering the matter. Encouraged, I convinced myself that there really was no alternative to disobeying orders. The trout should keep her occupied and out of mischief, so I set off along the corridor to make sure the meeting was indeed in progress. One should never assume, always check.

I put my ear to the door of the lounge. Ralph De la Haigh's cultured tones were faintly audible through the solid oak.

'The good news is that we've checked with the police, and provided guests and actors stay together, we've been given permission to continue with the next stage of the tour.' Murmurs indicated a favourable reception. 'Where will you be staying? At a private house that has an association with Mary Queen of Scots. From there it's a short distance to Loch Leven and the castle on the island, Mary's prison for almost a year. There you'll enjoy another of our re-enactments.'

Things were working out well. The tour was still on. The guests had to stay together and I was one of the guests. The actors might not like it, but they couldn't do anything about Shelagh Macbeth sitting in the audience. The police order had to be obeyed.

I lingered outside the door for a few moments longer, trying to ascertain if Arabella was in the lounge with her husband as she'd said she was going to be. It would be disastrous if I encountered her while snooping in her apartment. But all I could hear was Russell droning on about Loch Leven and its link with Mary Queen of Scots. I'd have to risk it.

When I returned to my room, G had satisfied her first hunger pangs, and like all cats, had left a portion for later enjoyment. I'd timed it right to entice her from her snack.

I held up the collar invitingly. 'Work, G!'

She glanced at the remnants of trout, then at the collar, clearly thinking, 'Will it still be there when I come back? But if I agree to do the easy sniffing work you've got in mind, and pretend it's difficult, I'll get to play with my mouse and be given more food.' Purring, she allowed the collar to be placed round her neck.

How much time did I have before the meeting finished? There was no way of telling. The De la Haigh's apartment was my priority, but it wouldn't take more than a couple of minutes for a quick look in the Templeton's room.

G followed me along the corridor to the honeymoon couple's door. The 'Do Not Disturb' notice hung on the handle, as it had from the moment they had arrived. This was no indication, however, that they were actually in the room. Had they gone to the meeting, or judging by their previous behaviour, were they taking this last opportunity for romance in the luxury double bed?

One way to find out. I knocked loudly and waited. No response. The bedroom doors in the Shooting Lodge were not fitted with locks, so I could now open the door to snoop. But never assume… I knocked again, more urgently this time and put my ear to the door. Nothing, not a sound. I was reaching for the handle, when to my consternation, it turned and the door edged open just wide enough for Tony's face to appear in the gap.

'What is it now?' His growl made it clear that my visit was ill-timed.

Recovering quickly, I cried, 'The meeting's just started! Mrs De la Haigh sent me to ask if you were coming.'

'I told that cow Arabella that we've something much more interesting to do here. Can't she take no for an answer? Now, sod off.'

The door began to close. The gap was narrow, but not too narrow. I put my foot in the door and nudged G forward, a signal to search. With a twitch of her tail she slid in and my foot slid out, just before the door slammed shut.

Almost immediately, piercing shrieks penetrated the thickness of the wood, followed by a string of oaths and Tony's muffled shout of 'Bloody cat! Get out of that effing suitcase!'

Confident that Tony and Val's attention was otherwise engaged, I eased open the door a fraction, the better to hear.

'Why is the mog making that funny sound, Tone? It's not about to shit, is it? Get it off the suitcase! Do something! Sling your shoe at it!'

G had done her part. Their suitcase had, as I'd thought, been used to carry drugs. That was all I needed to know. A gentle push and the door opened wide enough to facilitate her escape 'Come here at once, Lady!' I called out. 'I'm so sorry she's being a nuisance. She's very inquisitive. An open door and she's in!'

Sad to say, my apologies fell on deaf ears. 'Sod off the pair of you! And don't come back!' G shot out into the corridor just before Tony crashed the door shut.

I stroked G. 'That was close. Another millisecond and you'd have been a Manx cat with no tail at all. Good girl! That's a job well done'.

She purred in self-satisfied acknowledgement as we set off for the second objective, the De la Haigh's apartment. At the foot of the stairs I stopped to call out, 'Hello? Mrs De la Haigh?'

There was no reply. Ready with a convincing excuse for seeking her out, I advanced up the stairs to a half-landing and called out again, listening for the creak of a floorboard that would indicate that somebody was up there. The measured tick of a grandfather clock on the landing above was the only sound. To make 'assurance double sure' in the words of Shakespeare's Macbeth, I sent G up the stairs ahead of me in a final test for Mrs De la Haigh's presence, banking that the sudden appearance of a cat would provoke movement or exclamation. I waited, and when there was no cry of surprise, followed her up. Several doors led off the upper landing, four ajar, revealing a bathroom, a bedroom, a small kitchen and spacious lounge. I sent Gorgonzola to search the bathroom and the bedroom. With time running out, I focused on the lounge where I'd possibly find a laptop, a writing desk containing private papers and a wastepaper bin – all sources of information for the experienced snooper.

The lounge was furnished with a couple of comfortable sofas

and high-backed armchairs, some dark mahogany occasional tables, and a writing desk of the same wood. One wall was lined with shelves of books, though on closer inspection those imposing volumes proved merely to be three-dimensional *trompe l'oeil* wallpaper.

Similarly designed at first glance to impress the eye, was a large oil painting of the type so beloved by Victorians, a magnificently antlered stag on a heather moor. The focal point of the room, it hung above the fireplace in its gilded wooden frame. Sunlight slanting across it, however, revealed the texture not of oil paint, but of printed canvas.

It was no surprise, therefore, to find that the writing desk was cheap stained pine rather than the expensive mahogany it purported to be. Somebody had gone to a lot of trouble to give the Shooting Lodge and its managers a veneer of solid upper-class respectability. Was the impressively aristocratic De la Haigh name equally phoney?

The De la Haighs had been a little careless. None of the drawers in the writing desk were locked, documents detailing the dates and itineraries of previous tours and the names of guests staying at the Shooting Lodge had been left open to the snooping eye. I'd hoped for something more incriminating, but the papers might prove useful to HMRC if they correlated with increased quantities of drugs circulating in different regions of Scotland. I laid them out on the desktop and took a close-up of each one on my mobile phone.

A quick flick through the rest of the papers in the drawers showed nothing of interest: the waste paper basket was empty, the laptop password-protected. Disappointed, I glanced at my watch. Fifteen minutes had flown by. Every extra minute I spent here increased the risk of being found by one of the De la Haighs.

When Gorgonzola wandered in from a negative search of bathroom and bedroom. I bent down to tickle her ears.

'You've not had much luck either, eh G? The last time you took it upon yourself to sniff up here, you found something, but it's been moved whatever it was. Oh well, better make ourselves scarce.'

But as I straightened up, I spotted something that made my heart beat faster. On the telephone notepad were faint impressions of a ballpoint pen. I carefully tore off the top sheet and angled it so the light fell on it. There appeared to be three words, and underneath them what might be a date.

It was when I was trying to decipher the writing that I heard loud whispering at the foot of the stairs.

'Should we risk it? Maybe somebody's up there.' Val, definitely nervous. 'I don't like it, Tone. What if we're caught?'

I froze, hardly daring to breathe.

Tony was made of sterner stuff. 'It's all right, I tell you. They're both still at the meeting.'

Where to hide? I stuffed the sheet from the notepad into a pocket and snatched up G. Bad move. Her startled squeak was alarmingly loud.

'I heard something, Tone! There *is* somebody up there.'

'Don't be daft, Val. But if it makes you happy, I'll–'

I didn't wait. Three strides took me out of the lounge onto the upper landing.

'Hello-o-o, Arabella. It's Tony and Val. Can we have a word with you?'

A few seconds was all I had. When there was no reply,

they'd be up the stairs like a shot. The nearest door was closed. What if it was locked? As the handle turned, another shout covered up the slight rattle and I slipped inside the room. Before I eased the door shut and total darkness descended, I saw I was in a windowless boxroom used to store packing cases, large cardboard boxes and a cabin trunk.

A few seconds later, I heard their muffled voices and Val's giggles. They must be standing just outside. The handle rattled. Holding G close, I pressed myself against the wall behind the door as it started to open.

They glanced in. 'Waste of time to look in here. It's only boxes and stuff. My bet is what we're looking for will be in the lounge.'

The door closed, but a thin sliver of light along the vertical edge showed the latch hadn't engaged. After a moment I put G down, pulled the door open a fraction more, and put my ear to the gap. From the lounge came the sound of drawers in the writing desk being hastily opened and closed.

'How much cash do you reckon, Tone?'

'50K. Got to be here somewhere. He'll have been given the cash last night. He won't have had time to pass it on.'

'But he won't have left that in a drawer, will he? There'll be a safe somewhere. How about behind that awful picture?'

'Just like a woman to make a stupid suggestion like that! Far too heavy to move every time you wanted to get into the safe. It's more likely to be in the master bedroom.'

Amateurs! A safe would be protected by a complicated combination lock, and even if they found it, why did they imagine they would be able to open it? Professionals can second-guess other professionals, but amateurs are loose cannons, you can't predict what they'll do next. They're dangerous. That worried me. The bungling Tony and Val would leave traces, evidence that an attempt had been made to tamper with the safe, alerting the De la Haighs. They would know then that someone had infiltrated the Act It Out set-up so those on the tour who weren't part of the organisation would be under suspicion, their every move watched.

The Templetons returned to the landing and were now talking loudly outside the boxroom, forgetful of the need for secrecy.

'You take that bedroom, and I'll take that other one. Look behind any small pictures and under the bed.' A minute later a call of, 'Nothing here, Val! Are you having any luck?'

The meeting must be over by now, and if Arabella was on her way to tell the absentees what had been decided, she couldn't fail to have heard Tony's shout. What plausible excuse could they produce for being in the De la Haigh's apartment? I was about to find out.

'Who's up there?' Arabella's voice from the corridor below, sharp and tense.

A scurrying from further along the landing and a panicky whisper. 'She's caught us! What are we going to do?'

'Leave it to me, Val. Don't say anything.' Then, a cheery shout, guileless, as if there was nothing to hide. 'It's only us. Tony and Val.'

Footsteps came hurrying up the stairs. 'May I ask what business you have up here, Templeton and Sedgewick?'

Templeton and Sedgwick, not Mr and Mrs Templeton.

Interesting. I'd been right – they were just acting the role of honeymoon couple with suitcases full of drugs, not going-away outfits.

I wasn't prepared for Tony's reply. 'Sorry to disobey orders, Mrs De la H, but the cat's gone AWOL. The Macbeth woman's panicking because if it's not found, she'll have to leave without it.'

Full marks for quick thinking, but disastrous if a search for the cat discovered me. I listened in dismay as Tony elaborated on his spur-of-the-moment lie.

'And we thought we saw its scruffy tail vanishing round the corner of the stair. So we chased it up here.'

Arabella De la Haigh was silent for a moment. 'Where is the creature, then?' Her lie-detecting antenna had flagged up 'Liar'.

Val panicked, forgetting Tony's instruction not to speak. 'Well, Tone and I were just– Ouch! That's my foot you're standing on, Tone!'

'Actually, we haven't had time to look in any of the rooms yet,' Tony broke in smoothly. Full marks again. Least said, soonest mended. Don't volunteer information that might trip you up.

'We'll soon see if the cat's up here,' Arabella was making it clear she didn't believe them.

They moved off along the landing. I was trapped. When they didn't find Gorgonzola in any of the other rooms, they'd inevitably look in the remaining one, the boxroom. And when they switched on the light, they'd discover Gorgonzola. The Templetons would be off the hook, their story corroborated, but what credible explanation could I give for hiding in the boxroom? None.

Chapter Fourteen

G took that moment to squirm out of my arms and leap lightly to the floor. I made a grab for her, then let my hands drop to my side. As soon as they opened the door to investigate the boxroom, she'd rush out. She was already hooking her claws round the edge of the door, eager to leave the confined space. When they made a grab for her, she'd dash downstairs, followed equally rapidly by Tony and Val who'd be only too glad to make themselves scarce from a decidedly awkward situation. Satisfied, Arabella would close the door. G would be my 'Get Out of Jail Free' card.

But first I needed somewhere to hide… Using the light of my mobile, I surveyed my surroundings. The cardboard boxes were too small; the packing cases were big enough to crouch in, but had no lids. The cabin trunk was the only possible hiding place. I heaved up the lid. The scent of an aromatically spicy moth-deterrent wafted up from the heavy velvet curtains that half-filled the trunk, leaving plenty of room for me. I climbed in and lowered the lid, wedging it open with a fold of curtaining just thick enough to ensure a small air gap. In the confined space, the cloying spicy scent was overpowering. I put my nose to the air gap telling myself I'd be out of the trunk soon.

They were standing outside the boxroom door.

'So… no sign of the cat. Tell me, Templeton, what's the real story?' Arabella De la Haigh's voice, coldly menacing. 'All a big lie, wasn't it? Snooping. That's what you were doing!'

'No, honestly, we–'

'*Aaaah!*' Val's scream made me catch my breath. 'The door's further open than it was before. There's something in that room!'

'Absolute nonsense! The cat can't possibly be in there.' A puzzling tension in Arabella's voice.

'You're right, Val. Let's look in the boxroom.'

Click as the switch was pressed. A line of light appeared along the gap wedged open between lid and trunk.

Miaow.

Sounds of a scuffle.

'Got it! Shit! The brute's bitten me.'

'You've let it go, Tone. It's got away! Don't just stand there looking at your hand, stupid! Come on!'

Feet rushed down the stairs. *Thump thump thump.*

The trunk was hot and airless and despite painful pressure on my hip from something hard beneath the folded curtains, I didn't dare shift position. The line of light between lid and trunk from the open door indicated that Arabella De la Haigh might still be standing in the doorway. I'd wait till I heard the light switched off and the boxroom door close. When I was as sure as I could be that she wasn't coming back, I'd creep out and open the door ever so slightly. If I heard movements from the kitchen or the lounge, there'd be the chance to take a couple of steps to the top of the stairs, making it appear I'd just come up from down below. I'd call out, 'Mrs De la Haigh!' and explain that Tony and Val had told me that my cat had strayed into her apartment. An apology and offer to pay for any damage caused should put me in the clear.

The light went out, the door closed. I counted slowly up to a hundred, then pushed up the lid and climbed out of the trunk. What a relief to stretch my cramped arms and legs and escape from breathing in that cloying scent. The relief didn't last long. I was in mid-stretch when I heard low urgent voices on the other side of the door. Unmistakably the De la Haighs.

'…found our honeymoon couple snooping in our apartment with a fancy story about looking for the Macbeth woman's cat. Didn't believe a word of it. Oh, the cat was up here all right, they probably brought the brute with them. It was in the boxroom.'

A sharp intake of breath from Ralph. 'The trunk!' A pause. 'You don't think they'd been in there and looked inside the cabin trunk, do you?' That same tension that I'd heard just now and a few minutes ago in Arabella's voice.

'No, I'm sure about that. We're quite safe. When the cat clawed the door open, that silly Sedgwick girl gave a shriek. If she'd seen what was in the trunk, she'd have been running down the stairs screaming. The whole Lodge would have heard her and come running.' Her tone sharpened. 'But that's no thanks to you, Ralph. You said, "Leave it all to me. I'll have the trunk moved to the garage right away." And that was a couple of hours ago'

'Stop nagging, woman! After what happened this morning, I had to make arrangements at very short notice. Anyway, what chance was there that someone would come up here snooping?'

A pretty good chance, I thought. To my certain knowledge, three people had done just that.

'If something *can* happen, it will. Just keep that in mind,

Ralph.'

'Ok, ok, ok. I'll go right now and get two of the lads to come up and move the trunk. Just you make sure you do your bit and organize everything for the Loch Leven re-enactment.'

They moved away, still sniping at each other as they went down the stairs. I didn't have much time before the men came to move the trunk. Common sense dictated that I should slip away while I could, but if I didn't investigate what was in the trunk, I'd never get another chance. A few seconds, that's all it would take.

I made sure that the door was closed before I switched on the light, then darted over to the cabin trunk and lifted the lid. The overpowering smell of the moth-deterrent once more engulfed me as I leaned in and pushed the heavy velvet curtains towards the back of the trunk, exposing a layer of finer material, black and silky. On top of this, glinting in the harsh glare of the overhead light, lay a heavy gold cross, attached to a set of gold rosary beads.

I gazed down at them stunned, brain at first refusing to accept the significance of what I was seeing. That rosary with its distinctive three-pearl gold cross had hung from Marie Stuart's waist. She'd fingered the beads as she'd read her prayer book in the Act It Out bus speeding on its way to the Shooting Lodge, and as she'd knelt, weeping, in King James the Fifth's bedchamber at Falkland Palace. I slid both hands under the heap of curtaining and heaved the heavy folds onto the lid of the trunk.

Marie Stuart lay on her side in the foetal position. The pleated ruff was no longer round her neck, but torn off and cast on top of the body, exposing the livid bruises on her throat, evidence that she had been strangled. I closed my eyes, suddenly faint. I had been lying on top of her body, my face separated from hers by only a few inches of cloth.

Recovering, and all too aware of precious seconds rushing by, I pulled the mobile phone from my pocket, took a picture of her body lying in the trunk, pulled the curtain material back into place and closed down the lid. With fingers that trembled slightly, I switched off the light.

I didn't have to resort to explanations and apologies, for there was no sound or movement from the other rooms in the apartment and I made it safely down to the corridor below without meeting anyone. A couple of minutes later, I was quietly closing my bedroom door. Voices and approaching footsteps told me I was just in time.

De la Haigh was saying, 'The trunk's quite a weight, but you should manage it between the two of you. If you take it out the fire exit, it's not far across the courtyard to the garage.'

On the other side of the door, I leant against the wood, limp with relief at my narrow escape.

A few minutes later, a loud thump and muttered curses accompanied by grunts of exertion from the pallbearers, gave notice of the progress of Marie Stuart's makeshift coffin on its way from the boxroom to its temporary resting place in the garage, en route to her body being dumped in an unmarked grave. I sighed. I hadn't been able to prevent her murder, but I'd do my best to make sure that whoever had killed her paid the penalty. For the moment, Operation Red Grouse took priority.

A glance at my watch told me there was only half an hour before the minibus left to take us to our new base, the private house associated with Mary Queen of Scots near Loch Leven.

Mind busy, I stuffed my clothes into my trolley case. Why had someone taken the dangerous step of killing Marie Stuart? Though a plausible explanation for her absence would fool her fellow guests, the police would not be so easily satisfied at the sudden disappearance of one of the group. What had she seen or heard that had driven someone to take such drastic action, thereby focusing police attention on the Shooting Lodge and the De la Haighs? Could she, somehow, have witnessed the murder of Rizzio and said something that alerted the murderer? If only I'd had the chance to speak to her yesterday afternoon when G and I got back to the Lodge. I had knocked on her door, but there'd been no response so I hadn't liked to intrude. If only, if only...

I zipped and locked my case, then turned my attention to G's holdall, now half-empty of her gourmet tins. She demanded the best. I counted the tins. There were enough left for the rest of the week, but not if the police extended our stay.

I'd expected to find Gorgonzola sitting on the sill outside the bedroom window after making her escape from Tony and Val. But she wasn't looking longingly through the glass at the holdall of tins. Was she keeping lookout from her favourite spot on one of the lower branches of the Scots pine on the front lawn? Yes, that's where she'd be.

After a last glance round at the tartan splendour of the Clan Campbell room, I made my way to the entrance hall, one hand wheeling my trolley suitcase with G's holdall perched on top, the other carrying the empty cat carrier. There were, as yet, no other suitcases in the oak-panelled entrance hall ready for the departure of the minibus. There was still time to find her.

I stood under the Scots pine looking up through the dark

needles. No sign of G crouched on the lowest limb, but when she'd shot off from the boxroom with Tony and Val in hot pursuit, she might very well have raced up its fissured trunk, higher and higher, and be hiding out of sight. My heart sank. Trying not to think about another nightmare visit from the fire brigade, I cupped my hands and shouted up into tangle of branches.

'Lady!' No response. In desperation I hissed, 'Gorgonzola!'

Still no answering miaow. No rustle of branches, no scatter of twigs as she made her way down the tree, or tried to, in response to my call. But if she wasn't up the tree, where was she? If I failed to find her, the police stipulation that Mr Russell and the guests must stay together meant that there'd be no question of being allowed to stay behind to search for her.

Only five minutes left to departure time. If she was within hearing range, the ultrasonic cat whistle was a sure way to get a response. One blast of it and G would come out from wherever she was lurking. I felt in my pocket. No whistle. Not in that pocket – or any other. I always carry it with me, even when wearing sixteenth-century clothes at Holyrood Palace. And I'd made sure it was returned to me with my other belongings before I left the police station. I must have left it in my room.

With only four minutes to go, I was wasting precious time. I raced back to my room, pulled open every drawer, looked in the wardrobe, peered under the bed. No trace of the whistle. Was it in the pocket of the trousers I'd been wearing this morning when I'd hidden in the cabin trunk? I'd decided that the spicy scent clinging to the trousers would make it clear to the De la Haighs that I had investigated the trunk, so I'd packed the trousers in the suitcase now in the entrance hall. Maybe there'd still be time for me to rummage for the whistle.

A door opened along the corridor and suitcase wheels rumbled past my door.

Tony was saying, 'Not so fast, Val. Remember they're supposed to be heavy, full of wedding gear.'

Their voices died away. Another confirmation, if any was needed, that they had indeed been recruited as undercover drug couriers. But who was giving the orders? Were the De la Haighs, too, merely a link in the chain of command? That was what I had to find out.

As I set off along the corridor, Hermione emerged from the Clan Robertson room holding Gorgonzola, front paws draped over her shoulder. She was patting and caressing G as if she was a baby in need of burping. A light maternal pat to G's back elicited not a burp, but a contented purrr.

'Ah, there you are, Shelagh. I knew you'd be looking for Lady.' She advanced towards me, a disconsolate Meffy at her heels. 'You'll be wondering why Lady's with me. Half an hour ago I heard that young pair of lovey-doveys making a racket in the corridor. I poked my head out to see what all the fuss was about, and there they were, chasing poor Lady! Some silly game or other, I presume. When I scooped her up, her little heart was thumping fit to burst.' Another caressing pat to G's back, elicited another contented purrr, and a plaintive you've-forgotten-me whine from Meffy. 'I soon put a stop to those high jinks of theirs! Gave them a good telling-off that sent them scuttling back to their love-nest!'

'Oh, thank you so much, Hermione.' I lifted a noticeably reluctant G from her shoulder. 'I couldn't think where she'd got to. With the minibus about to leave, I was getting quite frantic.'

She smiled. 'We pet-lovers must look after each other's treasures.' She turned to go back into her room. 'Mustn't we, Meffy?'

An unambiguous growl from Meffy. In his opinion there was only one treasure – and that was himself.

Out on the forecourt, Ralph De la Haigh, suave, urbane, and as immaculately attired as ever, was supervising Gordon Russell loading suitcases into the minibus. Arabella De la Haigh, the perfect hostess, was bidding the Templetons, Rob MacGregor, and Brad Peterson a gracious farewell. Both she and her husband seemed untroubled by the Shooting Lodge's grim secret, the body in the cabin trunk.

I opened the door of the cat carrier, expecting G to express her usual objection to it by bracing her feet and arching her back, but she was, after all, a little shaken by the experience of being the hunted rather than the hunter, for she allowed herself to be put in without any fuss. I was securing the catch when Hermione appeared with the wicker dog basket clutched in one hand and Meffy struggling under her arm.

'I'm afraid Meffy's being a bit of a trial. Be a dear, Shelagh, and collect my suitcase from the room. Can't think what's got into him.'

When I returned, Ralph De la Haigh seized Hermione's suitcase from me. Had those same manicured hands closed round Marie Stuart's neck and squeezed the life out of her? He handed the case over to Russell.

'Here you are, Gordon. This is the last. Now you can get on your way. You're already behind schedule.'

Arabella turned to our little group. 'It's been such a pleasure having you with us.'

I certainly wasn't going to point out that Marie was about to be left behind, interesting as it would have been to see the De la Haighs' reaction, hear the story they'd spin to explain her non-appearance. It might re-ignite any suspicion they had about me if I drew attention to Marie's absence, give them the idea that I, as well as the Templetons, had been in the boxroom snooping. Arabella had found my cat in the boxroom, and if I too had paid the boxroom a visit, what might I have seen? The mission had to come first. I kept my mouth shut and said nothing. The right decision as it turned out, for Hermione drew attention to Marie's absence.

She frowned. 'Where's Marie? We're leaving without her! Can't do that.'

Brad grinned. 'She's probably still mumbling away over that stupid prayer book of hers. Drove us crazy all the way back from Holyrood.'

The De la Haighs exchanged a quick look.

Arabella cleared her throat. 'No need to worry!' She waved a carefree hand. 'Ms Stuart will be travelling with the actors. When we heard that a re-enactment could take place at Loch Leven, I suggested that she might like to take the part of Mary Queen of Scots as she is rowed away in her escape from the castle. I have to say that Marie thought it an absolutely wonderful idea.'

Quick thinking. Ralph must have been proud of her.

To distract from any further discussion of Marie, she added, 'You'll find on your seat a little booklet about Lochleven Castle and Mary's imprisonment there. I recommend you start reading it right away so that you have all the background information before the re-enactment this evening. Now if you'll just take your seats…'

Tony and Val rushed onto the minibus, in their haste bumping into Hermione as they passed. *Yip yip yip*. The wicker basket shook and swayed, threatening to twist itself out of Hermione's grasp.

As she struggled to control Meffy's frenzy, Brad took the basket from her. 'Let me help you with that. I know how to handle dogs. I've quite a reputation as a Dog Whisperer, you know.'

He thrust his face close to the grid in the basket. His lips were moving but whatever it was he was saying to Meffy merely had the effect of provoking a burst of even more strident barking. *Yip yipyip. Yip yip yip*.

Seeing her chance to join in the fun, G let out a long wailing *y-ow-ow-l* that far outdid Meffy on the decibel scale.

Threatened with losing face, the Dog Whisperer redoubled his efforts, goading Meffy to an even more strident *YIP YIP YIP*.

Hermione took charge with a sharp command, 'That's quite enough of *that*, Meffy!'

It had instant effect. Meffy fell silent, just as Brad's lips moved again. His whispered words came out loud and clear. 'Sharrup, you scrawny little weasel!'

A distinctly self-congratulatory *purrr* issued from the cat carrier.

Hermione snatched back the wicker basket, hissing, 'Dog Whisperer indeed! Charlatan!' She ground the heel of her shoe into his soft trainer. 'Excuse *me*!' Ignoring his yelp of pain, she elbowed him aside and took her seat in the bus.

Brad studied his once-white trainer, now besmirched by

the black imprint of Hermione's wedge-heeled sandal, and for once was silenced.

Impatient to set off, Russell revved the engine. As the minibus made its way down the drive, I turned in my seat to look back. The De la Haighs were standing on the steps of the Shooting Lodge, the diamond bracelet at Arabella's wrist winking in the sun as she semaphored farewell. It was too far away to make out the expression on their faces, but it would be one of satisfaction. They'd got away with it.

I patted the pocket that held the mobile phone with its damning photo. Unknown to them, Marie Stuart *was* with their guests on the minibus.

A few minutes after midnight, the fire exit door at the rear of the Shooting Lodge opened. Shadowy figures flitted across to the garage. The key turned in well-oiled locks *click click click.* The figures vanished inside. An owl hooted in the surrounding woods, dried leaves rustled across the flagstones. The black Mercedes crept out of the garage... wheels crunched on gravel. The headlights flicked on only when it had rounded the curve of the drive. Once again night took possession of the Shooting Lodge.

Two hours later the Mercedes slid silently through one of the entrances to the Duke of Buccleuch's East Lothian estate. Off to the east, the lion shape of Arthur's Seat, a deeper shade of black against the moonlit night sky, rose above the twinkling lights of Edinburgh. The car crawled up a stony track on Carberry Hill, trees pressing in on each side, their tops lost in the darkness beyond the headlights. Engine cut, headlights died, doors opened. In the dim glow of the courtesy lights the driver took a small collapsible spade from the boot, waiting impatiently as his two companions struggled to lift out a tarpaulin-wrapped bundle.

The three set off, ducking under low branches, the leader probing the way ahead between the trees with a powerful torch. Grunts and muffled curses marked their slow progress on a narrow path. Bare patches of earth were slippery dark holes worn in its threadbare green carpet of moss; gnarled roots poked up from the soil, snares for the unwary foot; waist-high nettles waged war on hands unable to shift their hold on the tarpaulin-wrapped body.

Abruptly the leader veered off the path. Panting and swearing, his men lurched after him through the tall grass, trampling nettles and seedling sycamores, catching feet in tangling briars and tenacious sticky willow. Halfway up the hill the burial party staggered to a halt, dropping their burden onto the wet grass. With a groan one sank down, the other drew an arm across his sweating forehead and lit a cigarette. The fiery tip glowed as he sucked greedily at the nicotine fix, initiating a fit of coughing startlingly loud in the silence.

Their leader pulled an Ordnance Survey map from his pocket, studied it in the light of the torch, then shouldered his way through the undergrowth and was lost to view in the darkness, the beam of the torch appearing and disappearing as he moved through the trees.

Five minutes later, the torchlight came dancing back. The half-finished cigarette was flicked away. A gob of spit landed on a dock leaf. At a signal from their leader, they shouldered the tarpaulin bundle and set off along the path he'd trampled in the undergrowth. At a small clearing, the leader stopped and played the beam of the torch in a semi-circular sweep ahead of him. Moving forward a few inches at a time, he drove the edge of the spade into the ground. Again… again… again. A *clunk*, unmistakably metallic. With a nod of satisfaction, he attacked the vegetation, shovelling off dried leaves and clumps of grass until he'd exposed a rusty sheet of metal.

The dark hole of the well-shaft swallowed up the beam of the torch long before it reached the bottom. The heavy bundle was dragged forward till one end was hanging over the lip of the well. With a faint sigh of tarpaulin against stone, the body slid down, down, down to its final resting place, a well so deep that though the three men listened for it, they heard no splash.

Mary Queen of Scots, reincarnated as Marie Stuart, had returned to Carberry Hill, the place of her capture five hundred years ago and the start of the journey that was to end in her execution.

Chapter Fifteen

Our first sight of the Red Tower came as a bit of a disappointment to me after the Scotch Baronial grandeur of the Shooting Lodge. Originally a red-sandstone defensive tower house with tiny windows set high up, alterations over the centuries had not been in the best of taste. In Victorian times, an extension had been added in Scotch Baronial style complete with the obligatory turrets topped with conical roofs in grey slate. A twenty-first century addition was the white pseudo-Victorian uPVC conservatory attached like a malignant growth to the five-hundred-year-old stone base of the tower.

Hermione sniffed. 'So this is purported to be one of the many private houses in Scotland associated with Mary Queen of Scots. In this case, I fear, the link is tenuous in the extreme.'

This time there were no welcoming words on the doorstep. In fact, there was no sign of the owner or anyone else in charge. We stood about while Russell unloaded the luggage, swinging out the Templetons' cases as if they weighed next to nothing, presumably having forgotten that they were supposed to appear as heavy as the others.

'Right, folks.' He set down the last suitcase. 'Due to the short notice, Mr Fotheringham-Green is unable to be here to greet you. But rest assured, arrangements have been made for your accommodation.' He consulted a sheet of paper. 'The evening meal will be at seven o'clock. After that, about eight-thirty, we leave for the floodlit re-enactment at Loch Leven. Your rooms are on the ground floor of the Victorian extension to the tower. This week the group is small, so rooms have not been allocated by name. You are free to choose your own. If anyone needs help with their luggage,' he indicated the Templetons' huge suitcases, 'just say the word.'

Cue for Val to squeak, 'Ooh, yes please. Tony can't manage two heavy cases.'

Brad grinned. 'So it's first come, first served. A Le Mans start, eh?' He made a dive for his holdall and loped off towards the front door.

'Come on, Val! If we want a good room, we've got to be quick.' Tony grabbed up both suitcases and pounded after him, overdoing the huffng, puffing, and staggering required to carry a heavy load. I smiled to myself. I was a hundred per cent sure that by the time of our departure these cases would have regained the weight they'd had at the start of the tour.

'Thank you so much, Mr Russell. I'm most grateful for your offer.' Hermione picked up Meffy's basket and set off after them, leaving Russell to lock up the minibus and follow with her suitcase.

Rob picked up his bagpipe case with one hand and his holdall with the other. 'Sorry, Shelagh, I'd help you if I could, but not enough arms...'

That left me juggling with my trolley case, G's holdall, and the cat carrier. When I caught up with the others, they were bunched jockeying for position in front of the still firmly closed front door.

Russell called out over the raised voices, 'They're expecting us. The door's not locked.'

Brad removed his thumb from the bell push, turned the handle and rushed into the small encaustic-tiled entrance hall, brushing past a large aspidistra in a cream ceramic pot on matching pedestal. In his haste to follow, Tony misjudged the width of the doorway, lost his grip on one of the suitcases, and had to turn back to retrieve it.

Muttering, 'More hurry, less speed,' Hermione edged nippily past him. She peered into the nearest room. 'This will do us fine. There's a double bed, that's a third for you, Meffy, and two-thirds for me. Just put my luggage in here, Mr Russell.'

'Get a move on, Tone.' Val hopped agitatedly from one foot to the other. 'The old biddy's just nabbed a room with a double bed.' Outraged that they'd been outsmarted, she didn't bother to lower her voice.

Flustered, Tony fumbled for the handle of the suitcase. As Rob pushed his way impatiently past, the light suitcase swung forward and up, missing the potted aspidistra but hitting Rob a glancing blow that dislodged the precious bagpipes from under his arm.

Rob snatched up the bagpipe case and hurried along the corridor, calling over his shoulder as he disappeared round the corner, 'These pipes cost a bleeding fortune! If they're damaged, guess which careless bastard will be footing the bill.'

Val grabbed one of the suitcases from Tony, all pretence of weight abandoned, and flung open the door of the room across the corridor from Hermione's.

'This one's no use! Crappy single beds.'

'Try the next one, Val.'

Flinging open each door as they came to it, they careered on.

I wasn't so choosy. I manoeuvred case, holdall and carrier into the nearest rejected room and threw the holdall onto a bed. 'This will do us fine, G.'

Brad, the Templetons, Rob, and even Hermione, had been caught up in the greedy rush to lay claim to a particular room. I sat on one of the beds stroking G and trying to work out the reason for this frenzy. Tony and Val's dash into the house to have first choice of room was probably driven by sheer lust, eagerness to find a room with a double bed. Hermione's motive was clear enough – she wanted a wide enough bed to share with Meffy. Rob had understandably rushed off, impatient to check if any damage had been done to his precious bagpipes.

But Brad Peterson's haste couldn't be so easily explained. Until now I'd put him to the bottom of my list of suspects, thinking of him as a harmless show-off, a genuine member of the public recruited to the tour to camouflage the drug-running activities. Now I'd have to give him a lot more thought. He claimed to be an actor. Hadn't I heard him say to Hermione that he'd once been in the same stage show as her? I closed my eyes in concentration. How had the conversation gone? Had she confirmed this? No, she hadn't. She'd laughed it off as you do when someone claims to have met you before and you don't remember who they are. He knew her surname was Fielding, but that didn't prove anything. If he was involved with the drug organisation, he'd have had ready access to the guest list. The more I thought about Peterson's behaviour, the more my suspicion grew. He had rushed straight past at least three rooms and disappeared round the corner, as if he already knew what lay inside each room, suggesting that he was familiar with the house from a previous trip. I thought back to the start of the tour. Russell had announced and checked off the names of the guests on a prepared list, but had given no name to the delayed guest who would be joining us at the Shooting Lodge. Was that significant? If Peterson was a regular 'guest' on tours run by Act It Out, was it under a different surname each time.

'We've a lot to think about, eh G? Could I be adding two and two and making five?'

Her long-drawn out *miaow* and fixed stare at the holdall indicated first things first, the only thing on her mind at present was food.

I opened a tin for her before sitting on the bed to compose an encrypted text to Gerry, something there'd been no time to do before we'd left the Shooting Lodge. I'd give him my new location and inform him of the murder of Marie Stuart and attach the photo of her body in the cabin trunk. I switched on the phone. On the screen the message, 'Cannot connect to network.' No signal. I'd have to go outside to send the message.

I took out my frustration on G. 'It's your fault for going missing at the Shooting Lodge,' I hissed, staring at her accusingly. 'If I hadn't spent hours looking for you at my wits' end with worry,' exaggeration is allowable in time of stress, 'while you were enjoying being pampered and petted by Hermione, I'd have sent that important text two hours ago. Do you hear me? Two *hours* ago.' I ranted on…

She paused briefly in mid-nibble at a piece of chicken to stare back at me with hurt copper eyes that said, 'Haven't I had the most *awful* experience? You tried to force me to get into a trunk with a dead body. And where were you when I was pursued through the house by maniacs intent on who-knows-what? If I hadn't been rescued by Meffy's kind provider...' Shaming broadside delivered, she resumed her gourmet meal.

Chastened, I set off along the corridor in an attempt to locate the room Peterson had chosen, my rubber soles making no sound on the thick pile of the carpet. The nearest two rooms were unoccupied, their doors flung wide-open by the Templetons in their headlong rush. Round the corner were three more bedrooms before the corridor ended in a tall, arched window. No need to put my ear to listen at the first of the doors. Sounds of a heated altercation penetrated the thick mahogany.

'Silly cow! You should have elbowed your way past the old dame and thrown yourself on the double bed.'

'That's right, blame me, you prick! If you'd tripped up that cocky show-off Brad with your case instead of dropping it–'

'Quit yapping and help me push the beds together! We've only got an hour to...'

I moved on. In the next room Rob was playing a few experimental notes on the chanter, ascertaining if there had been any damage to his precious pipes. No sounds came from Brad Peterson's room, but a thin sliver of light showed under the door.

I walked past and stood at the end of the corridor looking through the arched window at a wide expanse of lawn bordered by dark-leaved rhododendron bushes. The sun had already set, and in the rapidly dwindling light all colour had drained from the scene. Peterson's eyes would be adjusted to the lighted room. Outside would seem darker in contrast, so anyone in the grounds would be difficult to spot. If he hadn't drawn the curtains, it would be possible to see into the room. I'd put G on her lead and if anyone happened to be watching from the house, they'd assume I was out for an evening stroll taking my cat a walk for toilet purposes.

I moved swiftly back along the corridor to my room. A little deceit was called for. G would come willingly only if she thought she was going to be let loose to hunt down the local rodent population. Keeping the lead hidden in my pocket, I carried her out under my arm. As soon as her feet touched the ground, I clipped on the lead and set off at a brisk pace, tugging the outwitted G in my wake.

The façade of the Victorian two-storey extension seemed extravagantly ornate in comparison with the simple structural lines of the adjoining tower. To keep up the toilet-walk pretence, I cut across the lawn to make a wide circuit of the house, stopping now and then and gazing casually round as G prowled along the line of rhododendrons. When a tug at the lead indicated she had heard an interesting rustle in the undergrowth, I allowed her to dart through a gap between the bushes and followed her in until I was screened by foliage, then took out my phone to send the encrypted message. Still no signal.

Thwarted again, I pulled G out onto the lawn with more force than was strictly necessary, then stopped to pat her and tickle her ears in way of apology. Two lighted windows on the ground floor marked the position of the rooms occupied by Peterson and the Templetons. As I wandered towards the side of the house, Tony appeared at the left-hand window wearing only a pair of striped boxer shorts and swished the curtains closed. A moment later the light went out.

Keeping my fingers crossed that Peterson wouldn't decide to close *his* curtains, I moved closer until I was twenty yards away. Now I could see clearly into his room. He was sitting on the bed with his back to me, from time to time jotting down something on a writing pad, a landline telephone receiver to his ear. There was no telephone in my room, or any of the bedrooms I'd seen. It couldn't be coincidence that he had chosen the only room with a telephone. Further evidence that this was not his first visit to the house.

The sash window was open a few inches. I crept forward. If I got close enough, I might be able to–

With unfortunate timing, a figure rounded the corner of the building. *Yip yip yip.*

'Hello-o-o, Shelagh. It is you, isn't it?'

No point now in trying to remain unobtrusive. I waved and started walking towards her calling out, 'You've had the same idea as me, I see, a stroll with our pets before we set off for the re-enactment.'

Behind me I heard the sash window close. The chance to find out more about Brad Peterson had been snatched from me.

Chapter Sixteen

The cold light of a full moon glinted on the dark waters of Loch Leven. A mile from where we were standing on the jetty, the rectangular tower and curtain wall of the castle were mere silhouettes on a wooded island. A beautiful scene, but poignant, slightly eerie, loaded as it was with its melancholy associations with the imprisonment of Mary Queen of Scots. I pictured the tragic queen, exhausted and depressed, sitting at her window in the tower, looking out over the water at the shore so near and yet so far, hoping against hope for rescue. My companions seemed to share my mood for they were talking quietly as they gazed out over the water.

Russell clapped his hands to gain our attention, and broke the spell. 'The castle on the island was the prison of Mary Queen of Scots. She was held captive for almost a year and it was there that she was forced to abdicate in favour of her son, James.' Then, as an afterthought, 'That is, James the Sixth of Scotland, James the First of England.'

My ears took in what Russell was saying, but my mind was trying to work out the real reason for Brad Peterson's absence. He had excused himself from the excursion, taking to his bed with a convenient migraine immediately after evening dinner. I recognised this for what it was, a ruse. Had I not used the same tactic myself to search the other guests' rooms instead of attending the talk on Falkland Palace? Mr Fotheringham-Green, the owner of the house, had not yet made an appearance – still unavoidably detained in London, according to Russell. While the rest of us were here watching the re-enactment, was Peterson discussing a drug shipment with the supposedly absent Fotheringham-Green? Or perhaps he was seizing this opportunity to fill the Templeton's empty suitcases with drugs.

Russell treated us to more historical background on Mary's stay at the castle, finishing with, 'Any questions?'

Hermione frowned. 'I'm a trifle disappointed. Did Mr De la Haigh not lead us to believe that the castle was going to be floodlit?'

'He said the re-enactment would be floodlit. Now, if you will allow me, I'll tell you more about the procedure for tonight.' Brusqueness an indication that he was on edge. Could it be that he knew Marie Stuart had been murdered? He took a deep breath, then, with a smile that was definitely forced, launched into his prepared introduction. 'A launch will be taking us to the island where the actors are waiting to bring to life the events of five hundred years ago. And it was felt that the experience would all the more memorable for you if one or more of you could participate in the action. With this in mind, Mr De la Haigh has approached Mr MacGregor to suggest he might like to play his pipes at a certain stage of the proceedings, and he has kindly agreed.'

Rob nodded. 'Aye, that's right. I've one or two tunes in mind. For instance–'

Russell swept on. 'And as Mrs De la Haigh has already mentioned, Ms Stuart was also asked to take part in the re-enactment, not as an actor, of course, but to relive the Scottish Queen's successful escape by boat from the island.'

From Hermione, a delighted, 'I'm really looking forward to this. Since she believes she is the reincarnation of Mary Queen of Scots, that will certainly add an extra dimension.'

From Tony a derisive, 'Reincarnation, my foot!' echoed by Val's, 'Pull the other one!'

From me, a murmur that could have meant anything. I was glad of the darkness to conceal my expression. If Marie Stuart had risen from the dead to sit in the boat and be rowed away from the island, it would be nothing short of a miracle.

As the launch chugged towards the island, I was only half-listening to what Russell was saying. Arabella De la Haigh and Russell had both made the astonishing announcement that Marie Stuart would act in the dramatic escape from Lochleven Castle by boat? Why? There could be only one reason for the pretence, and that was to make it seem that she was still alive. Russell and the De la Haighs would be in the clear if the body was eventually discovered. Clever.

Of course, after the re-enactment was over, they'd have to concoct a story to account for her disappearance. Tomorrow morning Russell would make an announcement, no doubt with an anxious frown. Something on the lines of, 'I have some worrying news. Instead of waiting to be picked up with the other two actors after her part in the re-enactment was over, Marie Stuart insisted on setting off by herself to make her way back to the minibus.' There'd be an ostentatious wringing of hands. 'I'm afraid that she has not been seen since.'

To make this work, it would be essential to secretly recruit someone to represent her in the rowing boat, someone homeless on the street, hired for this evening only, someone hard to trace. They'd only have to tell the Act It Out cast that Marie Stuart, one of the guests, had made a special request to take the part of Mary in the boat. In the dark, the cast would take it for granted that the veiled figure dressed in sixteenth-century costume sitting silently in the stern of the boat was indeed Marie. After tonight there would be no trace of her. The woman taking her place would be paid off and melt back amongst the anonymous down-and-outs of Scotland. The cast would confirm that Marie had indeed been present at the re-enactment and the police investigation into her sudden disappearance would come up against a blank wall. Any claim by me that at the time of the re-enactment Marie Stuart was dead, that she had been murdered, would be dismissed out of hand – and worse, blow my cover and kill off Operation Red Grouse.

From a distance, the tower of the castle had been a black rectangle half-screened by the surrounding trees. Now, as I stared over the bow at the rapidly narrowing stretch of water between launch and island, the bright moonlight picked out the rough squared stone in walls pierced on the side facing us by two narrow windows. But as we nudged into the jetty, Tony and Val were far from being affected by the brooding melancholy of the place. Once again they were amateurishly over-acting the part of newlyweds locked in a passionate embrace on a romantic boat trip in the moonlight.

'The entrance is this way.' Russell led us across a sweep of lawn towards the castle wall and through an arched doorway into a grassy courtyard enclosed by twenty-foot high ramparts.

'We have arranged four short re-enactments bringing to life the main events of Marie's imprisonment on the island.'

Flaming torches in metal stands set at intervals round the base of the walls transported us instantly back to the castle as it had been five hundred years ago. An actor in sixteenth-century dress stepped forward, swept off his cap, and bowed.

'Welcome, my lords and ladies, to Lochleven Castle, the home of Sir William Douglas. Your arrival is timely, for the noble lady, Marie Stuart, has just been escorted to her apartment in the Glassin Tower yonder. Please to allow me to lead you thither...' A flaming torch lit the narrow cobbled passageway at the entrance to the tower. The original wooden floors of the two upper rooms had long since gone, its roof now the leaves and upper branches of a tree. The lower chamber with its fireplace and oriel window overlooking the loch had been furnished with printed cloth hangings, cushions, a couple of seats and an oak table. Candlelight lent a suitably authentic sixteenth-century ambience. Half-turned from us, Sophie, playing Mary Queen of Scots, was seated in the embrasure of the oriel window, prayer book in hand. Strands of red hair escaped from the heart-shaped headdress that shadowed her face. Chloe, less richly clad as lady-in-waiting, sat warming her hands at the flames of the small fire.

'Please be seated, my lords and ladies.' The courtier-cum-gaoler indicated a bench set against the wall.

As we took our seats I noticed that Russell had slipped away as we crossed the courtyard, presumably to organize the escape by boat with its fake passenger, Marie Stuart.

Mary Queen of Scots sighed. 'It is only two days since they took me by force after the battle at Carberry.' Another heartfelt sigh. 'Let us hope that we are not long held here...'

She launched into a retelling of the events made familiar

by research for my undercover role – her surrender to the Confederate lords on Carberry Hill near Edinburgh and her imprisonment afterwards in Lochleven Castle.

'Alas, I am friendless and alone...' She bowed her head, racked with sobs.

The sobs died away. The actors froze into immobility forming a tragic tableau.

The courtier-cum-gaoler stepped forward. 'Five weeks have passed. My Lord Lindsay has ridden to Lochleven to force the Queen to sign a letter of abdication.'

He stepped back into the shadows. The two actors stirred into life. Mary picked up a frame of tapestry and began to sew. Her maid stood up and poured wine into a goblet.

'Your Majesty must keep up your strength for–'

There was a great jangling of keys and Tarquin strode into the chamber. His rich clothing and arrogant bearing marking him out as a powerful lord.

'Madam, I am come to escort you to the laird's tower to sign the document of abdication in favour of your son, James.'

'Never, Lord Lindsay, never!' Her cry of horror and despair echoed from the wall. She threw down her tapestry and put her face in her hands, seeming on the verge of collapse.

After a moment, she straightened. 'I am Queen of Scotland. I will not abdicate. I will not sign such a paper. No, my Lord Lindsay, I will not go with you willingly, you will have to drag me.' She gripped the arms of the chair.

He pulled her hands roughly away. 'Believe me, lady, you *will* sign. If you value your life, do not resist. The stakes are high, madam. The Lords will not be gainsaid.' He put his face close to hers. 'Accompany me willingly and sign. Refuse, and they will slit your throat.' He walked to the window and stood looking out. 'The loch is deep, my lady, if you understand me.' Abruptly he swung round, strode across and seized her arm. 'Come with me now. We've tarried enough.'

Once again the actors froze into a silent and motionless tableau.

'The loch is deep.' Lord Lindsay's words hung in the air. Perhaps Marie Stuart's body would be dumped in the loch. They'd rely on it being too decomposed to tell the means of death by the time it was discovered. The verdict would be 'accidental death' or 'suicide while the balance of the mind was disturbed'.

'Very moving, don't you agree, Shelagh?' Hermione rose to her feet, clapping enthusiastically.

'Couldn't be better! Brings it all to life,' I agreed, joining in the applause.

'Bravo! Very convincing. You know, if I hadn't made a fuss and prodded De la Haigh into questioning that police order, we'd have been stuck at the Shooting Lodge and missed out on this.' Rob nodded in self-satisfaction.

There was no reaction of any kind, however, from Tony and Val. Tony's drooping eyelids betrayed that he, like Val, was half-asleep. This afternoon's bedroom activities seemed to have been particularly tiring.

I gave him a nudge.

'Er… what?' He roused himself with a start. A loud yawn.

'Time to clap,' I hissed.

'Oh, right!' He poked Val awake. Their lethargic handclap was embarrassing, but fortunately cut short by the courtier-cum-gaoler holding the door open to usher us across the courtyard to the Douglas family's tower house for the next stage in the re-enactment.

Russell was waiting outside. 'Time for you to take part in the re-enactment, Mr MacGregor.'

The entrance to the tower was on the second floor, reached from the courtyard by means of a sturdy wooden staircase. Leaving Rob unpacking his pipes in the courtyard, we filed through an arched doorway. As in the Glassin Tower, the upper floors and roof of the room were missing, but Act It Out had again hung the walls of the chamber with printed cloth. Four high-backed chairs befitting the one-time grand hall of a noble family had been arranged along one wall as seating for us. There were only four chairs, again confirmation that Brad Peterson's absence had been pre-planned.

Silent and motionless as statues, four courtiers were sitting at an oak table set with goblets and a pitcher of wine. When we had taken our seats, the scene came to life. One reached for the pitcher and poured wine for the others.

'Didn't take us long to force her hand. She signed the abdication parchment soon enough, once we piled on the threats.'

'Aye, my Lord Moray, she's plain Marie Stuart now. There'll be no more of that Queen of Scots nonsense. The new king's but a one-year-old bairn. When you're made Regent, you'll have the power till he comes of age, eh.' He held up his goblet. 'Drink a toast to our new king. This night I've ordered the castle's guns to be fired and bonfires lit in the courtyard to mark his crowning at Stirling.'

Raised goblets and a chorus of, 'Long live James the Sixth!'

'I'll give the signal for the celebrations to begin.' He seized a candle and moved to one of the two windows, then turned and beckoned to us. 'Come, behold the fires that signify the end of a queen's reign, the start of a king's.'

Small-cannon fire boomed out over courtyard and loch. Sound effects, of course, but nevertheless realistic. Tony and Val, who had again shown signs of nodding off during the speeches, leapt to their feet, suddenly wide-awake, and moved smartly across the room to claim prime position at the window. Too slow off the mark, Hermione and I had to be content with peering over their shoulders with a less than perfect view of the proceedings.

Down in the courtyard, the surrounding darkness pressed in round the flames of two bonfires that sent a yellow light flickering over the faces of a handful of people in sixteenth-century costume. From the shadows rose the triumphant skirl of bagpipes as the actors who had taken part in the scene round the table joined those already in the courtyard.

Losing patience with being forced to crane over the Templetons' shoulders, Hermione dug a sharp elbow into Tony's back. 'Excuse me. Time's up, you two.' She pushed between them. 'My turn now.'

Behind us, serving-men had quietly entered and were clearing the table to set down new goblets, pitchers of water and red wine, and a large pewter charger piled high with chicken legs. The appetising aroma of roast chicken drifted towards us. Tony and Val immediately lost interest in what was happening below and darted across to the table.

'I'm starving!' Tony snatched up a couple of chicken pieces and handed one to Val, showing a great deal more excitement over the food than any of the touching scenes that had been played out before them in the castle.

'This is a bit messy.' Val licked her fingers. 'What do we do with the bones?'

'This!' He finished gnawing a leg and tossed the bone over his shoulder onto the floor. 'Always wanted to do that.'

Engrossed in the scene in the courtyard, Hermione let out her breath in a long sigh. 'What must Mary have felt seeing these people celebrating the end of her reign! Full marks to Act It Out for their realistic re-creation of those long-ago events.'

I murmured agreement, though I couldn't forget that the only purpose of this re-enactment must be to cover up the murder of an innocent woman who had seen or heard something she shouldn't. Watching the living Sophie as Mary Queen of Scots in the Glassin Tower, I hadn't been able to suppress the image of the dead Marie Stuart lying in the cabin trunk, a twenty-first century Banquo's ghost.

The sound of the bagpipes faded and died, pails of water doused the flames of the bonfires, the people in the courtyard below melted into the shadows. This part of the re-enactment was over.

I poured myself some wine from the pitcher. When the pile of chicken legs had been reduced to a heap of bones, and the wine pitcher drained to the last drop, thanks mainly to Tony and Val, the courtier reappeared. He bowed.

'My lord and ladies, please to leave the hall and follow me up these stairs.'

At the top of a narrow steeply ascending spiral staircase, he paused. 'A year has now passed. It is the second day of May in the year of our Lord fifteen hundred and sixty-eight.'

He stood aside as we passed through a low-arched doorway

onto a wide wooden gallery that replaced part of the original floor and overlooked the hall below. Through a small window we could see part of the walled courtyard, and beyond that, waves lapping against a tiny jetty half-screened by trees.

A cry of alarm rang out from the dark stairway behind us. 'My lord! The prisoner Marie Stuart is not in her chamber!'

One floor below, feet thudded on the wooden treads of the entrance stair to the tower. This time Hermione and I reached the window first. Down in the courtyard, voices barked orders as dark shapes scurried to and fro holding aloft flaming torches.

A floodlight sprang into life, lighting the nearby shore. Three people, one hooded and cloaked, hurried towards a rowing boat moored at the tiny jetty. Oars dipping in the water, the boat pulled away with the cloaked figure huddled in the stern. As it passed from our line of sight, the floodlight switched off, bringing our attention back to the courtyard. The activity there was now more frantic, the cries more panic-stricken.

'The boats at the jetty are holed and one is missing!' In the night air the shout carried clearly from somewhere near the loch.

From the hall below, a light played on the opposite wall twenty feet away, shifting our attention to a small window level with the gallery. With perfect timing, the moon glided out from behind a bank of cloud. A silvery path shone across the dark water, as effective as a theatrical spotlight. Caught in its beam was the small rowing boat, in the stern, a slight figure shrouded in cloak and hood.

'Our own Marie must be going through a conflict of emotions,' Hermione murmured. 'The sixteenth-century part of her will be so excited at escaping after a year of being cooped up on the island, yet at the same time afraid of pursuit and capture, don't you think?'

'But the twenty-first century part of her will know that her escape ends in twenty years imprisonment and execution by beheading.' I heaved a sigh, all too aware that the twenty-first century Marie Stuart was incapable of feeling anything at all.

We followed the progress of the boat, a black speck on the moonlit path till the moon moved back behind the bank of clouds and the window showed only darkness.

Hermione dabbed at her eyes with a paper tissue. 'Very moving, very powerful.'

Tony looked at his watch. 'What time will we get back? There's a replay of a match I've got to see.'

'But, Tone, there's not a TV in our room. I've a better idea, a much better idea. We'll go to bed early.' Val put an arm round his neck, pulled him to her and whispered in his ear.

Behind me, Hermione sniffed and muttered, 'Insensitive Youth!'

Someone, by the sound of it, was making heavy weather of climbing the spiral stair. Red-faced and breathless, Gordon Russell paused in the doorway.

'I really must congratulate you and the actors,' I said. And I meant it. 'Those re-enactments from the life of Mary Queen of Scots were absolutely marvellous. It was masterful, the use of the window over there to frame the escape by boat.' Then added casually, 'I suppose Marie will be meeting up with us at the minibus.'

Hermione conveniently helped me pile on the pressure with, 'Marie and I had a long chat last night about the murder of Rizzio. She was in such a state that I'm surprised that she felt able to take part now.'

Russell turned a splutter into a cough to give himself time to think, and managed to avoid a direct reply. 'Yes, indeed. Very fortunate… We're running a little behind time, so if you'll now make your way back to the boat…'

As we prepared to board the launch, I said, 'Where's Rob? Is he not coming with us?'

Russell steadied Hermione as she stepped over the gunwale onto the wooden seating. 'Like Ms Stuart, he'll be coming back with the actors in their minibus.'

The boatman untied the mooring rope, leapt nimbly on board and moved to the cockpit to start the engine. As the launch curved away from the island, the castle faded from sight. Under a thick layer of cloud, the water was a featureless black expanse ringed by hills. Ahead, a mile away, but to the eye deceptively close, a cluster of lights marked the position of the small town of Kinross, the jetty, and the waiting minibus.

Hermione half-stood to crane round the curve of the cockpit. 'When we catch up with the rowing boat, I'll wave to Marie and take a photo as a souvenir. This camera's got a great zoom so I'll get a lovely close-up.'

A close-up that would reveal the woman in the boat was not Marie. How would Russell react?

To my surprise, rather than looking uneasy, he smiled and said, 'We'll catch up with the boat in a couple of minutes. I'll tell you the best moment to take the photo.'

Strange. It was essential for them to establish that Marie was still alive and thus avert any suspicion that she had been murdered at the Shooting Lodge, so why so calm about a close-up photo that would scupper that plan?

Another odd thing. They'd have to land 'Marie' on the shore to fit in with their plan. The closest point to the island was a mere quarter of a mile away, but where was the light guiding them to a landing point on the nearby shore?

'There's the boat, ahead on our right!' Russell blocked off the view through the forward window as he stood steadying himself by holding onto the edge of the cockpit roof. 'Ready with the camera, Mrs Fielding! You'll get a better shot if you stand up.'

I peered into the darkness, but could see no sign of anything in front of us. Feet apart, Hermione braced herself against the motion of the boat, raised the camera and peered expectantly through the viewfinder.

Just then, Russell shouted, 'Look out! Floating object! Change course or we'll hit it!'

Engine pushed to full throttle, the launch heeled in a violent swerve. Still clutching the camera, Hermione teetered, lost her balance, and pitched headfirst into the loch.

Chapter Seventeen

The deafening roar of the engine drowned Val's scream and my shout. In an attempt to get Russell's attention, Tony leapt up, staggered and fell on top of Val. She clutched the gunwale, letting loose another ear-piercing scream. The launch sped on, every second taking us further from Hermione.

I shrugged off my coat, kicked off my shoes, and jumped into the loch, disregarding the danger of the launch's slicing propeller blades. I surfaced, treading water, and turned slowly, hoping to pinpoint where she was.

The drag of my clothes hardly registered, as fuelled by adrenalin, I ploughed through the water in the direction of a *splash splash* and a cry abruptly cut off. Off to my right, a gasp and a gurgle. I reached her just as the pale blob of her face sank below the surface. I made a frantic lunge. My fingers took a firm grip of her hair. The black waters of the loch closed over my head.

Pulled under by Hermione's dead weight, we sank down… down… down. Lungs frantic for air, I kicked for the surface. At last I was on my back looking up at the night sky. I held her close to me, my arm across her chest and her head resting against my shoulder.

She choked and spluttered, struggling weakly in my grip. In

a desperate attempt to shock her into full consciousness, make her react, cough up the water she'd swallowed, I put my mouth to her ear.

'Hermione! You're safe now.' The reassurance in my voice calmed her.

Safe? Not true, not true at all. We would both drown if the launch didn't come back very soon. With sinking heart I had to accept that it might very well not. That tumble into the water had been no accident, but a deliberate plan to get rid of her, though I hadn't yet worked out why she, rather than myself, had been targeted.

The cold water was already sapping my strength and with it my morale. The shore was agonisingly close, but hampered as I was by Hermione's weight, not close enough. With the Templetons as witnesses, the launch would at least make a show of coming back to search for us. But only when it was too late, Russell would make sure of that. Tomorrow's headlines would scream: **TWO DIE IN BOATING TRAGEDY.**

Sound carries far over water at night. The rumble of the engine was distant and receding. Hope died. The launch must be continuing at full speed towards Kinross. The Templetons' link to the De la Haighs had made them unwilling to intervene. Why had I expected anything else? They were couriers for the drug organisation, so if Russell paid them enough, they'd support his story. After all, for them it was money that counted. Their unsuccessful attempt to steal £50,000 from De la Haigh's apartment in the Shooting Lodge was proof of that.

Water splashed over my face as Hermione's weight pushed me lower in the water. I, too, was going to be a casualty, caught up in the plot against her, someone in the wrong place at the wrong time.

'Meffy, where is he?' With a sudden twist, Hermione flung her arms round my neck.

We sank. To break her hold, I forced my arms inside her deadly embrace until the vice-like grip loosened. I pushed her away, kicked for the surface, and gulped in air. Mouth just clear of the water, she was beside me, hanging vertically, making no attempt to struggle or shout, hands paddling feebly – all signs that in a few seconds her lungs would fill with water as she drowned. I reached down, grabbed an arm, turned her on her back and kicked out in a sidestroke, pulling her unresisting body into a horizontal position.

She sucked in air, coughing and choking. Barely keeping us afloat, I swam on.

'The launch is coming back to pick us up. Won't be long. I can hear it,' I lied.

'So cold.' Her voice feeble, the words all but inaudible.

I moved slowly through the water, each stroke more and more of an effort.

'Boat… coming?'

'I think I can hear it now,' I said.

And this time I could. The beat of a boat's engine, faint, but getting louder, was unmistakable. Relief flooded through me, only to drain away as quickly as it came. Would they find us in time? The moon was hidden behind a bank of cloud. There'd be little chance of picking out the dark blobs of our heads, low in the water – especially if Russell didn't want to do so. A red navigation light indicated the launch was about to pass some distance off to our left. Cries for help wouldn't be heard above the noise of the engine. Our only chance was for me to flail the surface forcefully enough for the splashes to show white against the dark water in the hope the Templetons would see them.

'Don't be alarmed, Hermione,' I said. 'I'm going to slap the water as hard as I can so that they will be able to see where we are.'

With the last of my strength I hit the surface with the flat of my hand. *Splatt Splatt SPLATT*. Water fountained up, white against dark. For long, long seconds the launch continued on its course. I'd failed. Exhausted, I sank back with barely enough movement in my legs and arms to keep us afloat.

It slowly registered that the engine note had changed, the revs slowed, the navigation light was now green indicating that the launch had turned in our direction.

'What's happening?' Hermione's voice, faint, lips barely moving.

'They've seen us! They're coming back.'

Relief. Then an alarming thought: what if the launch headed straight for us, and deliberately ran us down? The last thing I'd see, a figure hunched over the wheel, a hand pushing up the engine rev lever to max, the sharp prow of the boat towering over us, blotting out everything.

Little more than a hundred yards from us, the launch slowed. A powerful torch swept its beam over the water.

'This way!' My shout was more of a croak.

The launch moved slowly forward. The torch beam swung in our direction – only to pass by, frustratingly close. Again and again it swept across the black water searching… searching…

'I can see them.' It was Russell, about to give the order that would direct the launch straight at us to finish us off.

When the torchlight moved not towards us, but away,

I realized that he had a more subtle plan – make a show of frantically searching until it was too late and there were no bobbing heads to find. For Shelagh Macbeth, posthumous praise as someone who died in a heroic attempt to save a drowning woman; for Operation Red Grouse, another agent dead in the course of duty.

My rage-fuelled *SPLATT*, shattered the smooth black surface of the loch.

'Over there!' Tony's shout.

The beam swung in our direction… passed by… 'No! Over there!'

It came back, steadied on us. The murder plan had failed.

The minibus sped towards the Red Tower as fast as the narrow roads allowed, perhaps even faster. I can't say that I cared if Russell was breaking the speed limit. Wrapped in tartan travelling rugs, our wet clothes in plastic bags, Hermione and I were slowly recovering.

'I didn't know what to do!' Val's hands shook as she handed us cups of warm tea from the vacuum flasks provided for the journey back. 'The boat driver and Mr Russell hadn't even noticed you had both gone overboard! It was awful! I screamed, but they didn't hear over the noise of the engine so–'

Tony couldn't wait for her to finish. 'So there was only one thing to do, 'cause with every second we were getting further away from where you'd gone in.'

'Tone sprang into action.' Val's eyes shone with pride. 'It was awesome. Just like James Bond in the movies. He shoved Mr Russell aside, reached over the boatman's shoulder and switched off the engine. Oooh, their language!' She giggled.

'Talk about the air turning blue, it was bright purple. Some words I hadn't heard before.'

The back of Russell's neck turned red. His grip on the steering wheel tightened till his knuckles showed white.

'Of course, once they realized what was wrong, they turned back.' She reached up and planted a kiss on Tony's cheek. 'Even then we wouldn't have found them without you, would we? We'd looked and looked and there was no sign, though Mr Russell was certain that we were in the right place. Got quite ratty about it when we wanted to look nearer the island. Then Tone saw the splash away off to the right, didn't you?'

Embarrassed by all this praise, Tony flushed. In the eyes of the law they were criminals, but there's good in everyone.

I reached over and shook his hand. 'Owe you one, Tony.'

I lay back and closed my eyes, suddenly very tired. What Tony and Val had just said proved the sudden swerve of the boat that threw Hermione into Loch Leven had indeed been no accident. There had to be a reason for wanting her dead. Like the Templetons, was she a drug courier, been greedy and tried to double cross De la Haigh? I'm a good judge of people, I have to be, and I was pretty sure Hermione was just an ordinary member of the public who had booked the tour for the reasons she'd given – to enjoy a holiday accompanied by her dog.

Then why did they want her dead?

An hour later I still couldn't get that question out of my mind. I snuggled under the duvet, gripped by an inner chill, cold despite a warm shower. What I needed was a hot water bottle or a fur coat like G's. She was trampling over the duvet at my feet, selecting, rejecting, and reselecting the perfect spot to spend the night. Meffy had jumped up onto Hermione's bed and burrowed under the duvet to be her hot water bottle. My thought processes being slow from the immersion in the cold waters of Loch Leven, it took me some time to realize that G would be only too willing to do the same. Past caring that I was setting a precedent I might come to regret, I folded back the duvet and patted the mattress invitingly.

'Here, G! Come and join me.'

For a moment she stared, unable to believe her good luck, then before I could change my mind, sprang up the bed to take possession of hitherto strictly forbidden territory.

'This is for tonight only,' I said into her ear as I covered her up and hugged her to me.

Warming up at last, I lay cuddling a purring G, the numbing cold of the loch a distant memory. My eyelids grew heavy and slowly closed.

A hand switched on the hall light. Soft footsteps padded past the bedroom doors and stopped outside Peterson's room. A light tap, the door opened and quietly closed.

'How did it go?' Peterson raised a questioning eyebrow.

Russell flung himself into a chair. 'Er… fine. They all swallowed the story that the mad-as-a-hatter Stuart woman had volunteered to re-enact her escape from Lochleven Castle. Yes, it was all going to plan. The launch was five minutes out from the castle on the return trip. I didn't even need to ask Fielding to change places with me. She played right into our hands by wanting to take a photo of Stuart in the rowing boat. Easy to suggest she would get a better shot of Stuart by standing up.'

Peterson smiled. 'Ah yes, the non-existent Marie Stuart!'

The smile faded. 'Wait a minute! Did you say she was going to take a photo? That means she must have seen right through our little scheme and suspected the woman in the boat wasn't Stuart.' His fist crashed down on the table. The two whisky glasses quivered. 'The minute we found the dog whistle beside Stuart's body in the cabin trunk, I knew she was Police or Revenue & Customs. And that confirms it.' A slow nod of the head. 'No way was she just a harmless old biddy with a yappy dog.'

Russell passed a tired hand over his eyes. 'You're damn right about the Fielding woman. When I went to collect them at the end of the re-enactment, she gave herself away, let slip that she'd spoken to Stuart about what happened at Holyrood Palace, "Had a long chat," was how she put it.'

'Doesn't matter now. You got rid of her as we'd arranged.'

Silence.

Peterson's eyes narrowed. 'You did, didn't you? You've just told me everything went fine.'

Russell shifted uncomfortably. 'Well, it did. I even suggested she should stand up to get a better photo. Then I gave Rick the code words to throw the boat about – and over the side she went, according to plan.' Russell's voice faltered. 'Then... then... it all went sort of pear-shaped.' He found himself lifted from the chair by the front of his shirt.

'What! There she was in the water, no life jacket! And somehow you managed to botch things when all you had to do was gun the engine. You'd have been away with not a chance of finding her by the time you turned back!' Peterson thrust his face close. 'Admit it! You bungled, staged the 'accident' too close to land and she swam to shore.'

'No, no! It wasn't like that at all.' Russell tried and failed to keep the whimper out of his voice. 'Even you couldn't have guessed that the Macbeth woman would jump in after her! But I'll have you know I kept my head, pretended not to notice, put the revs up and didn't look back – even when Templeton shouted and grabbed my arm.' He pulled himself free. 'You couldn't have done any more.'

'So what *did* go wrong? This had better be good.'

'Templeton, the bastard, shoved me aside, leaned over and switched off the engine. That's what went wrong.' Shakily, Russell righted the fallen chair and readjusted his shirt and tie. 'I went back and pretended to search, of course. Even then the plan would have worked if Templeton and Sedgewick hadn't kept insisting I was looking in the wrong place. Couldn't just ignore them, wouldn't look good afterwards. Put it off as long as I could, but eventually I had to go along with them, didn't I?'

'No, you bloody well didn't!'

'So, they drown, and at the inquest it comes out that I wasn't making a genuine attempt to find them, eh?' Then gaining confidence, 'Let me tell you, I took as long about it as I could.' He shrugged. 'But it was no use. Templeton spotted them. Another five minutes and there'd have been nobody to find. If you want to blame anyone, blame him.'

The two men glared at each other. After a few seconds Peterson turned away.

'There'll be another chance to get rid of her. So let's talk about how to arrange it.' He reached for the whisky bottle.

Chapter Eighteen

Huge waves were thundering down on the distant shore. I was swimming… swimming desperately across Loch Leven, but making no headway weighed down by Gorgonzola on my back. A wave reared up, its foaming crest curling to come crashing down on me. Marie Stuart, unseen till now in her black gown, floated up from the depths of the loch. Her white hands reached out, gripped me in a deadly embrace and held me fast, pulling me down… down into the dark waters. Lungs bursting for air, I thrust up, kicking for the surface.

Y-ow-owl… Thud. Suddenly the weight lifted from my back.

I could breathe. I opened my eyes to find myself sitting up in bed. In the grey light filtering through the curtains, G's stricken face peered up at me from the floor, her wide eyes clearly asking, 'What did I do to deserve this?'

I reached down to pick her up for a consolatory cuddle. She backed away, then having made her point – that her feelings of betrayal were still too raw – stalked to the door. It was clear that an early morning cat-hunt for rodents would be the only way for me to show genuine contrition.

What time was it? Not yet seven o'clock. An expedition with Gorgonzola would give me a chance to continue my investigation of the grounds and any outbuildings. That last snoop at the Shooting Lodge had led to a breakthrough with the discovery of the body of Marie Stuart and might even lead to the arrest of someone high up in the drug organisation. If we moved, either back to the Shooting Lodge or to a new location, there might not be another opportunity to investigate here. I pushed up the bedroom window and followed Gorgonzola in her stroll through the grounds. While she roamed in hopeful search of four-legged prey, I'd nose around to see what I could ferret out.

A low mist was drifting through the shelterbelt of larch trees, its wispy grey tendrils caressing the yellowing needles and coating them with fine droplets. The temperature had dropped overnight, depositing a film of moisture over the lawn revealing G's tell-tale paw prints heading purposefully across the grass towards the shrubbery, a warning to me that human footprints leading from the bedroom window would be a giveaway. If someone happened to remark to De la Haigh that they'd seen me and the cat wandering outside in the early morning, he might recall the two visitations G had made to the private apartments of the Shooting Lodge, and suspect that where the cat had strayed, I had too. I'd keep to the paved path round the house.

What I was hoping to find on my stroll was evidence of drugs, and the quickest way to do that was by using G's sensitive nose. Where had she got to? I felt in my pocket for the cat whistle, only to remember that I hadn't found it in the pocket of the trousers I'd been wearing when hiding in the trunk.

'G!' I hissed.

No stir of a rhododendron leaf, no rustle of dried leaves

in answer to my call, no alarmed chirp from a bird to pinpoint her position. It had been a mistake not to put her on the lead. With so little time to investigate, I couldn't afford to wait here till she chose to put in an appearance. I rounded the corner of the house. The path led behind the line of rhododendron bushes I'd seen through the arched window at the end of the bedroom corridor. Their height had hidden from view a roofless tumbledown cottage, its ruined walls shrouded in ivy, the gable wall leaning inward at a perilous angle.

Beside the cottage was a black Mercedes. Strange place to park a car... Anything out of the ordinary attracts me like a moth to a light. I walked round it. The number plate was different from De la Haigh's Mercedes, but a chip in the glass of the nearside rear indicator light was identical to the one I'd noted at the Shooting Lodge. A false number plate and the fact that it had not been parked in front of the house were signs that the driver did not wish his arrival known.

I peered through a side window. Lying on the front passenger seat was a road atlas open at a page showing the Firth of Forth, the East Lothian coastline and the network of roads radiating from Edinburgh. Highlighted in yellow marker pen was a minor road south east of Edinburgh. In hope of a closer look, I tried the car doors. Locked.

With no more information to be gathered, I moved quickly on towards my main objective, the conservatory, not an unusual attachment in Victorian times. This one, however, didn't date from that era, being constructed of gleaming white uPVC rather than wood or wrought iron. It would be big enough to cultivate hundreds of very lucrative cannabis plants. What better place for a cannabis farm – an isolated house with extensive grounds, no nosey neighbours, no prying eyes? The conservatory would definitely be worthy of a snoop.

Its door, too, was locked. It was impossible to see in, as the windows were misted up and running with condensation, evidence of the high temperature inside needed for tropical plants, not necessarily cannabis, of course.

I applied my picklocks to the door, locking it behind me, then walked between the three rows of staging, trying without success in the low light to spot the toothed leaves of cannabis amid the tightly packed plants. Trying to single out that distinctive smell, I stopped, eyes closed in concentration, breathing in damp earth… a chemical pesticide, lingering and slightly unpleasant… the peppermint scent of the geranium I'd brushed past a moment before… and, just detectable, flowering jasmine. Disappointingly, nothing seemed out of the ordinary in the humid air of the heated conservatory

I took another deep sniff. Could that be the faintest trace of sickly sweet cannabis, or was I fooling myself? If Gorgonzola had been with me, I'd have known for sure. But a scent so faint would indicate there were only a couple of plants in here, possibly grown by the gardener on the sly. And that was of no interest to Operation Red Grouse. I was wasting time. I turned to go.

Outside, quite close, Hermione's voice. 'Where are you, Meffy?'

In answer, even closer, a *yip yip*, and a snuffling at the conservatory door.

She'd mentioned that she was a keen gardener. If she peered in, as I was sure she would, the condensation on the glass might not be enough to hide that someone was inside. She would demand loudly to be let in. I ducked down and crouched under the staging. Just in time. From my hiding place I saw her forehead press against the glass of the door.

'I do love plants, and you do too, don't you, Meffy? Can we be nosy and look inside?' The handle rattled. 'Locked. What a shame. I wonder if there are orchids or bougainvillea.' Another rattle of the handle. 'So frustrating not to get in.'

A whine from Meffy whose sense of smell, though inferior to Gorgonzola's, had obviously detected my presence. *Yip yip yip… yip yip yip.*

'Shut up, Meffy. People are still sleeping. Do be quiet! There, you see! Mr Peterson's come to tell you just that.'

Brad Peterson. It could be no coincidence that he had turned up at the conservatory just as Hermione was peering in and trying the door.

'Thought it was you when I heard the dog, Hermione, but what the heck are you doing out here? After what you went through last night, you're one tough old bird to be taking the dog out on such a damp morning.'

'Now I take that as a compliment, Brad,' a light laugh, 'but not so much of the 'old', my lad. I'd have to be very under the weather not to take Meffy for his constitutional. Haven't missed a morning yet – and that's been two years. Not bad for an "old bird", don't you think?'

'What I think is that you should go inside out of the cold right now.'

'Oh yes! I'd love to see inside the conservatory, but it's locked. Do you happen to have the key?'

An impatient, 'Of course not. The owner obviously wants it locked. Forget the bloody conservatory, there'll only be a few dying plants in there at this time of year.'

Hermione was undeterred. 'Well, do you think Mr Russell could ask the owner to give his permission?'

'Fother-something-Green is still in London as far as I know.' An exasperated sigh. 'Come on, Hermione. I meant we should go into the house for breakfast beside a log fire. You can let me in on what you've been doing since the time we shared a stage together. Come on, I insist.'

A last frustrated rattle of the door handle. 'Yes, that would be fun reminiscing about our acting days. Now what was the name of that producer who...' Their voices faded as they walked away.

I didn't move. I wasn't risking that Peterson might return on some pretext or other. We hadn't seen him when we'd arrived back at the house last night, so how was it that he had known about her ordeal? He'd stayed in his room, undisturbed by our excited chatter, pretending to still be suffering from the 'migraine attack' that had prevented him from joining the rest of us at the Loch Leven re-enactment. And that comment of his, 'There'll only be a few dying plants in there at this time of year' was untrue. Did he know little about plants, or was it a tactic to ensure she lost all interest in the conservatory? Did this conservatory in fact hide a secret?

I looked at my watch. There was still time before breakfast, so I'd take another walk round the rows of staging, this time looking for something unobtrusive, something inconspicuous, that wouldn't attract attention and might conceivably have another purpose.

I nearly missed it. I'd made a full circuit and found nothing.

Last night's ordeal followed by a disturbed sleep had taken its toll. I yawned, and it was then I noticed that the faint scent of jasmine was stronger, much stronger. I frowned. There was something not quite right. The source of the perfume filling the air would have to be a big plant, one covered with flowers. And I hadn't seen one. I wandered round the staging again and came back to where the scent had been so strong.

A *squissssss*, barely audible. Curious, I moved in that direction. *Squissssss*. It seemed to be coming from a line of black tubing ending in a spray nozzle of the type used to humidify a greenhouse rather than a conservatory. *Squissssss*. The nozzle released a fine vapour into the air – and with it an intense waft of jasmine.

So it was an air freshener rather than a humidifier. There *was* something to conceal in here, the strong smell emitted by plants in a cannabis nursery. And they must be growing in an underground chamber. I switched on my pencil torch and played it on the floor under the staging, searching for tell-tale gaps that would betray the edges of a trapdoor. No luck. The flagstones fitted snugly together, green outlines of algae the proof that they hadn't been disturbed.

In the centre of a small clear area beyond the staging was a massive stone water trough, the paving to one side of it muddied with earth that had drained out of pots dipped in its pool. The trapdoor, if there was one, could only lie under the trough. But such a heavy object, even if it was emptied of water, could only be moved aside with some kind of mechanism. There was no sign of such a device.

I studied the trough and the surrounding flagstones. As with the scent of jasmine, the muddy paving could be a means of disguise. Why was the earth wet only on the paving at the left-hand side of the trough? Surely pots dipped and carried back to the staging would leave an earthy trail on all sides?

I seized a handy watering can, half-filled it in the trough, and watered the paving. With the earth washed away, long scrape marks on the stone were revealed, indicating that the seemingly immovable water reservoir had in fact moved a couple of feet to the left. I placed my hands on the edge and shoved. With a faint scrape as rollers passed over grit, the trough slid smoothly away from me. Taken by surprise, I lurched forward and fell on my knees onto a metal trapdoor.

I hooked my fingers under the recessed handle and heaved up the trapdoor to be met by the harsh glare of fluorescent lights, a blast of warm air, the hum of fans, and the distinctive smell of cannabis. I was looking down into a concrete-walled chamber filled with a sea of green foliage stirring in air from the powerful fans. Mission accomplished.

I lowered the trapdoor, pushed the trough back into position, and carefully set about muddying the flagstones. I didn't make the mistake of throwing down handfuls of earth and sprinkling with the watering can. The fine silt that drains out of plant pots could only recreated by repeating that action, so it took more time than I'd anticipated to hide all evidence that the trough had been moved. After that, it was essential to ensure that nobody was around to see me leave the conservatory. When all seemed safe, I slipped out, locked the door, and strolled casually back towards the house.

I'd half-expected Gorgonzola to come bounding out of the shrubbery to greet me, though I hoped she wouldn't be bearing the gift of a mouse or, worse still, a small bird. Where was she? If only I'd found the cat whistle, I could have called her to me right away. As I was already late for breakfast I certainly didn't have time to go in search for her now. Well, the bedroom window was open. She'd come back when she was ready, hunting desires satisfied, to burrow under the duvet and resume her sleep so rudely interrupted when I'd hurled her to the floor. And when she did deign to return, I'd point out that while she'd been on the loose enjoying herself, it had been my nose, not hers that had made an important discovery.

I didn't want anyone to know I'd been out, so the next decision to be made was how to get into the house. If I was seen climbing in through my bedroom window, there would be even more notice taken and questions asked. I'd have to use the front door, but mustn't look as if there was anything furtive about my approach. I strode confidently across the paving, pushed open the door and stepped into the hall.

'Been doing a spot of gardening before breakfast, Shelagh?'

Brad Peterson was standing in the shadow of the potted aspidistra as if he'd been waiting for me.

I didn't have to pretend surprise. 'Gardening? What made you think that?' I'd expected a remark such as, "Had a stroll before breakfast?" Could he have seen me crouched beneath the staging or leaving the conservatory? My heart was pounding. He was far too near the truth.

He smiled. 'Take a look at your trousers.'

I glanced down to discover the knees mud-stained where they'd made contact with the trapdoor, and the legs marked with earthy splashes from my efforts with the watering can. I'd been unforgivably careless.

'Oh dear, that's my cat's fault.' I feigned exasperation. To give me time to think, I made an ineffectual attempt to brush away the mud stains. 'She pestered me till I let her out this morning, but didn't come back. I was worried about her wandering too far away, so I went out to look for her. Spotted her in the shrubbery, made a grab, missed, and landed on my knees. Cats can be so infuriating.' I gave a final quick brush at my trousers. 'Well, she can come back when she likes. I'm not missing breakfast on her account.' Had I convinced him?

He grinned. 'I know all about cats and their manipulative ways. Had one of my own. Don't want to worry you, but there's a real danger of her getting lost. Cats that find themselves in an unfamiliar place try to make their way back to somewhere they know. She could be trying to return to the Shooting Lodge.'

'Oh!' I feigned a stricken expression. There was no risk of G getting lost. She knew exactly where her gourmet food tins were to be found. To her, the thrill of catching a skinny mouse came a poor second to feasting on chunks of the best quality salmon, trout, chicken or duck.

I turned to rush out again, as if panic-stricken, 'You're right. How could I be so selfish as to put breakfast before making sure she was safe!' My eager anticipation of tucking into a heaped plate of sausages, bacon, eggs, and black pudding was fading fast.

He put a restraining hand on my arm. 'No, no, I'll go and look for her. I insist.' Something in the way he said it, told me that he was only half-convinced by my story. 'I've just heard from Hermione that you were a bit of a heroine last night. You deserve a good breakfast after that.' Then, his turn to select a suitable expression. 'If only I'd been there instead of floored with a migraine. But don't worry. *If* Lady's out there, I guarantee

I'll find her.'

Definitely a stress on the 'if'. He didn't believe me.

At that moment a satisfyingly dishevelled Gorgonzola, twigs and earth adhering to her coat, poked her head round the half-open door.

'Ah, there you are, Lady!' I cried in genuine relief that my story now had the ring of truth.

Ignoring me, she made a beeline for Brad, and crooning the drug-detecting croon rubbed against his trouser legs.

'She's certainly taken to you, Brad!' I scooped her up and rushed off to my room. I wasn't going to miss breakfast, and neither was she.

Chapter Nineteen

I was looking forward to 'the hearty Scottish breakfast', but even more to hearing the explanation Russell would give for Marie's non-appearance. The dining room was decorated in Victorian style: dark wallpaper, dark furniture, dark varnished woodwork, dark velvet curtains tied back with tasselled cords. Even on a sunny day, all that would have had a gloomy effect. On a dismal morning like this, the overhead light had been switched on, though its thick shade and fringes did little to brighten the room, and the pale flames licking round the logs burning in the grate contributed atmosphere but not much heat. Seven places had been set at the rectangular mahogany table. It seemed that Marie Stuart and the mysterious owner of the Red Tower, Mr Fotheringham-Green, were not expected to attend.

Most of my fellow guests had arrived before me. Rob was busy at the buffet piling high his plate, not missing out on even one item of the traditional Scottish breakfast. In his MacGregor tartan trousers and waistcoat, he was the very embodiment of a Victorian shooting party host. Tony and Val, instead of the usual show of holding hands and inflicting love-talk on the rest of us, this time ate in unaccustomed silence. A lover's tiff?

I helped myself to a bowl of porridge and sat down opposite Hermione. She'd tied her hair up in a scarf and made an attempt to conceal with make-up the dark circles under her eyes, but it was clear that she had been more than a little shaken by her narrow escape from death.

I reached over and patted her hand. 'Didn't expect to see you at breakfast. How are you feeling?'

She clasped my hand in both of hers. 'I'll never be able to thank you enough, my dear, for saving my life. As to how I'm feeling… I've felt better, I have to admit. But then, it's thanks to you that I'm feeling anything at all.' She released my hand and picked up her fork. 'You know what's bothering me, and it shouldn't really, is my hair. My expensive perm's gone all frizzy and we're nowhere near a hairdresser.' She poked doubtfully at a piece of black pudding. 'Not at all sure about this. Meffy'll enjoy it more than I will.' She plucked a scrunched-up paper napkin from the egg-stained plate next to her and wrapped up the offending Scottish delicacy.

Was it Russell or Peterson who had already breakfasted? 'Who was the early bird?' I said, pointing to the used plate and the half-empty cup of cold tea beside it.

'That was Russell, and all I could get out of him was a grunt.' Rob set down his laden plate on the table and sat down beside me. 'The guy just finished and went off saying he'd be back to tell us what has been arranged for today. Must have felt responsible for the accident last night. Heard all about that from Tony when the actors dropped me off here.' He resumed the demolition of the pile on his plate.

I could understand that Russell had wanted to get away from the breakfast table before somebody asked about Marie. He was probably sitting in his room rehearsing what he was going to say.

But Brad's absence made me uneasy. What was he up to? In spite of G's timely arrival to corroborate my story, had he gone to check the conservatory? That's what I would have done in his place.

I'd finished the porridge and wandered over to the buffet to make a selection from the long-anticipated high cholesterol feast, when behind me I heard the door open and close. Suddenly Brad was standing at my elbow.

With my fork I pronged a plump sausage browned-to-a-turn. 'Not many of these left. It's better to get here before Rob demolishes the lot! I thought you'd be here before me. What's kept you?'

He took a plate from the pile. 'I had a call from my agent just after you went off with the cat. You know how it is, some people take twenty words to say what could be said in five.' A conspiratorial wink. He transferred two fried eggs and four tomatoes to his plate. 'But the offer of work takes precedence over a rumbling stomach.'

'You're right there,' I said.

Thoughtfully I made my way back to my seat. That reference to the phone call was clever: he'd not revealed that it was in his room, let me assume that it had been on his mobile or, if I knew there wasn't a signal, that he'd been summoned to the house phone. His manner was relaxed, the story plausible – but in reality had he spent the time investigating the conservatory for signs of entry and of any suspicious interest in the trough?

On my next visit to the buffet I discovered the answer, wet earth on the carpet just where he'd been standing. Not much, but it told me that he had just come back from checking on the conservatory. He didn't want me to know, so he'd lied. Was this mere caution on his part? Or did it mean that he still had suspicions of me? As I spread marmalade on my toast, I tried to visualize the trough and the ground beside it. Had I covered up all evidence of my visit? It would have been all too easy to overlook some detail. I was not in the clear.

Half an hour after we'd finished breakfast, there was no sign of Russell returning to tell us the programme for the day. Rob was staring gloomily out of the window at the dank mist creeping down from the hills.

'No chance of playing the pipes outside on a foul day like this. How about if I fetch them and give you a little tune or two in here?'

Noticing Hermione's wince, I said, 'Hermione's a bit fragile today. Loud noise – however pleasant,' I added hastily, 'won't do her any good. Anyway, wasn't Russell coming back soon after breakfast to tell us what's happening?'

Brad leapt to his feet and made for the door. 'That's right! I'll go and look for him.'

I heard Tony mutter, 'I should have thought of that excuse.'

Val turned her back on him. 'Too late, once again.' The lovers' tiff was still obviously in operation.

We waited in silence, the only sounds the loud tick of the mantelpiece clock, the crackle of logs in the fire, and the drip of water from a gutter downpipe leaking onto the paving outside. What the others were thinking, I could only guess. By now, I was pretty certain Brad Peterson knew all about the attempt to get rid of Hermione, perhaps had even organized it. I was trying to work out why he was so keen to speak to Russell. Had Peterson gone to tell him the secret room beneath the conservatory might have been discovered? I had seen for myself that Russell handled stressful situations badly. I didn't have long to wait.

Brad flung open the door, bounding in with a cry of, 'Found him! Here he is.'

Russell followed him in and took up position, back to the fire, swallowing nervously, rubbing and twisting his hands, obviously apprehensive about his ability to handle the announcement of Marie Stuart's disappearance. I sat back. This was going to be interesting.

Hermione leaned towards me and whispered, 'Reminds me of a surgeon scrubbing up for an operation!'

He cleared his throat. ' I... I... er...'

'Are you're going to tell us something's gone wrong?' A clever prompt from Brad.

Russell pulled himself together. 'I've just had a phone call from Arabella De la Haigh. There's bad news about Marie Stuart.' He cleared his throat. 'I'm afraid she's... she's...' An unfortunately long pause as he struggled to remember his script.

Hermione gave a little scream. '*Dead!*'

Precisely what they *didn't* want us to think. Brad would be seething at Russell's incompetence. Far from covering up Marie's death, he was drawing attention to the very thing they were trying to conceal. I was enjoying this.

'No, no, she's not dead. It's just that she's disappeared. She asked to be taken back with the actors to the Shooting Lodge, where we would meet up with her again today. But when the rowing boat came to shore, it seems she said she would walk back round the lake to meet up with our minibus. But... but...' Seeing Brad's frown, Russell staggered on with their pre-planned script. 'Arabella has just told me Marie's bed has not been slept in. She'd left a note on her pillow saying she was going back to France after the re-enactment.'

'Ooh! A note on a pillow. Just like in a novel.' Val wriggled in her seat with excitement.

'You mean she's just upped and gone?' Rob's question helped out the struggling Russell.

'That's just what I asked.' More confident now. 'Naturally, Arabella has informed the police, but as everybody thought Marie was with the other group...'

He waited tensely for our reaction.

Brad's snort conveyed male contempt for the weaker sex. 'Hysterical female, talking all that bilge about reincarnation! The murder of the Rizzio chap must have sent her over the edge.'

'That's a bit hard. If only she had come to me for help, poor soul.' Hermione looked genuinely stricken.

'Oh dear!' I sighed. 'The thought of visiting Loch Leven where she... er... where Mary Queen of Scots was imprisoned must have been too much for her, but it was very silly of her to go off like that. The police might well think she had something to do with the murder. I do hope she'll realize that and come back.'

Murmurs and nods of agreement from the others. Russell and Peterson exchanged a covert glance. It must have seemed that after those first hiccups, all was well.

To bolster Peterson and Russell's confidence that their story was accepted, I said, 'Leaving that note on her pillow before she left the Shooting Lodge with the actors for the re-enactment means that Marie must have planned to disappear.'

Russell nodded. 'Just what I was thinking. Looks as if she's deliberately misled us. I'll phone the police and let them know. It will probably take a couple of hours to find out how this will affect the tour. After lunch we will be returning to the Shooting Lodge, but meanwhile I'll leave you to spend the time as you wish. I'm sure you'll find your own entertainment.' Restored to his pompous self, Russell trotted off.

Hermione sighed. 'Two hours more sleep. Wonderful!'

The Templetons, sudden truce declared, hurried off to make the best of the unexpected opportunity, double bed or not.

Rob cast a look out of the window muttering, 'It'll give me the chance to clean the pipebag and the blowtube, and try out a new pibroch on the practice chanter. I'll be in my room.'

I crossed to the window and gazed out as if deciding what to do, but in reality wondering how I could get in touch with Gerry. More than enough time had passed without informing him of developments, but after the immersion in Loch Leven my mobile was useless. This morning I'd opened the case and left the parts out to dry in the hope that I could get it working and find somewhere with a signal – both equally uncertain. Too risky to use the landline phone in Peterson's room.

At that moment he came over to join me at the window. 'Weather's a bit nasty for a walk this morning, but I'm an outdoor guy. I can walk in all weathers. Better than hanging around doing nothing.' The dining room door banged shut behind him.

A few minutes later, I saw him cross the sweep of the drive, unlock the conservatory door and disappear inside. He'd played right into my hands. My mind was made up. I'd take the risk of using the phone in his room.

I wasn't surprised to find his bedroom door had a lock. A turn of my picklock and I was inside, relocking the door behind me. Mindful of how easy it had been able to see into the room from outside, I didn't make the mistake of striding over to pick up the phone on the bedside table, nor did I sit on the bed to leave a tell-tale indent on the duvet that had been hastily pulled up to the pillow. I crawled across the carpet and lying on the floor, reached up and lifted the old-fashioned receiver off its rest.

My heart sank. No dialling tone. Instead, Russell's voice on a linked house phone. I'd counted on making the call to Gerry and being out of the room in a couple of minutes and couldn't afford to wait until he eventually got through to whoever was in charge of the police investigation.

I was about to replace the receiver when I heard a squawk of anger at the other end of the line.

'Are you telling me she isn't dead yet?' Unmistakably, the refined tones of Arabella De la Haigh.

Russell was making the phone call to the Shooting Lodge, not to the police in Edinburgh as he'd said. 'Er… er… The plan to get rid of her failed. Circumstances beyond our control.'

An apprehensive intake of breath at the other end of the line. 'Does the Fielding woman suspect it wasn't an accident?'

Russell, hurriedly, 'No, no, not at all. Definitely thinks her misadventure last night was her own fault. But here's something else you won't like. Peterson caught her trying to get into the conservatory this morning. So what do we do now?'

Arabella, coolly, 'Well you'll just have to try again. Second time lucky. I'll see what Ralph can suggest. Phone you back.'

Click. Russell replaced the receiver. I waited till I was sure that Arabella, too, had disconnected, only then did I put the receiver down at my end.

Now I was faced with a dilemma. How long should I leave it before making the call to Gerry? If I did so right now and Russell picked up the phone to dial Police HQ while I was on the line, he would overhear everything I said. That would mean the end for me, and for Operation Red Grouse. I could listen till he came on the line speaking to the police, but I'd have to wait to contact Gerry till he'd finished, and every minute spent in this room increased the risk of discovery.

Decision time. Russell was irresolute and indecisive, but at the same time desperate to appear confident and in command. My guess was that he'd lift the phone only after a thorough rehearsal of what he was going to say. I'd phone now. Heart beating faster, I made the call.

The vital thing now was to get back to my room without being seen. Criminals are on high alert for anything that might threaten their activities. It wouldn't take much. If Rob saw me coming away from Brad's room, it would only need a remark to Brad, such as, 'So, you were entertaining Shelagh in your room, eh?' A knowing wink. 'Taking tea, I think they called it in Edwardian times', and I would join Hermione on their hit list. But as I passed his door, judging from the short bursts of musical scales emanating from the room, he was still tuning his bagpipes.

The tension draining out of me with every step, I'd almost reached my room when I heard, 'Really! So *rude!*' Hermione, pink in the face and somewhat flustered, came rushing through the front door slamming it behind her. I'd never seen her so worked up.

I stopped, alarmed. 'Oh! What's happened? I thought you were in your room catching up on your sleep?'

Her flush deepened. 'Sleep! That was my intention. I'd just turned back the duvet and crossed to the window to pull the curtains, when I saw–' She paused to catch her breath.

I frowned. 'Er... you saw Meffy up to no good?'

An impatient shake of her head. 'I saw Brad and Mr Russell going into the conservatory.'

Genuinely puzzled, I frowned. 'I don't quite...'

'It's what happened afterwards.' She beckoned me into her room. 'I've just got to tell someone about it.'

Anything to do with the conservatory was of interest to me, and even if all I was going to hear was a good piece of juicy gossip, what woman can resist that! I followed her in like a shot.

'You take the seat, Shelagh, I'll sit on the bed.'

Meffy already had possession of the bed, curled up, one eye closed, the other watching us sleepily. She pounced on the astonished dog and dumped him unceremoniously on the carpet. A startled yip was met with a fierce, '*Quiet!*'

Before he could react with more yips, she pulled open a drawer and tossed him a doggy chew in the shape of a frankfurter sausage. 'Kept for emergencies. But, for ourselves, something more palatable, a little more restorative'. She rummaged in her suitcase and held up a bottle of sherry with the triumph of a magician producing a rabbit out of a hat. 'Two tumblers from the bathroom and we're sorted.' She half-filled each glass and handed one to me. 'You see, when I saw them going into the conservatory, all idea of taking a nap went out of my head.' She sat down heavily on the bed and launched into her tale, punctuating each sentence with a sip of sherry. 'I thought, now's my chance to see inside! When I poked my head into the conservatory, what a surprise! So many gorgeous plants and such a lovely scent of jasmine! Brad was so mistaken in saying that there'd be only dead plants to see. Can't think why he'd want to look inside if that's what he thought. I didn't call out, though. Wasn't taking the risk of being told straightaway by Mr Bossy Boots Russell that I didn't have the owner's permission to be in there. I crept around, quiet as a mouse to see as much as I could before they spotted me.'

Much alarmed, my own intake of sherry increased. This was exactly the sort of behaviour that would spur on the drug organisation to make a second attempt on her life as soon as possible.

Spotting my empty glass, she picked up the bottle. 'A top-up?' She refilled her tumbler and mine.

'How long before they noticed you were there?' A casual question, as if it were mere chat, not a matter of life and death.

Hermione's hand paused, tumbler halfway to her lips. 'We-ell, it must have been about five minutes, I suppose, while I was gradually working my way towards the end of the conservatory. I didn't hear them talking, so I thought that there must be another door at the back and they'd gone out that way. All the better for me, of course, if they didn't know I'd been there. No tiresome lectures from Bossy Boots like that time at Falkland palace when–'

'But they suddenly appeared and gave you a telling off for being there? That's what upset you?'

'Yes and no.' She paused while she thought about it, then came out with an exasperating, 'Or do I mean no and yes?' Another nerve-racking pause, another sip of sherry. 'I heard voices behind the plants at the far end of the greenhouse. As I've said, I didn't want them to see me, so I moved cautiously forward and peeked through the leaves of a very fine rubber plant.'

The trough hiding the entrance to the underground chamber was at the end of the greenhouse. I ran my tongue over suddenly dry lips. 'And?' I croaked.

'There was Mr Russell pushing at a great heavy stone trough and Brad, hands in pockets, watching him. A strong young man like him doing nothing to help! I just couldn't help myself. I called out, "Don't just stand there, Brad. Give him a hand before he has a heart attack!" '

The sip of sherry I'd intended to take became a gulp and a splutter.

Hermione handed me a tissue. 'Calling out like that was my big mistake.' She pressed her lips together as she visualized the effect of her action. 'Mr Russell got a terrible fright, went quite purple in the face and collapsed across the trough. The impact pushed it a couple of inches across the floor. "Oh, my God, he's had a heart attack!" I screamed.'

The blood must have drained from my face, for she reached across to pat my arm.

'No, no, dear, don't worry! It turned out he'd just got a fright and tripped. But, of course, at the time I didn't know that. I rushed round the corner of the staging and yelled at Brad, "At Falkland you told us you were a doctor. Do something!" He took his hands out of his pockets all right. But it wasn't to give first aid to poor Mr Russell, would you believe it! He grabbed my arm, and the swear words, I've never heard the like!' She took a deep breath.

I took one too. This was worse, much worse, than I'd at first thought.

Pink with indignation, she continued, 'Mr Russell, as you know, is quite portly, so it surprised me how quickly he got to his feet. Then he too started shouting at me, something along the lines of, "You've no bloody permission to be in here!" It was awful, I just turned and fled!'

'Oh dear!' I said. 'What can I say?' A question not just to her, but to myself.

Meffy raised his head from an enthusiastic chewing of his doggy sausage. The intermittent low growls, designed to warn off any thieving challenger from his treat, suddenly stopped. He stared at me as if he too were pondering the matter.

Hermione's face crumpled. A wail of anguish, 'How can I face them at lunch?' Two tumblers of sherry hadn't had the desired restorative effect, rather the reverse, rendering her tearful rather than empowered.

It was vital to suggest something she could say that would lead Russell and Peterson to believe that she had no knowledge of the underground chamber.

'No need to worry,' I said. 'Russell was shocked by his fall and will be regretting that he lost his temper with a guest, so he'll be more than a little embarrassed. The best form of defence is attack, so get your word in first!' I leaned over and tickled behind one of Meffy's very large ears. 'Just say to Russell, "Someone of your age and unfitness should not have been trying to move a heavy piece of stone that would take four men to move even an inch." And then switch your attack to Brad.'

She brightened. 'Well… what if I said something like… like…'

'Easy. Complain about the swearing,' I prompted. 'You were an actor, weren't you? Once an actor, always an actor. Think yourself into the part.'

She closed her eyes in concentration, took a deep breath and snapped, 'And as for you, young man, your language was absolutely uncalled for! There you were, standing hands in pockets! Surely you could see what Mr Russell was trying to do was quite impossible and a danger to his health.' Then with an abrupt change of tone, 'Think that'll do, Meffy?'

Yip. He turned his attention back to the sausage.

'Just what's needed, Hermione,' I said. 'A convincing display of outrage.'

I hoped it was. I'd done all I could. If her acting was good enough to convince them that the secret of the stone trough was safe, I'd bought time for her. If they weren't convinced, the next attempt to silence her could come in a matter of hours.

There *would* be another attempt on her life. That was certain.

Chapter Twenty

At lunchtime Hermione's act of outraged indignation went as planned: she received Russell's and Peterson's sincere apologies, just as sham, of course, as her apparent outrage. Judging by the relief and easing of tension in the glances the two men exchanged afterwards, they seemed to accept that the secret of the underground chamber was safe. The necessity for killing her would not now seem quite so urgent.

We were sitting over after-lunch coffee in the lounge when we heard the sound of a car drawing up on the gravel outside.

Tony went to the window. 'Guess who? It's Arabella.' Hermione put down her cup. 'Maybe there's news of Marie.'

Rob looked up from studying the sports page of yesterday's paper. 'Maybe she's coming to tell us the police have lifted the restriction keeping us together.'

We waited expectantly. The door opened and Arabella came into the lounge waving a piece of paper.

'I'm afraid we haven't yet heard from Police HQ, but we can't have you sitting around bored, so at short notice I've managed to arrange an exciting excursion for you. Tomorrow you'll stand under the branches of an amazing thousand-year-old yew tree, in the very spot where Bothwell, the Earl of Morton, and other conspirators are thought to have plotted the revenge murder of

Lord Darnley!' A self-congratulatory smile at our exclamations of delight. 'The tree's on the Whittingehame estate not far from Edinburgh. And, to make the visit even more memorable for you, something to keep and treasure, Ralph will take a group photograph in the secret room formed under the branches of the yew.'

Even Brad seemed pleased. And that should have alerted me. But my only thought was that tomorrow Hermione would be safe in the company of the other guests. So, the very next day, when the attempt on her life was made, I wasn't expecting it. It came – not under the cover of darkness, not when she was alone, not in an obviously dangerous setting such as a narrow path along the edge of a cliff, but on the 'exciting excursion' organized by the De la Haighs to the Whittingehame Yew.

Arabella gestured towards two imposing, ornately carved red sandstone pillars that marked the entrance to what had once been the carriage drive of the fifteenth-century Whittingehame Tower. 'A short walk through the avenue of trees and we'll be at the Yew.'

Val looked down at her flimsy, diamanté-encrusted sandals. 'Ooh, I thought there would be a proper path.' She made a face. 'It's all mud and ruts.'

Hermione shook her head in mild disapproval. 'Shoes like these are not at all wise for walking in the country, my dear.' Adding in a whisper to me, 'The folly of youth!'

'Don't think I'm going to carry you. Just pick your way across the grassy bits.' Tony strode ahead to join Arabella, making it clear that he meant what he said.

The rest of us followed in a little procession, a motley

baggage train trailing behind two intrepid explorers: Hermione clutching Meffy's wicker basket, me holding G's carrier, Rob gripping the bagpipes snugly under his arm, Brad lugging a heavy picnic hamper, Val in her tights gripping her precious shoes by the straps, Ralph bringing up the rear, collapsible tripod under arm, digital camera round neck. A progress soon marked by the plaintive notes of Rob's pipes and Val's squeals.

After five minutes Arabella pointed off to the right. 'There it is!'

I had imagined the old yew as being a tall tree, its thick trunk topped by a cone of foliage. Instead, it was a round, low tree, an unremarkable leafy mound, its branches drooping almost to the ground.

Arabella forestalled any disappointed muttering. 'Yes, I know it doesn't look like much from here, but I guarantee you'll never forget what you are about to experience.' She bent down to pass under the skirt of outer branches. 'Follow me into the heart of this thousand-year-old tree. We'll have a little picnic and take the group photo inside the yew itself!'

I peered into the long low tunnel that stretched ahead towards the centre of the tree. Rusty iron frames held back the dark tangle of branches, thick as trunks, interlacing at each side and above my head. Holding the weight of the cat carrier, I shuffled forward in the semi-stooped posture of Neanderthal Woman towards the darkness at the end of the tunnel. Judging by the gasps behind me, Hermione was having equal difficulty with Meffy's basket. I thought with some satisfaction that Brad was going to find the heavy picnic hamper very awkward indeed.

I straightened up at the end of the tunnel and stopped in

astonishment. Splashes and streaks of sunlight were filtering through a tracery of interlaced branches, giving the effect of standing beneath a giant upturned bird's nest. The fluted column of the trunk stood anchored by massive roots in the centre of this bowl, its top lost in darkness high above. Through the mesh of branches the *cheep cheep* of birds and a faint burble of the river percolated from the valley below.

'Move aside, Shelagh. Bending like this isn't good for me, a lady of mature years!' Hermione set down Meffy's basket in the surprisingly large space formed by the drooping branches. 'These roots, Shelagh! They're like fat pythons writhing over the ground.'

Arabella allowed a couple of minutes for exclamations of amazement, then, 'Plenty of time to admire later!' With somewhat irritating efficiency she set about organizing us for the photo shoot. 'If you'll all just come over here and stand beside the trunk while Ralph's setting up the tripod and camera.' Head on one side, lips pursed, she stood for a moment surveying us critically. 'As I've said, we don't want the souvenir photograph of the tour to be too formal. So...' She pointed to Rob, kitted out for the occasion in red and black MacGregor tartan kilt, black jacket and Glengarry bonnet. 'You're quite tall. I want you there on the left, at that end of the line.'

'Yes, ma'am.' He marched obediently into position, bagpipes under arm.

'Now can I ask you to be playing the pipes.' A command rather than a question. 'The blowpipe to your lips, that's right.'

He puffed out his cheeks. The pipes emitted a thin wail that set our teeth on edge.

'No music, please.' A forced smile. Her feelings betrayed by a tone a little too sharp. 'Just *pretend* to be playing the pipes.'

He dug his elbow sharply into the bag to produce a fart-like groan. Her smile faded. His message was clear.

She turned her attention to Tony and Val. 'Now, Mr and Mrs Templeton, gaze into each other's eyes, hands intertwined. Perfect.'

No objections from them, I thought.

She positioned Brad to lounge against the thick trunk, hands in the pockets of his camouflage-pattern cargo pants.

'Next to Brad, you, Shelagh.'

I moved to stand beside him with Gorgonzola dozing in my arms. Our contribution to the souvenir aspect of the group photo was the spiky collar round her neck.

'So that leaves Mrs Fielding at this end of the line.'

Hermione had taken a lot more care over her appearance than I had, her silver hair heavily sprayed to thwart any mischievous breeze that might spring up. She took her assigned place, the Papillon earrings and the gemstone rings glinting in a splash of sunlight filtering through the net of branches. Her choice of pose was to smile serenely down on Meffy sitting quietly at her feet with his large ears pricked and eyes fixed calculatingly on Gorgonzola.

Arabella nodded her head in satisfaction. 'How does that look, Ralph?'

He stooped to peer at the screen and adjust aperture and focus. 'If you could just move a little to the left, Mrs Fielding. That's it. Now, everybody stay quite still. This will need a time exposure to compensate for the lack of light and get the full ambience of the place.

Click. He studied the screen. 'Mrs Fielding, look up at the camera.' *Click.* 'Good. You can all relax.'

Arabella undid the straps on the hamper. 'Now for our picnic. Choose a root to sit on, and when everyone has some slices of bruschetta on their plate and a glass of champagne, Ralph'll take another photo.' She lifted out a pile of plates. 'If you could give me a hand, Brad…'

I sipped the quality champagne, and from my plate balanced on one of the broad roots selected a slice of bruschetta topped with tomato and feta sprinkled with oregano. This last-minute addition to the tour, our visit to this remarkable tree with its historical connection to Mary Queen of Scots, measured up to any of the previous Act It Out re-enactments. And to round it off with a champagne picnic in this peaceful location, in perfect weather for the time of year, I had to admit, was a triumph.

The De la Haighs had planned well. In such a setting, and surrounded by her fellow guests, an attempt on Hermione's life was the last thing on my mind.

Chapter Twenty-One

'Go on, take it. It's the very last one. Nobody's looking!' Smiling, Brad slipped the remaining bruschetta slice onto Hermione's plate.

She hesitated. 'I've had four already. Must watch the waistline, you know. But, then, they *are* irresistible.'

I saw Meffy's nose twitch. He was lying quietly on the ground, head on paws, eyes riveted on her plate.

She broke the slice in two, put it in her mouth and stretched out her hand for the other half. 'Mmm. Delicious.'

I sensed what was going to happen next. 'Look out! Meffy's about to–'

Too late. Tempted beyond endurance, he'd launched himself at the tasty morsel with the velocity of a basketball player leaping for the net. Hermione jerked the plate away and Meffy's jaws snapped on air. The object of desire sailed into the air, dropped into a gap between two snaking roots, and disappeared from sight.

From Meffy, a frustrated yip. From Hermione, a furious cry,

'That was the last piece! Back into the carrier with you!' She bundled him into the wicker basket and slammed shut the door, leaving the crestfallen Meffy pressing his nose against the wicker bars.

His mournful yip... yip brought out the worst in G. She got up, slowly extending her front legs, bottom in air for better stretch, the said bottom carefully positioned in the direction of the miscreant in the basket. Now that she had his attention, she strolled provocatively over to the gap between the roots, sniffed, and put out an exploratory paw.

'Cheese not allowed!' I shrieked, foreseeing feline gastric upset and diarrhoea. 'Into the carrier with you too!'

Ralph de la Haigh waited till I'd finished dealing with G, then lifted out a bulky paperback from the depths of the hamper and opened the book at a marked place.

'The murder of Darnley at Kirk o'Fields was by tradition plotted under this very yew. There's an enthralling account of the five-hundred-year-old crime in this biography of Mary Queen of Scots by Antonia Fraser.' He looked slowly from one to other of us. 'How the plan was carried out, the actual murder, I think you'll agree, would fit into a modern crime novel. Darnley was discovered in his nightshirt in the garden, strangled, just after a gunpowder bomb demolished the house to a pile of rubble.' He started to read.

He finished. The sunlight had gone, leaving a chill and decidedly sinister gloom under the yew's honeycomb of branches. We made our way sombrely back down the avenue of trees to the minibus, my thoughts not on the Darnley murder plot but on a twenty-first century one being hatched against Hermione. What form would it take and what could I do to prevent it?

Something had woken me from a deep sleep. Moonlight was

filtering through the curtains of my bedroom at the Red Tower.

Tap… tap. A sound so faint I couldn't decide where it was coming from. Curled at my back on the duvet, Gorgonzola stirred. She had heard it too. I raised myself on an elbow and stared into the darkness. *Tap tap.* I reached over and switched on the bedside light. *Tap tap tap.* More urgent this time. Somebody was tapping. But not on the door.

I threw back the duvet and stood in the centre of the room, looking round to pinpoint the source of the sound. There it was again. It was coming from a point low down on the bedroom wall. Still half-asleep, it took me a moment or two to realize that Hermione in the room next door was calling for help.

Instantly wide-awake, I rushed out into the corridor and flung open her door. The bed was empty. Then in the soft light of the bedside lamp I saw her lying in a crumpled heap on the floor. The hand stretched out towards the wall was holding an empty tumbler. With a whine Meffy leapt up from where he had been sitting beside her. He ran towards me as if urging me to hurry, then scurried back to stand guard over her.

'Hermione!'

She didn't react. Was it too late? Had the attempt on her life succeeded? I dropped to my knees beside her. I was relieved to detect a pulse, but it was slow and irregular. As I turned her into the recovery position, she groaned and her eyes fluttered open. 'Shelagh… so much pain… been so sick…' She clutched her stomach. Her eyes closed.

Food poisoning? Possibly, though we had all eaten the same food at breakfast, on the excursion to the yew, and at dinner this evening.

I pulled the duvet off the bed and tucked it round her while

Meffy looked on anxiously, then licked my hand.

With no mobile signal to summon the emergency services, I tried to think what best to do. I'd have to be very careful not to betray that I knew there was a landline phone in Brad's room. When he opened the door, perhaps I'd catch a glimpse of it and express surprised relief at the discovery. Rehearsing what I was going to say, I rushed along the corridor followed by Gorgonzola, curious to know why her sleep had been disturbed in the middle of the night.

Thud thud thud. I pounded on Brad's bedroom door. *Thud thud thud.*

A sleepy voice called, 'What's up?

I didn't reply. A shouted conversation through the door would risk being fobbed off with, 'Nothing that can't wait till morning. Give her some bicarb.'

I banged my fist on the wood again. *Thud thud thud.* 'Brad! Brad! Wake up.'

The door was wrenched open. He stood framed in the doorway, effectively blocking all view of the room's interior and the tell-tale phone.

He peered at me. 'Bloody hell, Shelagh! It's three o'clock in the morning. This had better be good.'

'Hermione's collapsed!' I cried. 'Food poisoning, I think, but there's no mobile signal to phone for an ambulance. What are we going to do?'

He squeezed his eyes shut as if dazed with sleep. 'Phone... phone? Russell used the house phone to contact the police yesterday morning, but last night he told me the line had developed a fault and he couldn't get through to the Shooting Lodge.'

No mention of the phone in his room.

'What can we do?' I cried. 'She's in a bad way.'

'Food poisoning, you say? Fortunately I've some medical training.' Probably another lie, and whatever his 'diagnosis', it would certainly not be in Hermione's best interest. My mention of food poisoning had played right into his hands. 'I'll take a look at her.' He emerged from his room, closing the door quickly to prevent me seeing in.

As we passed Rob's door, it opened. His tousled red head appeared. 'What's wrong? Somebody been taken ill?'

'It's Hermione,' I said, 'and it's serious.'

We hurried to catch up with Brad. She was lying as I'd left her with Meffy standing guard.

'First thing, the pulse.' Brad bent over her and grabbed her wrist.

In a flash Meffy's sharp little teeth closed on his hand. 'Shit!' He jerked his hand away and eyed the two small puncture marks. 'Bloody brute!' He aimed a kick at Meffy's ribs.

Fast as lightning, Meffy leapt aside, sank his teeth into Brad's muscular calf and darted out of reach.

'*Yaoow!*' Brad danced up and down, clutching his leg.

Rob grabbed Meffy's collar, swept him up in one swift movement, and ignoring the frantic struggles, tucked him under his arm as easily as a set of bagpipes.

I shut my ears to the shrill *yip yip yip* and Brad's inventive swearing, and knelt down beside Hermione to take her pulse. Slower. And more irregular.

At my touch, she opened her eyes murmuring, 'Such a headache.'

I sat back on my heels, puzzled. A slow and irregular pulse, a severe headache. These were not the normal symptoms of food poisoning. She must have been deliberately poisoned, so they'd have made sure the landline phone appeared to be out of order.

I jumped to my feet. 'I'll ask Russell to drive her to hospital in the minibus.'

Brad shook his head. 'He isn't fit to drive. We emptied a bottle of whisky between us tonight, so he'll be over the limit.' He stood looking down at Hermione. 'Anyway, she's only suffering from a touch of indigestion and a dizzy turn because she got out of bed too quickly.' A shrug. 'She'll be fine in the morning.' A quizzical half-smile implied I was merely a hysterical female. 'I'm off to bed.' He limped out, tripping over G who chose that very moment to cross his path. Brad's attack on Meffy had not gone unobserved.

Tony appeared in the doorway. 'Oh! What's up with the old girl? Anything I can do?'

'Hermione's very ill.' I looked from him to Rob. 'Either of you licensed to drive the minibus?'

Rob nodded. Now all I had to do was ask Russell for the keys.

But somebody had thought of that possibility too. The drug organisation was one move ahead.

Chapter Twenty-Two

I found Russell lying snoring on his bed, fully clothed and smelling strongly of whisky. An empty bottle and two glasses on the dressing table appeared to bear out Peterson's story.

'Gordon!' I put a hand on his shoulder and shook him roughly. 'Mr Russell, where are the keys for the minibus?'

No response.

I shook him again, shouted in his ear, 'The keys... for... the... minibus.'

A snort, a gurgling snore. His eyes remained firmly closed.

I studied the prostrate figure. He was a pompous little man for whom image was all. It didn't seem likely that he'd let himself get as drunk as this. He would find it distressing and humiliating to be seen to be hung over when he met with his clients in the morning to tell us about the travel arrangements, so was this drunken stupor just pretence, a masterly piece of play-acting backed up with essential props of bottle and glasses? There was one way to find out. I jabbed my forefinger hard into his diaphragm. No movement. No cry of pain or protest. Gordon Russell really *was* out for the count. I made a quick search, but found no keys.

When I rushed back to Hermione's room with the bad news, Val was cradling the whimpering Meffy trying to calm him, and Tony and Rob had wrapped Hermione in the duvet with a sling fashioned from a sheet to carry her out to the minibus.

Rob looked up expectantly. 'Got the keys?'

I shook my head. 'We'll have to think again. He's blind drunk and sleeping it off. I've searched and I can't find them.'

Whether Russell had intentionally made himself drunk or whether his drink had been spiked, it was no coincidence that the keys of the minibus were missing. No coincidence at all. Provision had been made for all eventualities. We wouldn't be able to get her to hospital. And that was just what the drug organisation had intended.

But there was one eventuality they had not foreseen. And that was Tony Templeton's shady past.

He grinned. 'If they've left the bus unlocked, we're in business. I can get it started, no problem.' A knowing wink. 'Tony Templeton, hot-wiring a speciality.'

The minibus door wasn't locked. Once we found that out, everything went without a hitch. Val grabbed Meffy's favourite pink rat and a bag of doggy treats and swept him off to her room. Using the bed sheet as a makeshift stretcher-sling, Rob and Tony carried Hermione out to the minibus wrapped cosily in her duvet. Excitement over, G retired to my room to enjoy, as I later discovered, an untroubled sleep on strictly forbidden territory, my pillow.

'Hold the torch, Shelagh.' Tony lifted the engine cover. 'This is an old model, so we're in luck. Now all we need is a screwdriver and jump leads from the toolbox, and…'

In next to no time the engine fired, Rob took the wheel, and we were on our way. Our headlights cut into the darkness ahead, briefly spotlighting tree trunks… grassy banks… thorny hedges… drystone walls… and once, a pair of tiny diamond-bright eyes.

The Red Tower was situated somewhere deep in the countryside and none of us had paid particular attention as to how we'd got there. After several wrong turnings and a frustratingly long time, I grew increasingly worried. I calculated it would take another hour after we reached the main trunk road before we could get to Edinburgh Royal Infirmary with its ability to test for obscure poisons. At Accident & Emergency, they'd want to rule out food poisoning. To save valuable time, I jotted down a list of what she'd eaten in the past twenty-four hours: at breakfast, porridge, toast and marmalade; for picnic lunch, feta and tomato bruschetta; at dinner, onion soup, lamb casserole, apple tart. But we'd all helped ourselves from the same dishes on the sideboard at each of these meals, some taking two helpings, so how had the poison been administered? I closed my eyes the better to visualize each mealtime and whether she'd eaten anything different from the rest of us. As far as I could remember, she hadn't.

I tried tackling it from another angle: motive and opportunity. Russell, Peterson, MacGregor, the De la Haighs, the Templetons, all had had the opportunity. Motive narrowed it down. Who might want her dead? The Templetons and Rob were doing their best to save her life, so that left Peterson, Russell and the De la Haighs.

Brad Peterson! I had a sudden memory of him approaching Hermione as she sat on one of the snake-like roots under the interlacing branches of the Whittingehame Yew. Remembered him offering her a slice of bruschetta and saying, 'Go on, take it. It's the very last one. Nobody's looking!' He'd smiled as he'd slipped it onto her plate.

Yes, that's how it must have been done, but as to the actual poison… I cast an anxious glance at Hermione lying along the back seat. She was, if possible, even paler, and was that a blueish tinge to her lips? I reached over, took her hand and felt the tremors.

'Go as fast as is safe, Rob,' I said, my voice calm, heart racing. 'Just get there.'

Hooaa hooaa hooaa. The siren startled me from my thoughts.

Rob swore. 'There's a police car behind us with a flashing blue light. What does he expect me to do? On this narrow road there's nowhere to draw in to let him pass.' He swore again. 'My God, he's impatient! Can't go any faster than this.' He gripped the wheel and peered through the windscreen concentrating on taking the bends.

I twisted round to look through the rear window. The police car was now flashing its headlights. 'They're not trying to pass, Rob. They're ordering us to stop!'

As we braked to a halt, the police car drew in behind. The doors opened, two burly officers got slowly out and put on their uniform caps.

Tony leaned forward to slide open the window. 'Guess the landline fault's been repaired. Brad's had another think about how ill Hermione is and he's phoned the police to give us an escort.'

If he had indeed phoned the police, I thought grimly, it would only be in the hope it would delay us so that Hermione would die before we got her to hospital.

A face appeared at the driver's window. 'Can I ask you to switch off the engine and get out of the bus, sir.' Command, not question.

Rob sighed, then, 'I can certainly do the one, but not the other.'

The face remained impassive. 'And which would it be that you can't do, sir?'

'Switch off the engine.'

'Indeed, sir, and why might that be?' More than a slight edge in the voice.

The burlier of the two wrenched open the passenger door. 'Everyone out!

Tony and I stepped down onto the grass verge. Rob climbed out from behind the wheel onto the road. The engine purred on, loud in the early morning silence.

'Told you to cut the engine, didn't I? He reached towards the dashboard. 'No key in the ignition. My, my, my!' He raised his voice above the noise of the engine. 'Van reported stolen. Here's the confirmation, Mike.'

Mike joined him. Judge and jury, they stared at us accusingly, then sentence of guilt delivered, their hands moved to their equipment belt, ready for a hostile move on our part.

'Excuse me, officer, did you say it was reported stolen?' I frowned to indicate how preposterous the whole idea was.

'Indeed, madam.' He pulled a notebook from his top pocket and opened it with a flourish. 'Minibus reported stolen from the Red Tower estate by a Mr Gordon Russell at 0440 hours this morning.' He closed the notebook with a snap and returned it to his pocket.

I gave an exaggerated sigh of relief. 'Oh dear, I'm afraid it's all been a most unfortunate misunderstanding. Mrs Fielding, one of our fellow guests, took violently ill in the middle of the night with severe abdominal pains. We couldn't phone for an ambulance because there was a fault on the landline. In desperation, we decided to take her to hospital in the minibus…'

Sceptical glances. 'And this? Engine running without a key in the ignition.' Mike slapped the flat of his hand down on the vibrating engine cover.

Rob shrugged. 'Mr Russell had celebrated a bit too much with the whisky, and as we couldn't find the keys, we had to… er…'

Mike glanced at his partner. 'Credibility rating, Bob?'

'Two out of ten, and that's being generous.' A smile without humour. 'You're all under arrest and–'

A low moan from inside the minibus cut him short.

'That's Mrs Fielding!' I cried. 'You'll see for yourself that this is an emergency.'

One glance at Hermione was enough. They escorted us on our way, police siren howling, blue light flashing. As we rushed through the night, I pondered this latest move by Peterson. I was absolutely sure that Russell had been incapable of getting out of bed to report anything in the condition he was in. Peterson must have made the phone call, the 'fault' on the line having been conveniently fixed. He must have hoped the police would delay us enough for Hermione's condition to worsen. That meant that he knew the poison was fast-acting. Would we reach the hospital in time?

I stared at the doctor. 'Taxus poisoning?'

He nodded. 'Most parts of the yew tree are toxic even the

leaves, though the highest concentration of the poison is in the seeds. We are monitoring Mrs Fielding's vital signs and supporting her breathing. It would be most helpful if we knew the approximate time that she ingested the berry.'

'I didn't see her eat a berry,' I said, 'but we did picnic under a yew tree at lunchtime yesterday. I suppose something could have fallen into the salad.' And not by chance, I thought. Yew leaves chopped small would have looked very similar to oregano on the tomato and feta bruschetta.

He made a note on a pad. 'In these poisoning cases, the outcome for the patient depends on how quickly they are treated. You did well to bring her in as soon as you had concerns. Any later and we would not have been able to save her.' He hurried away.

So Peterson had miscalculated. By reporting the minibus stolen, he had increased Hermione's chance not of dying, but of living.

Dawn was breaking as I slid open the door of the minibus. Tony and Rob had chosen to wait there for me rather than sit on hard chairs in the noisy A&E. They sat up yawning as I climbed in.

'She's critical in intensive care, but thanks to you she's got a slim chance,' I said and buckled my seatbelt in readiness for the journey back. I kept to myself the fact that the doctor was hopeful she would recover. Safer for Hermione that way.

When we arrived back, hungry and more than ready for a late breakfast, Brad was alone in the dining room. Evidence that Val had eaten and gone was a side plate with a crust of toast beside a crumpled paper napkin smeared with lipstick. There was no sign of Russell.

Brad looked up casually, a tightening of the muscles in his cheek the only sign of inner tension. 'So you all overslept after that false alarm in the night? Me too – once I got to sleep thanks to the pain in my leg, that is.' He pushed away his porridge plate and limped ostentatiously towards the bacon and eggs on the buffet table. 'How is Hermione by the way? Take a tip from me – sodium bicarbonate's the thing if she's still queasy.'

Rob elbowed him roughly aside. 'Queasy? A load of rubbish! Some medical training, you've got, telling us there wasn't much wrong with her! She's in hospital on life support. A bloody lot of help you were last night.'

'Really?' Brad's consternation was plain. Tony and Rob would read this as dismay at how wrong he had been, but to me, it revealed alarm that she was still alive.

Rob motioned us forward. 'Don't hold back. There's enough bacon and eggs for the three of us.'

'Hey! Russell's not eaten yet. Leave something for him.'

'With the mother and father of a hangover, he won't be eating. You just want Russell's share for yourself.' Pointedly ignoring Brad's objection, Rob emptied the contents of the serving dishes onto our plates.

Brad watched in silence as we ate. He'd be wondering when we were going to bring up the reported theft of the minibus.

Speaking between mouthfuls, Tony eyed the vacant seat at the table. 'So Russell's lying low, not keen to face us, eh?'

Brad frowned. 'Russell? What's he done?'

'Bloody fool noticed the minibus was missing and reported it stolen. We were stopped by the police.' Tony's fork viciously speared the last piece of sausage.

Brad's feigned frown deepened. 'You've lost me. Minibus?

Police? Ah! Now I get it. You mean you actually took Hermione to hospital in the minibus?' He forced a laugh.

Rob pushed away his empty plate. 'Didn't you hear me? She's very poorly, might not make it.'

'Might not make it!' Brad's jaw dropped in pretend horrified surprise. A pause. 'Did the hospital say what was wrong?' Again, that tightening of muscles in his cheek.

I shook my head. How to put it so that he'd think the attempt on Hermione's life was about to succeed?

'The doctors were puzzled. They said she had ingested some toxin or other, so they washed out her stomach to remove whatever it was, but that didn't bring about the expected improvement, I'm afraid.' My heavy sigh implied that I feared the worst, that death would follow soon.

'That's terrible!' He shook his head as if he couldn't believe what he'd just heard. 'But you can't blame me for not diagnosing something that's got experts at the hospital baffled.' As he went out closing the door behind him, did I glimpse a quiet smile of satisfaction?

Judging by the tell-tale cat-body-shape impression left on my pillow, Gorgonzola had hastily vacated forbidden territory when she heard me opening the bedroom door. Eager to catch up on a missed night's sleep, I unceremoniously turfed her off the bed and turned over the pillow. Two hours' sleep should be enough. Then I'd take a stroll in the grounds past the ruined cottage to see whether the Mercedes with the false number plate was still there. Only pausing to take off my shoes, I threw myself down on the bed.

Not two, but three hours later, a light *tap tap tap* roused me from a deep sleep.

Val's voice called through the door, 'Wake up, Shelagh. Lunch'll be ready in half an hour and after that we'll be going back to the Shooting Lodge.'

Annoyed with myself that I'd overslept, I sat up, pushing away G who had made a stealth approach under the duvet to curl up beside me. There'd just be time for me to plant a tracking bug on the Mercedes in the half an hour before lunch.

But I was too late. The car had gone.

Our return to the Shooting Lodge was in fact delayed till late afternoon, ostensibly to call in a mechanic to check the minibus engine after the hotwire start, but I suspected that the real reason for the delay was to allow Russell to fully sober up. When he eventually appeared, red-eyed and unusually silent, he curtly turned down Rob's offer to drive. The only sign that he was still a little hung over and sensitive to noise was that the CD player and radio remained switched off. It was a mercifully music-free journey.

From the seat beside me, Gorgonzola glared balefully out of the cat carrier at Meffy sitting on Val's knee, free from the confines of his wicker basket while she whispered endearments into his heavily fringed ears and treated him to frequent strokes and pats as befitted an orphaned dog. If a dog could purr, and a cat could snarl... When we arrived at our destination, I knew that G would demand just as much attention, as well as compensation for being neglected.

Arabella De la Haigh was positioned on the steps of the Lodge to greet us. As soon as the minibus came to a halt, she rushed forward.

'Terrible news about Mrs Fielding! As soon as I heard,

I phoned the hospital, but all they would say was that her condition was giving concern.'

'Oh dear!' I said, biting my lip. 'I'm afraid that doesn't sound too good.' That should hopefully give the impression that Hermione was at death's door and not worth finishing off.

I was in my bedroom sitting on the window seat brushing Gorgonzola with long slow strokes and murmuring the expected soothing, honeyed words, when I heard the sound of a car engine. The black Mercedes nosed into the courtyard and drew up in front of the garage. The driver's door opened and Ralph de la Haigh got out. The number plate had been changed back to De la Haigh's from the one it bore at the ruined cottage. He drove the car into the garage and remained inside with the garage doors closed.

I was wondering what he was up to, when a sharp tap from Gorgonzola's paw reminded me I was neglecting my duties. I slowly resumed the brushing, my thoughts on where best to plant the tracking device in the Mercedes during the visit I'd planned for the early hours of tomorrow morning.

3 a.m. It was time. I pushed up the bedroom window. Wearing her spiky working collar, Gorgonzola jumped down onto the paving. I followed her out, careful to pull down the window till it appeared to be closed. I stood in the shadows, pressed against the building, eyes scanning for the slightest movement, ears taking in the sounds of the night – the soft patter of raindrops on stone, the *drip drip drip* from a leaking gutter, the mournful hoot of a hunting owl. Overhead, the moon was a hazy circle, its light barely penetrating the thick layer of cloud.

At last, satisfied that nobody was about, I darted across the courtyard to the garage, G at my heels. It took a few seconds to deal with the mortise locks, then we were inside with the door closed securely behind us and I could switch on my pencil torch. The Act It Out minibuses were parked one behind the other, but it was the Mercedes that I was interested in. G's check of the boot confirmed that the car had recently been used to transport drugs, presumably to the Red Tower. The thin beam of my torch moved across the car... Once again the number plates were those I'd seen at the ruined cottage. It seemed the car was about to make another mysterious trip.

Now to the purpose of my visit, the planting of the GPS tracking device. I leaned in the rear passenger door and reached for the lever that raised the hinged back seat, revealing the fabric designed to deaden road noise. I lifted the fabric and slipped the tracker device up behind the rear seat cushioning. Smaller than a credit card, it wouldn't be easily detected. The signal would transmit date, time, and the location of the car to HMRC so that Gerry would be able to track it on a computer via Google maps. I lowered the hinged seat, pressing it down till it clicked into place. Satisfied, I glanced at my watch. Time to get back. It would take a lot of explaining if anyone noticed I wasn't in my room. Mission accomplished, G and I left.

In blissful ignorance of the motion-activated CCTV camera that had been recording our every move from the moment we entered the garage.

Chapter Twenty-Three

'It's short notice, but we've managed to organise a visit today to the castle at St Andrews. Such a pity that Mrs Fielding isn't here.' Arabella shook her head and sighed. 'The actors have rehearsed a short re-enactment of a little-known but scandalous event in Queen Mary's life when a French lover burst into her bedchamber and...' she put a finger to her lips, '... but I say no more!'

'Ooooh!' Val gave a little scream of delight.

'Hwoar!' Tony winked knowingly at Rob who grinned back.

'How interesting!' I cried, and it was, because the visit must be a cover for another drug distribution.

'Looking forward to it! Can't wait!' Brad had never shown any particular enthusiasm for a re-enactment, so I should have taken note. But my mind was on how to follow whoever slipped away to make a delivery of drugs.

Arabella held up a hand to regain our attention. 'There's one other matter. Ralph and I both have business to attend to and will not be here at the Shooting Lodge to look after the delightful animals, so I must ask that they accompany you. Otherwise, I'm afraid, someone will have to stay behind to look after them.'

'It's no problem as far as Lady is concerned,' I said. 'I can carry her in my rucksack.'

A long pause. All eyes turned to Val, now acting as Meffy's carer. It was clear that none of the men were going to volunteer.

She pouted, then gave in. 'I suppose… it won't be too much bother to take Meffy in his basket. I'm certainly not going to miss out on royal scandal.'

'Good, that's arranged then.' Arabella consulted a small notebook. 'You'll leave here in half an hour, arrive in St Andrews about eleven o'clock, and after the short re-enactment you'll have the rest of the day for the Castle, lunch, and looking round St Andrews. The ruins of the cathedral are well worth a visit. The minibus will pick you up in the car park beside the Golf Museum at four o'clock. Enjoy your day.'

Surprisingly little remains of the Castle of St Andrews. Reduced to a mere shell by nearly a thousand years of storms and siege, the ruins stand high above the shore with its jagged reefs colonised by clusters of seabirds.

Russell led the way over the drawbridge and under the still-impressive entrance arch. 'As you can see, so few walls remain round the inner courtyard that there isn't anywhere sufficiently preserved to hold the re-enactment indoors. Act It Out have risen to the occasion, however, by holding an outdoor performance with the ruined four-storey Gate Tower as stage scenery.'

We sat on folding chairs in the grassy courtyard, Meffy on Val's lap, and Gorgonzola enjoying a snooze hidden in the rucksack at my feet, out of sight, out of mind of her arch-enemy. The Tower provided perfect stage scenery for the re-enactment with its glassless windows and wooden balustrade on the first floor. In front of the doorway at ground level, Act It Out had cleverly conjured up the impression of a room by providing a bed covered with a richly embroidered cloth, and draping velvet curtaining over the crumbling walls.

Russell stepped forward to address his tiny audience, now swelled by a group of curious tourists standing behind our seats. 'Ladies and gentlemen, the incidents in this re-enactment took place not in the castle itself, which was already half-ruined by French bombardment and therefore no place for a queen, but at the court in Aberdeen and in a house in South Street, a stone's throw from here. What you are about to witness is motivated by a plot...' he let his gaze move slowly from face to face in a theatrically melodramatic manner. '... a plot concocted to damage the reputation of Mary Queen of Scots in the eyes of her God-fearing subjects, and thus confirm her unsuitability to be Queen of Scotland! Behind the plot were the politics of sixteenth-century Scotland and France.'

Dressed in sixteenth-century costume, three of Act It Out's cast appeared on the first floor of the tower. Samantha stepped forward and made a deep curtsy to the audience. 'The year is fifteen hundred and sixty-three. It is long after midnight. Queen Mary has taken her court to Aberdeen where she is holding a conference with Lord Maitland...'

She moved aside as red-haired Sophie in the familiar black gown and ruff of Mary's portraits extended her hand to be formally kissed. 'My Lord Maitland, I bid you leave for England this very morning.'

Tarquin, as Maitland, made a courtly bow. 'Your wish is my command, madam. What is the message I am to bear?'

Lowering their voices, they moved towards the window

and stood looking out, leaving our attention to focus on the base of the tower. The door creaked slowly open. Minibus driver Jamie had sacrificed his designer stubble to play the role of a handsome young aristocrat. He peered cautiously into the space set out as a bedroom, slipped through the door and closed it quietly behind him. He took two strides, dropped to his knees, and rolled under the bed. The heavy coverlet fell down behind him, concealing him from view. A slight movement of the material and it was still.

After a few moments, male voices could be heard on the other side of the door. Two servants walked in. One was Allan carrying a long-handled copper warming pan, the other an actor I didn't recognise, presumably recruited to make good Act It Out's shortage of male actors.

Allan folded back the coverlet to expose the pillows. 'See if any of the Queen's enemies are skulking behind the tapestries, Tam, while I attend to the bed.' He pushed the warming pan between the sheets, turned away, then paused. 'Better check under the bed, I suppose. Who knows, a rat could be lurking under there!' He lifted the edge of the coverlet and stooped to look.

A sharp intake of breath from Val, a snigger from Tony.

'A rat, God's Blood! And a big un.' Allan seized the intruder's leg and dragged him out.

The two servants stood gazing down at the dishevelled young man lying at their feet.

'Methinks 'tis Lord Châtelard, the Frenchie. He's forever following the Queen around spouting poetry!' They looked at each other then heaved him to his feet.

'Perhaps my lord has imbibed too much wine. Sir, 'tis not

seemly for you to be in the Queen's bedchamber. We will escort you to your room.' Gripping him by the arms, they led him away.

Samantha stepped forward at the first-floor level. She was now alone. Mary Queen of Scots and Lord Maitland had gone. 'Some time has passed since the Queen learned of Châtelard's intrusion into her bedchamber and ordered him to leave the court. She is now staying in St Andrews.' A gesture directed our gaze back down to the bedchamber.

The door at the rear opened and Mary Queen of Scots came in chatting to two maids-in-waiting, played by the matronly Jacqui, and by Chloe, Goth attire replaced by a sixteenth-century gown.

Mary sat down on the bed and extended a foot. 'I shall retire early tonight. Pray, take off my shoes.'

Chloe knelt and was removing one royal shoe when the door burst open. Châtelard rushed in, pushed Chloe aside and seized Mary's stockinged foot.

'My lady, my Queen!' He smothered her foot with kisses, working his way slowly up her leg.

The shrieks of Mary and her ladies echoing round the courtyard had an unforeseen effect. For a couple of minutes chaos reigned. Tourists rushed out of the Visitor Centre, Meffy's high-pitched *yip yip yip* contributing to the commotion.

Yoaoowl, Gorgonzola, all too ready to be in on any action, forced the zip apart with her head and attempted to jump out of the rucksack, only to be thwarted by the spikes on her collar.

Yip yip yip.

Val made a grab for Meffy, too late to prevent him leaping off her knee and dancing up and down in a show of bravado.

I pushed G's head down into the rucksack and refastened the zip, keeping a firm hold of the rucksack quivering with a life of its own on my knee. Val pounced on Meffy, dumped him into his basket, and covered it with her coat, plunging him into darkness. The yips faltered and trailed off. Order restored, silence fell once more.

The actors, surprised into immobility, now sprang to life as if in a video replay. Once again Châtelard seized Mary's stockinged leg and re-applied the kisses, once again Mary and the maids-in-waiting threw their hands up in horror and opened their mouths, but this time miming the screams. The door at the rear was flung open by two servants led by a lord represented by Tarquin, this time wearing a beard to avoid being mistaken for Lord Maitland. He hauled Châtelard roughly to his feet and pulled his dagger out of its sheath.

Mary rose to her feet crying out, 'Plunge your dagger into his black heart, my Lord Moray! By my troth, he hath committed *lèse majesté* against my person.' She burst into hysterical sobs.

Châtelard fell to his knees and held up hands clasped in prayer. 'My Queen, I beseech you to show mercy to one who was merely expressing his heartfelt regret for the occasion when, overcome by wine, by mischance he fell asleep under your Majesty's bed in Aberdeen.'

'Enough!' Moray knocked Châtelard to the ground and pinned him down with his foot. 'Calm yourself, my dear sister. The knave shall stand trial before the people of the town, that they may judge the falseness of his tongue and see him executed in the market square.'

At a signal from Moray, the servants took hold of Châtelard and dragged him out.

As the actors froze to indicate the end of the scene, Samantha addressed us from the floor above. 'My lord Châtelard was held in the dungeons, and on the twenty-second of February in the year of our Lord fifteen hundred and sixty-three was put to death in the market square. On the scaffold, to the very end the romantic poet, he recited Ronsard's Hymn to Death.'

Châtelard's disembodied voice rang out eerily from within the ruined tower. 'I salute you, happy and profitable Death, since I must die either for the honour of God, or in the service of my Prince.'

Chunk. The sound of an axe blade biting into wood. A long silence.

Samantha spoke again. 'Ladies and gentlemen, 'I leave each of you to make up your own mind about the motives of the unfortunate Lord Châtelard. Was he a brave man sent on a suicide mission to blacken Queen Mary's reputation? Or merely, enamoured of his beautiful queen, a rash youth who paid a terrible price for his foolhardy behaviour?' She bowed and moved slowly out of our sight.

Judging by Val's watery sniffs of suppressed emotion and Rob's shout of 'Bravo!', I was not the only one to find the short re-enactment rather moving. Even Tony surprised me. His comment, 'My vote's for suicide mission,' showed that, for once, he thought sexual passion wasn't the only motivation for action.

Russell stepped forward, beaming at the success of the hastily arranged re-enactment. 'You have now till four o'clock to do your own thing. I remind you that the bus pick-up point is next to the Golf Museum.'

The others wandered off in different directions. That was what

I'd been waiting for. Today's drug courier would have to have a means of transporting a packet of drugs, so that narrowed it down to Meffy's basket or Rob's bagpipe case. It was not likely to be the wicker basket. What dog would tolerate sharing that confined space with a bulky item like a kilo of drugs? And the danger of sharp little teeth tearing open the wrapping would be too much of a risk. That left the bagpipe case, certainly large enough to accommodate several kilo packets.

I bent over the rucksack petting G, but keeping an unobtrusive eye on Rob, watching for him to make a move. I didn't have long to wait. Looking round, he strode off across the courtyard with the bagpipe case, climbed the steps to the crumbling rampart of the Kitchen Tower and stood looking out to sea, an ideal spot to be seen and approached by his contact. He swung the pipes under his arm and started to play, soon attracting a small cluster of tourists. Which of them was the contact? The mournful notes of the pipes drifted up to mingle with the cries of the gulls wheeling over the jagged reefs below, but nobody from the group climbed the steps to engage in pretend conversation as a cover for passing over drugs.

Slowly, one by one, the onlookers moved away. Either the courier hadn't made the rendezvous or… I'd been wrong about Rob. When I already had evidence that Val was a courier, why had I wasted time on him? And a little more thought would have told me that the dog carrier was indeed very suitable to transport drugs. A thin plastic container the width and length of the basket would be dog-proof and undetectable under its removable floor.

Cursing my folly, I looked at my watch. Ten precious minutes had passed. There was no sign of Val in the courtyard, but perhaps, just perhaps, the transfer of drugs had not yet taken place, so I might yet be in time to take a photo and establish another link in the chain. If she was still in the castle grounds, where would that be? Somewhere out of the way, where she could wait for the contact. Perhaps the Sea Tower with its narrow entrance and the steps leading down to the Bottle Dungeon? Val wasn't there. I returned to the grassy central courtyard and looked around at the sprinkle of tourists and Rob on the rampart playing his pipes.

The rucksack on my back thumped me in the ribs. Gorgonzola had had enough of being cooped up. The zip, left slightly open for air, was forced apart, two large paws hooked themselves onto my shoulder and whiskers tickled my neck. Feline feet scrabbled for leverage. She was about to climb out.

I shrugged off the straps. The paws detached themselves, the rucksack slid slowly to the ground and Gorgonzola leapt out with a not-before-time miaow. Russell was sitting on one of the seats overlooking the sea listening to Rob's pibroch lament. I clipped on her lead and wandered over.

'Would you have you seen Meffy and Val anywhere?' My question casual.

'Val? Let me think… I told her that the Mine and Countermine are well worth a look, so that's where she'll be.' He tilted his head back and closed his eyes, the better to appreciate the sound of the pipes. 'That music suits the sad history of the Castle, doesn't it?'

I muttered agreement and wandered off towards the Countermine and Mine. That tunnel would be ideal for a secret rendezvous. The sixteenth-century defenders of the Castle had dug the Countermine to intercept the Mine dug under the walls by besiegers. I stopped at the information board to study the illustration, but I'd only managed to read a paragraph before Gorgonzola was tug-tug-tugging at the lead. A particularly forceful tug pulled it out of my hand. She bounded down the steps and disappeared into the darkness of the Countermine with the lead bouncing along behind her.

'No soft duvet for you tonight!' Muttering the dire threat, I hurried down the worn steps and past a wooden door latched back against the wall. Lights fixed at intervals revealed a passageway curving out of sight as it burrowed under the castle walls. For the first few yards the roof was so low that a deep channel had been dug in the centre of the floor, but I still had to bend almost double, holding onto a handrail for support.

Slowed down considerably, I was just in time to see G's lead disappearing round the curve. I hesitated, doubts forming. Couch-potato Val definitely wouldn't go to such lengths to deliver drugs. This had turned out to be another time-wasting mistake. There might still be time to find out where she had gone, but first I had to catch G. With no cat whistle to call her back, I went on, head and knees bent, rucksack scraping against the ceiling.

I heard her before I saw her. *Hrwow*. Not a miaow of distress, but her triumphant drug-detecting croon. I rounded another curve – and there she was, crouched over a small plastic bag. Murmuring words of praise, but taking no chances that she might make another run for it, with one hand I grabbed hold of the lead and with the other pulled her rubber mouse from my pocket and dropped it at her feet.

I picked up the plastic bag while she played with her reward. One sniff caught the distinctive sweet smell of cannabis. G had been lured into the tunnel by a bag discarded by a drug user. That was all it was. Someone had chosen the Countermine for a fix away from prying eyes. I shouldn't have allowed Val out of my sight. Wherever she had gone, I had to accept that the transfer of drugs had long been made.

Gloomily I watched G playing with the mouse. I knew there was no chance at all of being quick enough to snatch it from her before she tired of it. When I judged the time was right, I gave a gentle pull on the lead, and as I'd hoped, G picked up the mouse and followed me back along the tunnel.

We must have been about half way back to the entrance, when all the lights went out bringing a darkness so sudden and intense it felt like a blow, pressing on the eyelids like a thick blindfold. I held my hand up in front of my face but still couldn't see my fingers. Keeping hold of the lead with my left hand, I released the other shoulder from the rucksack, allowing the strap to slide down my left arm and along the lead till the rucksack reached the ground. I scooped Gorgonzola into it, patting her head and feeling to make sure the mouse was still clamped in her jaws. She would be quite content zipped up inside.

Confident that whatever had caused the electrical fault would be remedied soon, I wasn't too worried. Till then, I had my pencil torch. After a few steps the rucksack on my back bumped and scraped against the low roof, drawing a squeak of protest from Gorgonzola, then the beam picked out the channel cut in the floor. Hampered by carrying the not inconsiderable weight of G in front of me in the rucksack, I made my way slowly over the uneven surface. My torch shone on the curve of the wall picking out shadows on the rough-hewn rock... Not far to go now.

I rounded the curve of the passage, expecting to see the grey of daylight. Instead, I was met with a wall of darkness. A few steps more and I discovered the reason. The torchlight shone on the rough wooden planks of the outer door to the Countermine. The custodians must have closed it early for Health and Safety reasons when the electricity supply failed. Or had a gust of wind slammed it shut? I lifted the latch. The door was definitely locked. I shouted, hammered on the door with my fists, my boots. Nobody heard. Nobody came.

G and I were trapped.

Chapter Twenty-Four

I sat down, back to the wall, and switched off the torch to save the battery. Surely it was just a matter of waiting till I heard voices, then all I needed to do was shout and kick at the door as hard as I could.

With nothing else to occupy my mind, I puzzled over the attempts on Hermione's life. How had she aroused the suspicions of the De la Haighs? Was it because she had brought a dog on the tour with her? Drug organisations know the danger presented by sniffer dogs. Suspicion would have become certainty when Brad had discovered her trying to get into the conservatory and appearing to spy on them as they operated the mechanism for the underground chamber. Yes, they would have been sure that they'd discovered an HMRC agent.

I must have dozed off, for when I switched on the torch to look at my watch, an hour had passed. Two nights of broken sleep tending to Hermione and planting the tracking bug in the garage had taken their toll. I wasn't too worried – when it came time for the bus to leave, somebody would be sure to come looking for me.

Then a sobering thought. What if Russell didn't say anything about sending me to look for Val in the Countermine, deliberately kept quiet about where I might be, had in fact been directing me into a trap? Trap, no, that was too fanciful. How could he be sure I'd go into the Countermine? I thought it over… I'd followed G when she had dashed into the mine. It was as if she had smelt the drug packet lying deep inside. But that was impossible – even her super-sensitive nose wouldn't have caught the scent at that distance. But what if… what if… someone had sprinkled a few specks of cannabis at intervals with the purpose of luring her, and therefore me, deep into the mine?

Then an even more sobering thought. Laying a drug trail would mean they knew that G was a sniffer cat. A sniffer cat is probably unique, so how could they possibly know? It could only be because I had aroused suspicion. That had to have been after the visit to Whittingehame, or both Hermione and I would have been fed a slice of poisoned bruschetta. So it must have been something I did or said yesterday.

I stared into the darkness… It could only have been that visit to the garage. Our every move must have been recorded on CCTV – they'd seen me planting the tracking bug in the Mercedes and G sniffing for drugs in the boot. Everything fell horribly into place. Being locked in the Countermine had been no accident, but part of the plan to get rid of me. Someone had got hold of the key kept in the Visitor Centre, locked the door and pinned on it an official-looking notice about closure. They'd come back when the Castle was closed. I'd hear low voices outside the door, the key being inserted in the lock. The beam of a powerful torch would blind me and…

But they wouldn't kill me here, wouldn't want Act It Out associated with another murder. They'd arrange my disappearance to look as if I'd gone on the run, just like they had with Marie Stuart, and plant evidence implicating me in the death of actor Mark Carpenter so that the police would concentrate on hunting me down. After all, I'd been held for questioning as the only one present in Holyrood Palace that night without an alibi. Police scrutiny would be lifted from Act It Out and the Shooting Lodge.

But I wasn't going to make it easy for them by sitting here and waiting for death. Perhaps, just perhaps, there was somewhere in the Mines to hide, somewhere they'd overlook. If only I could remember more precisely the layout from the guidebook Gerry had sent to brief me. The besiegers' end of the tunnel, originally a few yards outside the castle walls, was now under a house across the street. Though it would certainly be blocked off, it might be possible to attract the attention of someone in that house. It was the slenderest of hopes, but if I remained here, there was no hope at all.

I picked up the rucksack, switched on the torch, and made my way deeper into the Countermine. Once I was past the spot where I'd found the empty cannabis bag, the roof was higher and I could stand comfortably upright. I moved more confidently forward, only to stumble as the floor sloped suddenly down and the passage came to an abrupt end. In front of me was a wall of rock glistening with moisture except for a dark circular patch low down like the outlet of a drain. I shone the torch on it. It appeared to be a manhole with a metal ladder descending into a black void. This must be the spot where the Castle defenders in the Countermine had broken through the ceiling to the besiegers' Mine below. I climbed down the ladder into the unknown. It was my only chance.

I'd imagined the Mine would be claustrophobic, so narrow

and low in height that I'd be forced to crawl like a potholer squeezing through a split in a rock. To my surprise, it was about eight feet in height, floored with wooden boards and wide enough for the besiegers to have used pack animals to carry the rubble away. I could walk upright and carry G's rucksack on my back past two shallow alcoves. In a few yards, a flight of steps rose steeply up… up… the top out of range of my torch. I felt a surge of hope. The steps could only lead towards street-level and a possible means of escape from De la Haigh's trap.

The pencil-thin torch beam probed the darkness ahead – and fell on blocks of stone cemented together into a solid wall. I played the torch over the surface… from side to side… down to ground level… up to roof height. A dead end – in more ways than one. I tried my mobile. No signal. My last hope gone, I switched off the torch and in despair slumped to the ground, back against the wall. Eyes closed, I sat with G on my lap waiting for them to come for me…

From overhead, a sepulchral whisper, 'Anybody down there?'

My eyes shot open. The darkness of the Mine was tinged with grey from daylight seeping down a narrow vertical shaft in the ceiling. At the far end of the shaft was a circular grating pierced with pinprick-holes.

Clearly from above came a giggle and a child's voice, 'Do that again, Daddy.'

A man's voice, deeper and slower than before, 'Any-y bo-dy do-wn the-e-re?'

This was my chance and I'd only have the one. 'Hallo!' It came out as a croak from a throat suddenly dry. I tried again.

'Hallo-o-o-o!' This time my cry echoed satisfyingly off the

Mine's rock walls.

A wail from overhead. 'Da-a-ddy! It's a ghost!' Loud sobs.

'You should be ashamed of yourself, down there, frightening a child like that!' The angry shout boomed down the shaft. Then, in a soft and consoling murmur to his son, 'Just somebody playing the fool, lad.'

Desperate to gain this man's attention, I shrieked, 'He-e-elp! Get help! I'm locked in the Mine with my cat.'

I don't know why I brought G into it, stress I suppose, but instead of gaining his concern and sending him rushing for help, it had the opposite effect.

'Pull the other one!' His voice faded as he turned away. 'Come along, Harry, I'll buy you an ice cream.'

I tugged at the rucksack zip. As Gorgonzola poked her head out, I whispered desperately, 'Meffy! Is that Meffy?'

Miaow Miaow Mia-ow. She did a meerkat stretch of her neck, swivelling round to catch sight of him.

From above, silence. It was too late. In despair I buried my face in G's soft fur.

Then, down the shaft came a cautious, 'So you weren't joking? You really are trapped in the mine with a cat?'

'Yes, yes!' My voice trembled, and it wasn't an act. 'The lights went out and the custodians must have locked the door for safety reasons. Could you alert the Visitor Centre, and come back and tell me what's happening?'

'Be as quick as I can. Sorry for not believing you. Let's run, Harry. The ice cream can wait. There's a lady to rescue.'

I shone the torch on my watch. Three minutes to five o'clock, three minutes before the Centre closed for the day. The digital seconds flicked by. What if they'd already locked up, or ignored the man hammering on the door? And even if he did get there in time, was there a duplicate key? If not... I tilted my head to look up the length of the narrow airshaft, trying to judge the diameter. If I stretched my arms above my head, my body might just fit in the shaft for rescuers to drag me up. At least there would be no difficulty about them rescuing Gorgonzola. I wouldn't have to worry about her.

It seemed an age before I heard a scrabbling from overhead and the pinpricks of light in the grating were blotted out by a head. 'Got them... just as they... were locking up.' Breathless from running, his words came in gasps 'They said... you are to wait... till they get the lights back on...' A deep intake of breath. 'Then make your way back towards the entrance. They'll get the door open and send someone to meet you.'

Half an hour later I was settled comfortably in a nearby fish and chip shop. The Historic Scotland officials had been most apologetic about the 'prank' that had trapped me in the Mine. They'd insisted on compensating me for my ordeal with a restorative meal at a restaurant of my choice.

Over a very welcome fish supper and pot of tea, I calculated how much danger I was now in. Rather than making the long journey to St Andrews themselves, the De la Haighs must have delegated Russell or Peterson to spring the trap, steal the key, pull the fuse from the lights, and put a fake *Ministry of Works Danger Keep Out* notice on the Countermine door.

I wasn't in any imminent danger. The minibus would have left an hour and a half ago, so Russell and Peterson wouldn't know I'd been rescued. They'd come when the streets were as deserted as they ever would be in a university town, so I'd be safe until the early hours of tomorrow morning. They'd find the Countermine door locked, and though the *Danger Keep Out* notice had been removed, they'd assume I was still in there. That gave me time…

I fed G a tasty morsel of chip and pondered my next move. Should I go back to the Shooting Lodge, act as if I was the indignant victim of an unknown prankster? Far too dangerous, how long would I last before an 'accident' befell me? Yet, if I contacted Gerry to inform him my cover was blown, that would bring my role in Operation Red Grouse to an end and I wanted to see it through. I picked up a fat chip and bit into the soft potato. Perhaps I could simply 'disappear', leaving the De la Haighs wondering how much I knew and when HMRC were going to strike. The best form of attack is to make your opponent nervous, always looking over his shoulder. That's when he makes mistakes. I swallowed the last of the chip and licked my fingers. Disappear, yes, that's what I'd do.

Chapter Twenty-Five

I'd decided I wouldn't go back to the Shooting Lodge or contact Gerry, but in the end I did both. I'd come to the conclusion that a brief nocturnal visit to the Shooting Lodge would be useful. For that I'd need a car and that was why I had to make a phone call to Gerry.

'The most important information first, Gerry. When I broke into the garage at the Shooting Lodge last night, I made a serious mistake, the same mistake that our agents Grantham and Carpenter must have made. I didn't spot a CCTV camera in the garage. My cover was blown and as a result an attempt was made on my life this afternoon.'

His reaction was as expected. 'The information you have supplied so far has been most useful. However, I've now no option, I'm afraid, but to withdraw you from Operation Red Grouse. It's a great pity, but for you to turn up at the Shooting Lodge pretending you thought the Mine incident was all a childish prank would be a fatal mistake.'

'There's a high probability that the De la Haighs will be in St Andrews later tonight, Gerry,' I said, desperate to make one last contribution to Red Grouse. 'Having set the trap for me in the Countermine, they'll be sure to want the satisfaction of being in at the kill. In their absence, it will be quite safe for me to make a quick visit to the Shooting Lodge, investigate the safe in their lounge and plant a listening device somewhere in their apartment.'

A long pause as he thought it over, weighing the pros and cons. At least he was not rejecting my proposal outright.

I added quickly, 'I won't risk it if the De la Haighs are at home. Instead, I might have another go at concealing a tracking bug in the Mercedes, if I can do so without entering the garage. They'll have swept the car electronically and will now assume it is 'clean'. Operation Red Grouse will still be able to monitor the movements of the De la Haighs. I won't be tempted into anything else. Promise,' I added, hoping that would clinch it.

'Hmm…' His uncharacteristic indecision told me he was reluctant to expose me to extreme danger, but half-persuaded to agree.

In a final attempt to convince, I added, 'It's the one place the drug organisation won't expect to find me in the next few hours, so I'd be able to do all that without putting myself at undue risk.'

A sigh revealed the burden of responsibility he felt for putting the success of Operation Red Grouse before the life of an agent. 'I'll send a car. But on two conditions: that there's a tracking device on your car, and that you switch on the transmitter in Gorgonzola's collar and keep the collar in your pocket. I'll have it monitored as back-up. Contact me when you're clear of the Shooting Lodge.'

I knew I was in safe hands. Making assurance doubly sure, that was the way Gerry Burnside worked. Many of his agents owed their lives to what at the time might seem unnecessary precaution. I gave G a cuddle. I'd managed to convince him that

I still had a useful role to play in Operation Red Grouse.

At 2 a.m. I parked the car off the road a quarter of a mile from the Shooting Lodge. With no work for Gorgonzola, I left her in the car, rucksack invitingly open as a comfort-hole for a snooze. I held up the rubber mouse for her to see and dropped it on the back seat. Playing with her favourite toy would keep her occupied for the short time I was away.

I locked the car and walked off, then remembered Gerry's instruction to keep G's transmitter in my pocket. I hesitated. I'd be gone less than an hour. Would it matter? Probably not, but I did as he'd asked, went back to the car, unbuckled the collar, switched on the transmitter and slipped it into my jacket pocket.

'Back soon, G,' I said.

Ten minutes later I was sneaking up the drive of the Shooting Lodge using the rhododendron bushes as cover. The crescent moon provided just enough light for me to see without using my torch, and the strong breeze sighing through the branches masked any sound I made. In a word, for my stealth mission conditions were perfect.

The dark mass of the house loomed up. With my back pressed against the rough trunk of the Scots Pine, I studied each window. There were no tell-tale chinks of light. Avoiding the gravel of the forecourt, I moved round to the back of the house. All was dark there too. There had been no sign of the Mercedes, either in the forecourt or here in the rear courtyard. It might be in the garage, so I couldn't be entirely certain whether the De la Haighs were away from home.

The best way into the house was via my bedroom window,

avoiding the alarm fitted to the front door. Selecting a thin metal strip, I slid it between the upper and lower frames of the sash window to force the snib-lock aside, the work of a moment with my picklock kit. I pushed up the lower half of the window and climbed in.

I closed the window and switched on my pencil torch. Easing open the door a crack, I listened to the sounds of the house: the creak of old timbers settling, the faint tick of the grandfather clock further along the hall, and a slow rhythmic snore from Rob's room. Satisfied that no one was aware of my presence, I crept along the corridor and stopped at Brad's door. No sound from within. Had he gone off to St Andrews, one of those assigned the task of killing me and disposing of my body? I crept on. At the foot of the stairs to the De la Haigh's apartment, I paused to listen again, then made my way up, avoiding the creaking centre of each step, keeping close to the wall.

Near the top of the stairs, the hairs on the back of my neck prickled. I was not alone. A scraping sound as of something being moved out of position… a soft thud… a muffled curse. Someone was moving stealthily about the lounge. Why no lights, why this furtive behaviour?

I switched off the torch and tiptoed across the landing to peep round the frame of the door. A figure was standing in front of the fireplace slowly playing a torch over the *trompe l'oeil* shelves of books. He could only be looking for the tell-tale lines that would betray the presence of a safe. No chance now for me to find out if it was concealed behind the picture of the stag. No opportunity, either, to plant a listening device in the lounge, but rather than leave with nothing accomplished, I'd place the bug in the bedroom while the intruder was searching the lounge.

I didn't get the chance. *Creak... creak... creak.* Someone was coming up the stairs. I whirled round. *Creak... creak... creak.* A moment of silence at the half-landing. *Creak... creak... creak.* There was no time even for the two paces that would take me to the safety of the boxroom. My only chance was to go on the attack. Surprise would give me the chance to hurl myself on whoever was coming up the stairs, knock him over and make my escape. I switched on the pencil torch, aiming it to dazzle.

The bright beam shone straight into the face of Val Templeton. Before her squeak of alarm could be followed by an ear-piercing scream alerting the sleepers in the bedrooms below, I hissed, 'Shut up, Val! It's only me, Shelagh. We don't want to waken the others.' That should make it clear to her that I, too, was up to no good. I lowered the torch to light her way up the stairs.

Tony came rushing to the lounge doorway. 'Who's that, Val?' Panic in his whisper.

'It's me. Shelagh. I don't know who you're working for but I'm sure we can come to a suitable arrangement. My boss wants me to get hold of the papers in the De la Haigh's safe and I'll make it worth your while to do a deal.'

Greed – and relief that they hadn't been caught by the De la Haighs – might make them accept my sudden switch from apparent upright citizen to underworld crook.

They spoke as one. 'Cash?'

'Any money in the safe is yours. Is that a deal?' Consent was instant. We moved back into the lounge.

Once more Tony swept his torch over the *trompe l'oeil* shelves of books. 'Trouble is, the safe's too well hidden. We've been searching for ages. Can't find it.'

I went over to stand in front of the fireplace. 'Have you looked behind the painting of the stag? Give me a hand to take it down.'

The apparently heavy gilt frame was made of balsa wood. Light as a feather, it lifted off its hook, exposing the door of the safe.

Val held the torch steady on the lock. 'I said it was there, Tone! I was right. It wasn't a stupid suggestion like you said.'

'Maybe if you're so clever, Val, you know how to open it.'

Typical amateur criminals, bickering and forgetting the dangerous situation we were in.

'No time for argument.' I took out my picklocks. 'I know exactly what to do.'

In fifteen seconds the safe door swung open. The Templetons were in luck. Neat bundles of crisp banknotes filled the lower shelf. While they were frantically stuffing their pockets, Val's bra, and Tony's shirtfront, I reached into the safe and pulled out a slim wad of papers enclosed by an elastic band. I skimmed through them: names, addresses, dates and quantity of drug shipments, cash payments – everything I needed to bring Operation Red Grouse to a successful conclusion. I slipped the papers down the side of my boot where there was more chance of them being overlooked if I was caught and searched.

'That's it, guys. Time to go.'

'Just a mo', Shelagh. There's lots left. See if there's a carrier bag in the kitchen, Val.'

'That's enough! We're pushing our luck.' I slammed shut the safe door and turned the lock. 'Any minute now, the De la Haighs might–'

The headlights of a car swept across the ceiling, momentarily lighting up the room, the wallpaper of fake books and the Templetons' startled faces. We'd run out of time.

Chapter Twenty-Six

The Templetons stood as if turned to stone, paralysed, frozen with fear.

The time was past for speaking in low whispers.

'Quick, help me get the picture back on the wall.' Tony didn't react. 'Now! Now! If we can hide the fact we've been here, there's a good chance they won't look in the safe for some hours.'

As he leapt forward to take hold of the frame, I shoved the torch into Val's hand. With the picture back in position, I grabbed the torch back from her.

'Beat it, the pair of you!'

They scuttled off. I didn't follow immediately but took time to check the alignment of the picture. It had the slightest of tilts to the left, a tell-tale sign that someone had been at the safe. Though the few seconds it took to level it seemed to stretch for minutes, I didn't turn away till I was totally satisfied.

Now speed was the only thing that could save me. Heedless of creaking treads, I ran down the stairs. Anyone who heard would assume it was the De la Haighs. In the corridor leading to my room caution was more important than speed. I slowed to a quick and silent walk. No one must hear me pass by or detect the opening and closing of my bedroom door.

Once in the room, I eased the latch closed and leaned against the wood, heart pounding, trying to control my breathing.

Keeping out of line of the window, I crossed the room and scanned the courtyard. Nothing moved. The long dark shape of the Mercedes was parked on the far side. The De la Haighs hadn't taken time to put it inside the garage.

This was a golden opportunity to plant a second tracking device. The faint squeak as I slid up the sash window was a warning to take care. I stood waiting, back pressed against the stonework, ears straining for a sound that might indicate someone had heard and was coming to investigate. Waiting... waiting...

Taking advantage of a cloud obscuring the faint light from the moon, I darted across the courtyard to take cover on the far side of the Mercedes. The hiding place for the tracking device would have to be somewhere on the exterior. I crouched down, careful not to trigger the alarm system by jolting the bodywork and took from my pocket the real-time GPS tracker that would allow HMRC to trace the movements and location of the vehicle. The wheel arches and most of the chassis would be rubber-sealed against rust, useless for placing the magnetic tracker. I reached under the rear bumper, felt for the gap alongside the spare wheel housing and stuck the tracker firmly in place. Job done. With a sigh of satisfaction I half-rose, ready to make my getaway across the courtyard.

Low voices, close by – very close by – coming from inside the garage. In one quick movement I slid under the car. Lying motionless, the side of my face pressed against a cold flagstone, I heard the latch click and the hinges creak as the garage doors swung open, then a metallic clink as they were hooked back. The car was about to be driven into the garage. Into my narrow field of vision moved a pair of polished shoes and expensive tweed trousers, followed a few moments later by scuffed trainers and jeans.

My only chance, the slimmest of chances, to be honest not really a chance at all, was to make a run for it. A bullet in the back would be a preferable death to being crushed when the Mercedes began to manoeuvre. I tensed, ready to squirm out from underneath. I was too late. The driver's door opened, the trainers disappeared and the vehicle settled under the driver's weight as he got behind the wheel. With no clearance now between my body and the underside of the car, I let out an involuntary grunt as something bit hard into my back.

An exclamation. The pale blob of a face as someone peered under the car... the blinding beam of a torch. A hand grabbed my ankle and dragged me roughly out. The toe of a polished shoe hurtled towards my head. A moment of searing pain, then nothing.

Throbbing headache... I opened my eyes to darkness, the impenetrable black of the Countermine. I closed my eyes again, fighting the pounding in my head, trying to remember. G and I had been lured into the mine and trapped behind the locked door. I touched the side of my head and winced. Yes... that was what must have happened. They'd come for us, and as I'd run further into the mine, I'd knocked myself out on the low roof. They had decided the best way to dispose of me was to block the tunnel with a roof fall and leave us to die of hunger and thirst. Sudden panic. Where was G? I felt around me – no soft fur, no sound to indicate she was nearby. Had she run off into the depths of the mine?

Something was digging into my side, something in my pocket. My fingers closed round G's rubber collar and memory came flooding back... being dragged from under the Mercedes... Tony and Val stuffing cash from the safe into their clothing.... Were the papers, vital for the success of Operation Red Grouse, still in my boot? I sat up to reach for them – and hit my head on hard wood. More pain, intense pain. I fell back and stretched out an exploratory hand. I seemed to be lying, knees bent, on soft material in some sort of box. With both hands I pressed hard against the lid in a vain effort to push it up.

Exhausted, I lay back, aware for the first time of the low hum of an engine, its vibrations barely perceptible through the soft material on the floor of the box, a box too big to fit into the Mercedes, possibly one of the costume trunks stored in the garage. I must be in a large van – or possibly the minibus. They were taking me off to dispose of me, just as they had Marie.

My fingers closed again on the thinnest of lifelines in my pocket, G's rubber collar with its transmitter, reassurance that Control would be monitoring the moving black dot on the screen. I'd promised I'd restrict myself to the De la Haighs' apartment and the Mercedes. When I didn't report back, Gerry would know something had gone wrong.

A sudden jolt. The vibrations stopped. Muffled voices, the sound of the rear doors being opened, objects being shifted about. Thumps on the side of the trunk. A man's voice, very close, muttering something.

More thumps and bangs, then quite clearly, 'Found the petrol can.'

They intended to pour petrol over the trunk and set fire

to it. I lay there, heart racing, mouth dry, visualising a hand unscrewing the cap of the petrol can, fuel splashing out over the lid, running down the sides of my prison, a lighted match tossed through the air, an explosive burst of flame… The signal from G's collar would suddenly disappear, the dot pinpointing my location vanish from the screen, the message flash up, 'Alert! Transmitter inactive. Status of Agent?'

The operatives dispatched to my last recorded position would arrive to find charred bones. Violent death is an ever-present companion lurking at the shoulder of an undercover agent, but if death has to come, we hope for it to be quick. Weak from concussion and stiff from lying in a cramped position, even if the lid wasn't locked, I wouldn't manage to throw it back, climb out over the high sides, make a run for it and meet that quick death of a bullet in the back.

Voices, one a woman's. That would be Arabella De la Haigh. I heard the unmistakable gurgle of petrol being poured out of a can… I closed my eyes, fighting the urge to beg for mercy.

Instead of the scrape of a match and the crackle of burning wood, I heard a peculiar *snuffle snuffle* followed by *scratch scratch scratch*, first on the side of the trunk, then on the lid.

'Stop it!' A woman's voice, vaguely familiar, not Arabella's. Again, *snuffle snuffle snuffle scratch scratch scratch*.

'What *is* the matter, Meffy? Naughty boy! Come here! There's nothing in that box.'

Val! Hope flared.

'Grab the pin-brained mutt and let me close the doors, Val. I've filled the tank. We've got to get out of here with the loot before the Delly Haighs turn up.'

So the Templetons were making their getaway in the

minibus with the money from the safe. But even if the De la Haighs had not yet discovered the raided safe, they'd certainly come in hot pursuit as soon as they noticed the minibus with its incriminating trunk was missing.

Hope died. If I didn't attract the Templeton's attention, my reprieve from death would be temporary, for as soon as they reached the dual carriageway with its busy traffic, they'd be sure to hitch a lift with their loot, abandoning the minibus – and me – in a lay-by. When the De la Haighs spotted the parked minibus and the trunk, they'd finish me off.

Clang. One rear door had slammed shut. I'd only seconds before they shut the other door.

'Help!' The cry emerged as a squeak so faint they couldn't have heard.

Yip yip yip. High-pitched, excited yelps. Meffy's large ears had picked up the tiny sound. Claws *scrabble scrabble scrabbled* against the side of the trunk.

I drew my legs back as far as I could and thrust them forward to thump against the wood. Another cry for help produced merely a long croaking groan.

'Did you hear that, Val? There's a dog in there. Sounds big enough to be a Rottweiler.'

'It's trying to get out! Do something before it kills Meffy!'

'Take the other end, Tony, and we'll dump the trunk by the side of the road.' Rob's voice. 'Can't have the brute escaping into the van while we're on the road.' The Templetons must have sacrificed some of their loot to bribe him to drive the getaway van.

'One... two... three, heave.' Grunts. The trunk shuddered and slid a few inches.

The pursuing De la Haighs would be sure to recognise the abandoned trunk. Panic. I opened my mouth to shout. Too late. The trunk moved again, tilted, swayed.

'Look out! Watch yourself! Can't hold it.'

With a bone-jarring jolt the trunk crashed to the ground. Its side splintered, the lid burst open and I found myself sprawling, dazed, on the tarmac, dimly aware of Val's scream and Meffy's excited yelps. Hands pulled me free of the trunk, lifted me into the luggage compartment and propped me up against the back of the rear seat.

Val's face loomed in front of me, eyes avid with curiosity. 'There's blood on your head! Bet it was the Delly Haighs! They caught you in their flat, beat you up and stuffed you in the trunk. I'm right, aren't I?'

Tony's anxious face joined hers. 'Did they check the safe? Well, did they?'

'Yes, I'm afraid so.' True or not, that should impress upon the Templetons that there was no time to lose. To emphasise the urgency, I added, 'The next set of headlights behind could very well be theirs.'

Even in the dim interior light of the minibus I could see the colour drain from their faces. 'They'll kill us if they catch us, Tone.' Val's voice a whisper.

Implicated as co-conspirator, Rob looked uneasy. 'Don't know what's going on, but I'm not waiting around. Help Shelagh onto the back seat and we're off.'

A sudden jolt as the minibus hit a pothole brought me half-awake to hear the hum of the engine... the murmur of voices... Rob was concentrating on hurling the minibus along the narrow road, slowing fractionally as the headlights picked out each approaching bend. Hedges… trees… field walls and fences looming up, sweeping by.

Tony was sitting in the front seat poring over a road map. 'We're just passing along the side of a loch… only another ten minutes, I reckon, to the motorway. After that, the Delly Haighs won't have a clue which exit we've taken.' A snap of his fingers. 'We'll have vanished into thin air.'

Rob glanced in the rear-view mirror. 'Hate to tell you the bad news – the headlights behind are coming up fast. If it's them, they're going to catch us up before we reach the dual carriageway.'

I twisted round to peer back the way we'd come. Headlights on full-beam were clearly visible at the far end of the loch, perhaps a mile behind. We were travelling fast, perhaps faster than was safe, but the distance between us was narrowing. The driver clearly knew the road. Not necessarily the De la Haighs, of course, but…

Tony studied the map. 'Level crossing approaching.'

The headlights picked up a white X with red tips, the sign of an un-gated railway crossing. The minibus slowed to a halt.

'Why are we stopping? Don't stop! Don't stop! They'll kill us!' In Val's voice a rising note of hysteria.

Rob shrugged. 'Would you rather a train killed us?'

Possibly yes, I thought.

'Val's right.' Tony turned in his seat to squeeze her hand. 'Put your foot down, Rob. It'll only take a few seconds to cross the rails.'

Rob lowered the windows on both sides. 'Got a death wish? How far can we see down the track? A hundred yards? That's less than five seconds warning. Anyone hear anything?'

No whistle, no rumble of metal wheels on track, only the sigh of wind through the tops of the conifers. Satisfied, he revved the engine and accelerated across.

Less than half a mile ahead, a moving line of headlights marked an elevated section of the dual carriageway. Less than a mile behind, the lights of the pursuing car were closing the gap.

'Which way at this road junction?' Rob jammed his foot down on the brake, throwing us forward as the minibus screeched to a halt.

Tony peered at the map. 'Er... er....'

'Come on, *come on*. Make a decision. Right or left?'

'Well... er... the road on the right ends in a picnic area. So it's left, yes, definitely left.'

Rob swung the wheel. The minibus turned down a narrow road. Trees closed in on either side forming a long dark tunnel stretching ahead.

Tony folded the map. 'They'll not catch us now!'

Val threw her arms round Meffy and squeezed him in a bear-like hug. I craned round to look through the rear window and kept my misgivings to myself. Bump... bump. Our headlight beams lit up the rutted road... the tunnel of trees... treetops... and suddenly, as we rounded a bend, a metal sign.

Tony looked down at the map. 'That'll be the sign for the dual carriageway.' There was indeed a sign. *Forestry Picnic Area. No Through Road.*

No one spoke. After a few seconds, I said as calmly as I could, 'Looks like we should have taken the other road, Tony.'

'Tone! How could you be so stupid!' Val's voice rose to a scream.

'Sod it!' Tony shrugged. 'Don't you start on me, Val. Easy mistake to make. All we've got to do is go back. We've time before that car catches up.'

Rob swung the wheel to turn the minibus. Too late. Much too late. Coming rapidly towards us at the far end of the leafy tunnel was a set of headlights. Rob jammed his foot on the brake. Tony froze, staring through the windscreen, mouth open. Val put her hand to her mouth and whimpered, too terrified to scream.

I leaned forward and gripped Rob's shoulder. 'Switch to full beam *now*.'

In a crisis situation, a voice of confident authority gets instant response. Blinded by our headlights, the driver of the oncoming car veered to the left and steered into a clump of bushes.

'Everybody out while they're dazzled and their night vision's gone!' I put just enough urgency into my voice to galvanize rather than panic.

Fired with adrenalin, we threw open the doors of the minibus and ran for the cover of the trees. Even in my weakened state, I wasn't far behind the others.

'Separate!' I called after them. 'If one of us is caught, the rest will have a chance.'

Ahead of me, Val staggered and fell, victim of her designer heels. Meffy struggled out of her arms and bounded away, his white coat vanishing into the darkness under the trees.

I hauled her to her feet. 'Let him go, Val. His barking will only lead them straight to you.' I pointed off to the right. 'Keep off the paths and find a place to hide.'

Off to the side was the bulk of a recently fallen tree, root base in the air, branches embracing the earth. I burrowed beneath the tangle of branches and lay there hidden by the leaves, heart racing, listening to shouts from the visitor car park.

Yip yip yip. A shot, followed a moment later by the *yo-o-owl* of a dog in pain. A woman's scream. A second shot. Silence.

The need to find out what was happening overrode instinct and training. I crept from my hiding place, feet making no sound on the soft carpet of fallen pine needles as I threaded my way between the close-packed trunks. Near the edge of the trees, I dropped to the ground and squirmed forward on my elbows.

Headlights blazing, doors wide open, the Mercedes was drawn up in front of the minibus. Halfway between it and the edge of the trees, Val was lying face down on the ground. As I watched, Peterson ran forward and hauled her roughly to her feet. From the bloodstains on the front of her jacket it was clear that she'd been shot. Yet, far from hanging limp and motionless, she was struggling to break his grip, kicking at his legs ineffectually with her stockinged feet.

'Bastard, bastard, bastard ! What have you done to Meffy?'

She wrenched one arm free and clawed at his face.

'You bitch!' Peterson staggered back.

She flung herself down onto her knees in the long grass, snatched up a small white bundle and clutched it to her chest.

Recovering, he grabbed her by the hair.

'Leave her, Brad!' Arabella's voice rang out, sharp and authoritative. 'We'll deal with her later. It's the Macbeth woman we want.'

De la Haigh pointed his gun at Val. 'We know you're here, Macbeth! You've ten seconds to give yourself up or she's dead.'

Chapter Twenty-Seven

I remained silent, playing for time.

'Eight seconds... seven... six... five!' His voice calm, level, lacking any emotion. Mission Control counting down the seconds to rocket lift-off.

I'll never know how I would have reacted to De la Haigh's ultimatum – would I have stood up, revealed my position, waited for the bullet? Or would I have stayed hidden, silent witness to Val's murder, made up excuses later, mere justifications for saving my own life – with the inevitable aftermath of guilt.

I didn't have to make the decision. Without warning – startling, shocking, paralysing in their unexpectedness – the crescendo wail of police sirens blotted out the background hum of traffic on the nearby dual carriageway. The howling sirens and blue flashing lights were already turning off the elevated section, racing down the slip road we'd been making for, only to be lost to sight as they sped along the minor road towards its junction with the picnic area.

'Into the car!' Peterson flung himself behind the wheel of the Mercedes.

'There's still time for this.' De la Haigh took aim at Val.

'Payback time, Macbeth.'

'Get in, Ralph!' Arabella scrambled into the car pulling De

la Haigh after her.

The approaching sirens were louder, closer, but not close enough to save Val. As the car moved, he fired. Tyres spinning in a racing turn, the Mercedes roared off, leaving her lying face down, motionless. The tail lights glowed red as it slowed for the bend – and was gone.

'She's dead! The bastard's killed her!' Tony pushed me aside and ran to kneel down beside her. 'Val! Val!' He slumped over her, pressing his face into her back.

The note of raw emotion in his voice surprised me. Perhaps their over-the-top honeymoon behaviour hadn't all been an act.

'Gerr-off, you fool! With a sudden twist she heaved herself up, sending him sprawling. 'It's the dog that's been shot, not me.' She knelt back on her heels, cradling Meffy in her arms. His silky white coat was stained red by the blood welling up from a wound at his shoulder. His upright ears drooped, his eyes closed, he didn't make a sound. The signs weren't good. Shocked, I barely registered the sirens approaching on the minor road, passing by and receding.

'There's a first aid kit in the minibus.' Rob pulled off his coat, wrapped Meffy in it and laid him gently on the back seat. 'Ok, everybody, pile in. Let's go before the police decide to take an interest in us.'

We weren't quick enough. A police car, blue light flashing, no siren, was approaching at speed through the tunnel of trees. I'd forgotten about the transmitter in my pocket. It must be homing in on that. It screeched to a halt, the doors flew open and four men leapt out. Within seconds, they'd pinioned our arms to our sides. Val screamed. Tony and Rob swore. I said nothing.

A familiar voice said in my ear. 'You're looking a trifle the worse for wear, Deborah.' Gerry released my arms. 'Isn't it fortunate that for once you followed orders and put the transmitter collar in your pocket.' He nodded towards Tony, Val and Rob. 'How do they come into this?'

They were clearly panicking at the prospect of having to explain away the incriminating wads of banknotes on their persons. Val was on the verge of tears, Tony's forehead was beaded with sweat, Rob was biting his lip. I hesitated. A truthful report on Act It Out's drug-running would expose the Templetons as drug couriers, and Rob's presence here in possession of a large amount of cash would implicate him too.

I looked Gerry straight in the eye. 'They're just fellow guests on the Tour,' I said. 'I cadged a lift with them. They don't know anything about all this. Let them go. A dog's been shot and it's urgent they get it to a vet.'

I was confident that once they'd put sufficient miles between the police and themselves, Val's soft spot for Meffy and the prospect of a reward from a grateful Hermione would ensure they'd temporarily suspend their going-to-ground plans and seek out a vet.

'Hmm...' Gerry had them sussed. He turned to me. 'Whenever you look me straight in the eye like that, Deborah, I can be very sure you're not being totally on the level. But you will, of course, be able to justify it in your report, so I'll go along with it.'

That's what we undercover operatives in the field like about Gerry – he backs our judgement and doesn't insist on sticking rigidly by the rulebook.

He nodded to the police officers. 'These people are of no

interest to us. The dog needs a vet.'

Hardly daring to believe their good luck, Rob and the Templetons legged it towards the minibus, trying somewhat unsuccessfully to give the impression that they were upright citizens whose only concern was for a suffering animal.

A sudden violent BANG. The long-drawn-out scream of tortured metal shattered the silence of the night. The chilling sound of an impact.

'Christ!' Gerry sprinted towards the police car. 'Come with me, Deborah.'

Barely waiting for the doors to slam shut, the police driver sent the car hurtling down the tunnel of trees, siren howling. At the road junction where Tony had made his map-reading mistake, I expected them to turn left, towards a road accident on the four-lane highway. Instead, we turned right. I twisted round to peer through the rear window just in time to catch the rear lights of the minibus heading for the dual carriageway. The Templetons were making good their escape. In the front passenger seat Gerry was listening on an earpiece to Control.

I leaned forward to gain his attention. 'Why this way?'

'Bad accident on the railway crossing.'

Ahead, the red-tipped white X that marked the crossing was leaning at a crazy angle. Two police cars, blue lights flashing, blocked the road. In their headlights a pile of twisted metal, tossed to the side of the track by the speeding train, just visible on the edge of the pool of light. One wheel was still spinning. It was the only indication that the mangled wreckage might once have been a car.

As I watched, the revolutions of the wheel slowed... slowed... and came to rest.

Chapter Twenty-Eight

Hermione leaned forward to pick up the teapot. On the table for the occasion was her best eggshell-thin bone china tea service. 'Well dears, how do you like Earl Grey?'

Tony and Val, perched on the edge of the sofa opposite her, looked at each other, baffled. After a pause, Tony came up with an answer. 'Afraid Country and Western's not our kind of music.'

The perfect hostess managed not to smile. 'Silly me! I didn't make it clear I was referring to the tea.' She poured the pale liquid into their cups. 'With or without lemon?'

'Er… with.'

Hermione added the appropriate squeeze of lemon. Tony and Val took a tentative sip, repressed a shudder and hastily returned their cups to the saucers.

Hermione fed Meffy a morsel of cake. 'Thank you so much for looking after Meffy until I was out of hospital.' She leaned forward and patted Val's hand. 'I was in despair about what would happen to him on the rest of the tour. Shelagh would have done her best, of course, but dogs and cats don't get on. They had a fight, isn't that so?' That's why poor Meffy's been in the wars.' She dabbed at her eyes with a tiny handkerchief. 'Do tell me what happened.'

To gain time to think, Val forced herself to take another sip of that revoltingly scented tea, and nudged Tony to do likewise. Their eyes turned to the yellow iodine staining the white fur of the dog curled up beside Hermione on the sofa. Sensing their interest in him, Meffy played up with a weak *yip* and a feeble wag of his tail.

'Oh my poor darling! You'll have to build up your strength.' Hermione fed him another piece of cake.

'Well, what actually happened was–' Tony stopped short as Val administered a warning kick under the coffee table. In her opinion, the least said the better about that night's events at the Shooting Lodge.

She knew what to say. 'I'm afraid Meffy was a bit naughty He tried to eat out of Lady's bowl and naturally she objected. When she lashed out with her claws, he snapped at her. Shelagh and I didn't know what to do. Tony was so brave! He leapt forward, snatched Meffy up and lifted him out of Lady's reach. Didn't you, dear?'

Lost in admiration at her inventiveness, Tony was slow to reply. She administered another surreptitious kick.

'Oh… er… it was nothing, Hermione. We didn't like to tell you we'd taken him to the vet because you'd only have worried.' He fell silent, unable to think of anything else to add.

'Vet's bill and dog food, neither of them are cheap. I must reimburse you, and I'm going to add a little extra.' Hermione opened her handbag and took out her chequebook.

Val experienced a twinge of guilt. 'No, no, no. We can afford it, can't we, Tony?' And indeed they could when they'd just pocketed half a million pounds from the De la Haigh's safe.

'Nevertheless…' Hermione poised her pen. 'Tell me how

much I owe you.'

'A hundred pounds should cover it, but really...'

'No, I insist. Meffy means more to me than anything.' Hermione filled out the cheque and added a zero to the total.

Chapter Twenty-Nine

Already I was missing the adrenalin rush of an undercover assignment. I wouldn't be offered another one until the conspicuous bruise left by Peterson's boot on the side of my head had faded from its present greenish-yellow, and that would be another week at least. Agents can't afford to attract any attention or make themselves memorable in any way.

'*You're* not memorable, are you, G?'

She pretended she hadn't heard. In her opinion, sufficient amends had not yet been made for cruelly abandoning her in the car at the Shooting Lodge, then subjecting her to the horrors of the cattery while I was under medical care and then at HQ writing up my report. Two weeks had passed since, but she was still aggrieved. For these two weeks I'd had to put up with behaviour designed to challenge and annoy: the tell-tale dent on the forbidden pillow, the persistent paw demanding out in the middle of the night, the vigorous burrow under the duvet, the relentless parading up and down the bed while I was trying to sleep...

I sighed and made myself a sandwich and a mug of coffee, then turned my attention to today's mail, throwing the obvious junk in the bin. That left a letter, ostensibly income tax self-assessment, but in reality one of HMRC's means of communication with undercover agents. It was unlikely to be a new assignment, unless there was a sudden need for an agent with a bruised face.

The envelope contained a second envelope, one that had been opened and resealed with HMRC tape. It was addressed to Shelagh Macbeth c/o Historic Scotland, Edinburgh, ENGLAND and bore an American stamp. Intrigued, I slit it open.

Inside was a postcard featuring the slot machines of Caesar's Palace Las Vegas, overprinted in a glowing neon font with the invitation, 'TRY YOUR LUCK HERE!'

I turned the card over. On the reverse was written

We did! And we won!!! Thanks a MILLION!
Tony and Val xx

Lightning Source UK Ltd.
Milton Keynes UK
UKHW020642240821
389389UK00013B/1012

9 781843 965497